Tales from Christmas Town is the story of Santa Claus' adult children and their bumbling quests to find true love. When Santa and all of Christmas Town come down with the flu, his children have to step up and take over the "business". Jack Frost gets involved, a few innocent mortals, and Santa's motorcycle riding son Noel, who prefers to be called Leon. This four story anthology features authors Roni Adams, Allie Standifer, Bev Oz, and Betty Hanawa.

Tales From Christmas Town

Betty Hanawa
Roni Adams
Allie Standifer
Bev Oz

This is a work of fiction. Names, characters, places, and incidents are either the product of the author's imagination or are used fictitiously, and any resemblance to actual persons living or dead, business establishments, events, or locales, is entirely coincidental.

Tales From Christmas Town

Contact Information: info@thewildrosepress.com
The Wild Rose Press
PO Box 706
Adams Basin, NY 14410-0706
Visit us at www.thewildrosepress.com

Cover Art by *R.J.Morris*

Publishing History
First Faery Rose Edition, November 2006
ISBN 1-60154-023-X

Published in the United States of America

CONTENTS

NOT YOUR MAMMA'S REINDEER GAMES
Betty Hanawa

THE CHRISTMAS STAR
Roni Adams

JACK'S CHRISTMAS SPIRIT
Allie Standifer

FAR FROM SILENT NIGHT
Bev Oz

Not Your Momma's Reindeer Games

Betty Hanawa

Betty Glasgow Hanawa

Hot, sexy otherworld romance with hint of snark.

Enjoy being you

Betty Hanawa

www.bettyhanawa.com

Elf Queen Logo
© 2005 Amanda Hanawa

Chapter One

"But, Noel, truly you can't waste your Christmas wish from Father on a new motorcycle. Your Ducati is only two years old and still looks like new," his sister Christmas Spirit, known to the family as Krista, pleaded yet again.

Leon—named Noel at birth and doing his best, but not succeeding all that great, to get everyone to call him Leon—looked at the cards in his hand in the weekly guys only poker game.

"One card," he told the dealer who slid a single card across the table. He studied the card and wondered if the dealer again had a full house.

"Noel, be nice. Think of others."

"Princess, it's my Santa Claus wish and I can use it however I want," he said as patiently as possible. He was heartily sick of having this conversion starting at Halloween every freaking year. "The new model Ducati is coming out with a bigger engine and sleeker design. I want it." He took a deep drag of his cigar enjoying the smooth taste of the smoke swirling in his mouth.

Krista coughed and waved her hand in front of her face. With all four of the poker buddies relishing their cigars, Leon didn't have a clue how she thought waving her hand was going to freshen the air.

"You need to stop smoking. All of you," she chastised.

Leon blew out a stream of smoke and told her, "You get the Old Man to stop smoking his pipe and we'll consider giving up our once a week cigar night."

"That's a no-brainer," one of his poker buddies commented. "Can't envision Santa Claus without his stump of a pipe held tight in his teeth and the smoke circling his head like a wreath."

"Kind of like asking him to go on a diet and build abs," responded another.

Leon double-checked his own abs still as flat and firm as ever. He had an irrational fear of someday being stuck taking over the Old Man's job and having to carry around that big belly. In his ongoing effect not to inherit his dad's physique, Leon worked out every evening after a day spent taking care of the Christmas Town computer systems.

"Are we playing poker or not?" The dealer blew smoke rings at the ceiling. By the pile of chips in front of him and his nonchalant air, he probably thought he was going to win this pot, too.

"We're playing poker. Krista, do you see any females around here?"

Krista shook her head.

"Of course not. It's the guys' poker and cigar night. Now go away, Krista."

"But, Noel, please think about it. If we all wish for peace on Earth this Christmas, maybe Father will have enough magic to make it happen."

Leon set his cigar down and grabbed the trash can. The retching noises he made echoed in the small room.

"Gross."

"Damn, if I wanted to hear that, I would have stayed home tonight."

"Does this mean the game is over?"

"Oh, Noel, I hope you're not coming down with the flu like so many in Christmas Town."

Krista's sweet sympathy almost made his stomach turn for real. "Nope, just your give whirled peas a chance made me sick to my stomach."

He thrust the wastebasket with nothing in it but a couple of beer cans under her face.

She jumped back, then peered inside. She lifted her head and, for a second, Leon saw a flare of anger on his normally unflappable, always sweet sister's face. Then her smile reappeared and her partially closed fist eased into a pat on his shoulder.

"Your jokes are awful, Noel." Her laughter pealed like bells.

"Go away, Krista," Leon repeated. "We're got a game to concentrate on."

"Alright, but at least promise me you'll think about using your Christmas wish to help someone else."

"Bet," the dealer said.

"Call."

"Call"

"Bet's to you, Leon."

"Fine, Krista. I promise. Now will you leave?" Leon shoved a pile of chips into the pot. "Raise."

Christmas Spirit leaned over and kissed his cheek. "Have a good game. Oh, gee, Noel, you've got nothing but pretty hearts in your hand."

"Fold, fold, fold," echoed around the table from the other players while Krista gently shut the door behind her.

Leon scowled as he scraped the barely above ante pot to his stack. "Sisters are a pain in the ass."

"And you've got a bunch of them."

"Are we playing poker or not? Ante up, everyone."

Once again the door opened. This time his sister Holly traipsed through it.

"What part of guy's only poker night do you girls have trouble remembering?" Leon blew a stream of smoke into his sister's face.

Holly coughed, then smacked his shoulder. "Stop blowing smoke straight into my face. I knew I should have stopped by the infirmary and gotten a face mask. Hurmph," she snorted, "actually I need an oxygen mask in here. You males and your testosterone bonding over cards and cigars. Big whoopee-do. If you think I wanted to be in this stinky place, you can think again."

"Then why in the name of spoiled fruit cake did you come in? No one invited you."

"I'm delivering a message from the boss."

Santa Claus' number one helper and the family member all the others suspected was the Old Man's favorite—although he and Mom both tried really hard not to play favorites—had the efficient follow-through that made the Old Man's job easier. Leon didn't know why everyone automatically assumed he was going to take over the Old Man's job some day. Just because he was a male wasn't a good reason. Holly not only knew as much about the job as the Old Man, she also had the same air of command.

But on the other hand, Holly never left Christmas Town unless the entire family took a trip. It'd be kind of hard for her to make the Christmas Eve delivery run since she didn't like to travel. A thought occurred to Leon as he eyed his sister, her long gown swishing around her ankles as she dumped empty cans into the trash and cleaned ashtrays. When was the last time she even visited Christmas Town? He couldn't remember. Oh, well, not his problem right now.

"We'll clean up after ourselves, Holly," Leon said. "But thank you."

He placed his bet and tapped ash onto the clean ashtray. "What does the Old Man want?"

"Oh," Holly's eyes went round with surprise. "Not Dad. The message is from the Boss. She wants to see you ASAP."

"Damn!" Leon hastily pushed back his chair, snubbed out his cigar, and laid his cards face down on the table. "And you wandered around here cleaning without telling me immediately? Damnation. Anybody got any peppermint on them?"

"Number one on the Naughty or Nice list, that's our boy," chortled one of the players, coughing on smoke.

"Choke on your cigar. Here, Leon," Holly handed him a peppermint cane from her pocket.

"Your leathers and hair probably reek," one of the other players pointed out. "Everyone count your chips. Guess the game is over."

"Holly can play my hand out," Leon said. "The Boss in her usual office?"

"Of course," Holly sat down and looked at the cards. "Who's the bid to?"

"I'll be back." Leon took off down the hallways on a dead run, wondering if he ever mentioned to his poker buddies that Holly had their dad's perfect memory and counted cards. Of course, she'd claim all the winnings from the time she sat down until he got back, but then again she was the one to earn them.

Leon made a quick dash to his room, stripped and jumped in the shower, and shampooed as fast as he could. He jerked on a clean pair of black leather pants and a black silk shirt, while he crunched more peppermint between his teeth and swallowed. He shoved his feet back in his boots and hustled down to the kitchen, tying his wet hair back into its normal ponytail as he ran.

The combined scents of cinnamon, ginger, sugar, and vanilla warned Leon just before he got to the kitchens. He slowed down and took some deep breaths. Bolting into the kitchens like a scalded cat would play havoc with the image he was trying to cultivate. His breathing calm, although his heart still raced, he sauntered into the warm room bustling with the controlled madness of Holiday baking.

In the midst of elves stamping out cookies, folding together cake batter, and icing cupcakes stood The Boss. The Christmas cards and holiday songs touted the Old Man's job, but everyone in Christmas Town knew the true power behind the sleigh.

Not much bigger than the elves she supervised, his mom was as round as the snowmen they all liked to build. But unlike the creations made courtesy of the magic of Jack Frost, Mary Claus was warm, both in body and in heart. All long as you didn't get on her bad side because, where Santa and Holly had command authority, Mom had drill sergeant genes.

"Hi, Mom," Leon kissed her cheek. "Sorry I'm late.

Holly caught me during my work out." He reached for a glob of cookie batter.

His mom promptly rapped his fingers with a wooden spoon. "Stay out of that. Work out, my big toe. Working out your hands playing cards and smoking cigars with your buddies is more like it."

Leon blew on his fingers and flexed them. Nope, not even bruised. He wouldn't have any trouble with his motorcycle's controls. "You so don't have the ability to know when we're sleeping or when we're awake."

"I don't need to," she responded. "I developed eyes in the back of my head when my first child was born and a sixth sense to know what they're up to. Besides, Noel, you reek of those filthy cigars."

"Leon, Mom. Call me Leon," he begged "And I took a shower, washed my hair, and changed clothes so I wouldn't stink up your kitchen. How can you smell the cigars?"

"Please, *Noel*," she said with a sneer, "the smoke is in your lungs. All you have to do it talk and we can all smell it. And why does Christmas Spirit get to call you Noel and you get grumpy if the rest of us don't call you Leon?"

"He probably hurt her feelings when he got obnoxious insisting on Leon," his twin sister Joy said, carrying a fanciful frosted cake to their mom for her approval.

Hurting the feelings of someone as sincerely kind as Krista was as cruel as kicking a puppy. When Krista looked at him the first time he griped at her about his name, Leon knew he'd lost that battle. He didn't have that kind of cruelty in him. But he also wasn't going to justify himself to his sister.

"I don't like the name Noel," he stated yet again.

"I don't like the name Leon," Joy continued. "It reminds me of an old man who wears polyester slacks. Besides, we're Joyeux Noel. Not Joyeux Leon. I think you need to go back to Noel," insisted Joy. "There are worse names."

"Name one," he challenged.

"Junior," their mom said dryly. "Be grateful I talked your dad into Noel." After she approved Joy's cake and sent her away, she turned back to Leon. "Why don't you like your name, Noel?"

"Mom, it's a girly name."

"You're named after your Uncle Noel," she said tartly.

"Don't you mean my Aunt Noel who's living in a civil union with Uncle Charlie?"

Mary Claus' lips thinned. "Don't call him 'aunt' and there's nothing wrong with their relationship."

"No, Mom, I didn't say there was. I was just pointing out a fact to make my case. Plus this time of year, everyone thinks it's funny to sing 'No-el, No-el' at me. Like I haven't heard it ten thousand times before?"

Leon didn't like the sudden surge of understanding in his mother's eyes, especially because he saw a flash of pity.

"You're not still bother by all that teasing from Junior High, are you?" she took a pan of cookies out of one oven and shoved another pan in with her second hand.

"Mom," Leon grabbed a warm chocolate chip cookie off the cooling rack and bit it defiantly before she had a free hand to smack him with. He took the time to enjoy the hot sting of the fresh cookie in his fingers and the burn of the melted chocolate on his tongue. His twin Joy walked passed and handed him a cold glass of milk. He dipped in the cookie and ate a second bite, then finally answered, "I'm an adult. That whole thing upset you, Joy, and Krista more than it ever did me."

"Having our son come home with a black eye and a two week suspension did not make me or your dad happy. Of course," she finished taking the cookies off the pan, then began to prep another pan, "we were just as upset when our blond son suddenly became a brunet."

"I like it," Leon said before finishing his cookie.

"I don't," Joy tossed her head, shaking her white-blonde ponytail caught back in a hair net. Her eyes, identical to the ones he saw every day in his mirror, flashed ice blue sparks at him before she walked back to decorate another specialty cake

He drained the milk glass and wiped the milk mustache off with the back of his hand. He'd like to grow a mustache. But then he'd had to keep up on the dye for it the same way he did his eyebrows and hair.

"Mom, did you make me leave my poker night just so you and Joy could harass me about my hair and my name?"

"Of course not. We can do that any time. No, this is different. You know that flu that's ripping through Christmas Town?"

"Yes. Hard not to be aware of it."

"Well, it's been going through the United States, too."

"And your point?"

"Your dad's not getting adequate Naughty and Nice reports back."

"You want me to develop a computer program to extrapolate a curve based on reports coming in from the field? I can do that. All you had to do was swing by the Information Technology office in the morning and my staff and I would have jumped on it immediately." Leon managed to stifle his irritation. He already had his mom annoyed about his name change and hair. There was no point in grumbling at her more about interrupting his poker game with the guys.

His mom was shaking her head. Her white hair bounced in curls all over it. At least, he wasn't stuck with curly hair like a couple of his sisters.

"I'm not worried about a computer program. What you and your staff are doing now is quite sufficient. No, I want you to go to the States and do field work. Several of our field agents are down with the flu. We need someone to supervise and coordinate the data from our agents. And that someone is you."

"But, Mom," Leon protested. "I run the Technology department."

"For which you have a very well trained staff to handle any computer glitches or problems. Besides, if you want correct data for the Naughty and Nice list, then you go to the States and be a mall Santa and get the data. You can get it first hand from the children and gather the reports from other agents.

"Mom," Leon took a deep breath to keep from yelling. "I don't have to do field work for that."

"You're the one who's always spouting 'garbage in, garbage out' and complaining that without adequate data, you can't guarantee the results your dad needs to make sure he has the right number of toys under production. This is your chance to get the raw data and make sure it's what you need to fine tune your program. That program's been a big help for your dad in the past several years. It's taken away a lot of his stress."

"Mom," Leon said intensely under the bustling noise of elves baking and decorating, "please don't start with the guilt again."

"Face facts, Leon," his mom said with a sweet smile he didn't trust for a minute. "Your dad is old. Anything that helps him relieve his stress is a good thing. But sooner or later, he's going to step down and a new Santa Claus will be taking his place. You're the only son. Everyone is looking to you to step up to the plate. And in the long run, making his job easier now will make your job easier in the future."

Mary Claus beamed at him as though she'd found a logical way to persuade him.

"I don't want to be Santa Claus either at a mall or in the future as the real thing."

"Too bad," his mom said with a scowl he spent hours trying to master. The drill sergeant was now in command. "You're going to relieve some of your dad's burdens starting right now. I've had someone pack your bags. You get yourself to Chicago—."

"Chicago?" Leon yelped. "Mom, if I have to do field work, can't I at least go to Florida where it's warm?"

"Chicago," she said firmly. "Your bags will be transported to the apartment that's been rented for our agents in Chicago. If you want to take that motorcycle of yours, you'd better head out to the Transportation barn and get it. But tomorrow morning, you report to the mall office at nine o'clock. Don't you dare pull that Billy Bob Thornton's 'Bad Santa' imitation either. Go."

Leon got out of there.

"Where are you headed, Leon?" his sister Christmas Star asked when he got to the Transportation barn.

"Don't you ever wonder why our parents have such a lack of imagination when it comes to names for us? Holly, Joyeux, *Noel*," Leon managed not to spit. He rolled his Ducati from its stall and joined Chrissy to wait for the Transportation elf. "Then there's Christmas Spirit who we all call Krista and you, the Christmas Star, who we all call Chrissy. Don't you wish your name was something else instead of a Christmasy name?"

Too late Leon remembered who he was talking to. His sister Chrissy had been adopted by his parents after his dad found the orphaned baby girl during his Christmas Eve deliveries. "Oh, damn, Chrissy, I'm sorry."

"Hey, Leon, it's okay. I don't know what my mother might have named me if she'd lived, but I love being Christmas Star and having this wonderful family who calls me Chrissy. I'm sorry you don't like your name though."

"I suppose it's better than Santa Claus," he said glumly, dreading the day he was going to have to put on the Big Guy's suit for real instead of just the mall Santa his mom was making him do. He eyed Chrissy. "Hey, we need to get you girls all married off. Then one of your husbands can take over Santa Claus and I'll be off the hook."

"Ha!" Chrissy said. "Fat chance of that. I'm just looking forward to my vacation and maybe getting a date."

"Where are you going this year?"

"I've got two weeks of hot sun and sand and fruity, frosty drinks with my name on them at an island resort off the coast of Greece."

Leon stepped back and looked at his sister from the top of her head to the soles of her feet, then back up. "You did pack a one-piece bathing suit, didn't you?"

"Oh, sure," Chrissy said with the smile she'd learned from their mother. The smile silently said 'you're so full of reindeer poop, but I love you anyway.' "It's packed right next to my chastity belt. No, Leon, I've got the most gorgeous barely-there bikini. And, by the way, Holly's put a lock on Dad's 'Two Places at One Time' magic dust, so don't think you're going to track me down and scare away any possible dates. I've had enough of that.

"Besides, how are any of us supposed to get husbands to take over Santa Claus' job so you don't have to," Chrissy advanced on him, "if you don't let us date!" In one swift move, she grabbed and twisted his shirt collar until he was nearly choking. "Bother me on this vacation of mine and I'll spend the rest of my life making yours miserable. Got it?"

"Yes," he gasped out, afraid if he said anything else she'd knee him in his nuts.

Chrissy released him and he looked down at his shirt.

He coughed and cleared his throat, relieved he could still breath, much less talk. "At least you didn't tear my shirt."

"Aren't you lucky? Where are you going? Hot date?"

"Chicago. I'm going to do some field work to make sure the Naughty or Nice data is correlated properly."

Chrissy laughed at him. "I told you Mom was going to make you sorry you dyed your hair and eyebrows burnet. What did she do? Stick you as a mall Santa for the Season?"

Oh, double damn, he thought, he'd forgotten to ask how long he was going to be stuck down there. His life sucked.

“She did!” Chrissy laughed again.

Leon polished a few smudges off his Ducati’s gleaming black finish.

“You never have taken me for a ride on that,” Chrissy said, her giggles finally under control.

“Do you see a bitch seat on it?”

“Tsk, tsk. Your language, Leon. You could call it a ‘passenger seat.’ No wonder you hold first place on the Naughty and Nice list. How come you want a new motorcycle anyway?”

“He nearly lost to Donner in the last Reindeer Games,” the Transportation elf said, coming up to them with the traveling magic dust. “Are you ready, Chrissy?”

Laughing almost too hard to answer, Chrissy nodded and picked up her laptop and small traveling case.

“Hey, Leon,” she called, just before the sparkling powder zipped her away. She flashed open her coat to reveal a sundress that barely covered her body. “When you see me again, I’ll be tanned. All over,” she added with a wink. “Have a good time being a mall Santa in freezing Chicago. At least the uniform will keep you warm.”

“Ho...ho...ho,” Leon said as she disappeared. His life really sucked.

Chapter Two

Being a mall Santa sucked. In four hours on the job, Leon had a baby spit up on him, a toddler pee on him, and a whole bunch of kids screaming at the fat stranger in the red velvet suit, white beard and hair. He also discovered some extra heavy duties diapers weren't. He sponged the worse of the brown-yellow baby poop from the suit, but ended up having to change into another suit during the lunch break. He really disliked this costume. The damn red velvet suit, beard, and white wig suit were not only hot, but the appliance to make him fat was heavy.

The only bright spot to the job was his current "Mrs. Claus," Candice Craig. From her slim hands and delicate face, Leon suspected the "fat" dress she wore covered a knock-out body. The costume also didn't cover the dark honey-colored skin of her face and hands. The fake glasses only magnified a pair of dark brown eyes a man could lose his soul in.

Unfortunately, the only chance he had to talk to her was in the brief moments she passed his throne after she took a child back to the parents and was on her away to collect the next kid in line. He thought they'd share lunch together, but a friend of hers came by and the two of them talked the entire time they ate their salads. He ended up taking a power nap on the couch while they talked and ate—kind of reminded him of home with all his chatty sisters. He wanted, hell, he needed to get her away from all this madness and find out exactly what was hidden under her "fat" dress.

But first he had to take to yet another kid who thought Christmas was a time to extort the newest gadget on the market out of the Santa Claus.

"Princess, it's my Santa Claus wish and I can use it however I want. The new model Ducati is coming out with a bigger engine and sleeker design. I want it." With a wince, he realized he needed to apologize to both Krista and his dad. He'd email them when he got back to the apartment he shared with a couple of the other Naughty and Nice field agents.

But for now…

"Listen, Joshua," Leon told the kid on his knee, "you're six years old. You don't need a cell phone or an iPod. How about a bike?"

Joshua's eyes narrowed into slits. "You're supposed to be Santa Claus. You're supposed to get me anything I want."

"No, kid, that's not how it works. You're supposed to tell me what you want for Christmas. If—and here's the catch, Josh—if you're a good boy—and only Santa determines that—then maybe Santa will show up with a Christmas gift for you. And what you get depends on what he thinks is best for you. Now smile for the nice lady and let's get good picture for Mom and Dad."

Personally, Leon didn't think either one of them gave a damn. Mom was currently yakking away on her cell phone. Dad and a couple of other people had just celebrated a touchdown that took place during the pro football game where the score had been text messaged to his cell phone. Plus Dad has his iPod ear buds in. Leon figured old Joshua here just needed his own to talk to Mom and Dad.

"All my friends have cell phones and iPods. I want a cell phone! I want an iPod! You're a terrible Santa Claus."

"Too bad. Right now, I'm the only one you've got. Tell you what, Josh, do a real nice smile at the nice lady, and I'll think about it."

The kid finally turned his head to face the photographer and the Santa Helper, Candice, dressed as Mrs. Santa and looking absolutely hot and nothing like his comfortable Mom, stuck out her tongue at the kid.

Josh promptly laughed. The photographer toggled the button on the camera to get the picture. Candice came with a sucker for Josh and Leon bent his knee so the kid had nowhere to go but slide off.

Or so Leon thought.

Instead, Joshua grabbed a handful of suit jacket and hung on. "I said I want a cell phone and an iPod for Christmas. I smiled for the dumb picture. Now you have to get them for me."

"Not if you're not nice, I don't. If you tear my suit, you're going to be on the Naughty List forever. There's a bunch of kids waiting. You've had your turn, now go with the nice lady."

"Joshua," Candice began unpeeling the kid's fingers from Leon's suit, "asking for cell phones and iPods is kind of like asking for a puppy or a kitten. Santa," she continued with a warning glare at Leon, "has to get permission from Moms and Dads for those kinds of things. If your mom and dad tell Santa it's okay to bring you one, then he'll do it."

"Yeah. Uh. Yeah. That's right." Leon agreed, wondering why he hadn't thought of that excuse. He'd remember it for the next time. "Your parents have to let me know it's okay for you to have that kind of stuff. So, ask your parents and write me a letter care of the North Pole. And, remember," he added, "I'll know if you've faked their permission."

"You're not a nice Santa," Joshua said with another glare. "I don't like you." In one swift movement, the kid's foot shot out and landed squarely on Leon's thigh.

Leon gasped and managed not to deck the halls of the little brat. "You're on the Naughty List forever, kid!"

Candice hustled the kid from the Santa stall with Joshua screaming, "Mom! Dad! The Santa Claus is mean. Mom! Dad!"

The mall security guard came quickly. Candice started talking fast while Leon managed to not rub his thigh. Considering how close the brat had kicked to his groin, Leon was afraid if he touched it, all the parents and kids standing in line might think he was feeling himself up. He shifted in his throne and checked his watch. The end of the shift was too far away.

"You okay?" the photographer called.

Leon nodded. He really, really hated this job.

The security guard wrote something in his notebook and made the parents sign it. The parents looked a little pale when they took the picture of their darling from the photographer's assistant. Candice came back to the Santa throne where Leon sat drinking from a bottle of water and wishing it were vodka.

"You're not going to have to sing the soprano lead in 'The Messiah,' are you?" She asked while she handed him a piece of paper.

"It was a close call. What's this?"

"The parents' names and phone numbers. They were yapping about suing you and the mall for upsetting their kid's image of Christmas. I pointed out their child had kicked you and you could sue them for damages. Since we have witnesses to it and the boy was still whining about wanting a cell phone and an iPod, the parents backed off."

"I owe you, Candice."

"No problem. Part of my job. Ready for the next kiddo?"

"I guess. Want to have supper with me after the shift ends? I need a stiff drink."

"Sorry, sounds nice, but I already have plans for the night."

Her hips swaying under the long velvet skirt, Candice moved to the next child in line. She brought back a little girl with long dark curls tied back from her face with a big red bow. With her pretty Christmas dress, she looked like a specialty Christmas doll to be kept behind glass and treasured.

"This is Sabrina," Candice helped the little girl onto Leon's knee.

"Good afternoon, Sabrina. Can you smile at the

photographer so she can get a nice picture for your mom?"

The photographer clicked a fast shot and Sabrina's mom and the photographer nodded at the digital result.

"Very nice, Sabrina. So, tell Santa. What do you want for Christmas?"

Sabrina's mouth worked and Leon hoped she wasn't puckering up to cry. He really hated it when kids got scared and cried.

"Hey, Sabrina. You want to go back to your mom? You can always have her help you write a letter to Santa at the North Pole."

Her little mouth twisted and she nodded. She slid off his knee. As Candice handed Sabrina a sucker, the little child belched worthy of Donner after an oat pig-out.

"Tell Santa 'thank-you,' Sabrina," called her mother.

Sabrina turned from Candice to him and Leon saw panic in her eyes. "Hey, it's okay. You don't have to talk. You're welcome. Thank you for coming to visit."

Sabrina's mouth worked again and, without any more warning, she barfed all over Leon's red velvet pants.

"Don't people feed their kids anything nutritious any more?" Leon glared at the mess on his pants while he changed in the room the mall had designated for their changing and rest area. "Pepperoni pizza, ice cream, cola, peppermint cane, cookies. No wonder the poor kid got sick. Just look at this."

"I'd rather not," Candice said dryly. "The smell alone is about to make me barf, too. I'm calling the cleaning service and getting this suit, this morning's, and yesterday's picked up as soon as possible. I hate the thought of walking in here tomorrow morning and smelling this."

"Good idea." He crammed the suit into the dry cleaning bag and looked at the couple clean suits still on the rack. "Ask them to bring any they have already have cleaned when they pick up these rather than waiting until Monday and, if they don't have any ready, ask them to put a rush on them."

"Magic word," she sing-songed like he was a five year-old.

Leon swallowed his automatic "bite me" and said, "Please, Ms. Craig."

"Very good, Leon," she responded sounding for all the world like one of his elementary teachers, then her voice took on a more business-like tone. "You don't think the big bosses are going to have a problem with the extra cleaning expenses?"

"Not with my authorization," he said absent-mindedly while pulling a clean pair of pants over the damn fat belly appliance. He pulled the suspenders over his bare shoulders—he'd be damned if he wore a shirt under the fat appliance and the hot coat. He gagged at the smell still on his hands. He needed to wash them again. Hell, he needed a frigging shower. He hated kid puke.

He heard Candice finish the call, relieved to hear her thank them for scheduling to come right away. He knew extra cash always made people more cooperative. Besides, the puke smell was making him nauseated already, too. Like Candice he cringed at the idea of walking in this room in the morning after the smell had a chance to permeate everything.

"What's your position with Christmas Town Fantasies that enables you to casually authorize extra expenditures?" Candice asked as he came from behind the changing screen, carrying the heavy suit jacket and the wig and beard and headed to the restroom to wash his hands. The cool air against his mostly bare upper body felt good, especially since he'd been so hot in the velvet all day.

Working on the knowledge that telling the truth was less likely to be believed than a lie, Leon promptly answered, "I'm Santa Claus' only son. Next in line—unfortunately—to take over the Big Man's job when he retires. Hopefully, not anytime soon." He kept the washroom door opened while he soaped and rinsed his hands. "Right now I'm doing field work to collect proper data for the Naughty and Nice list because some of our regular agents are down with the flu."

From the mirror, he saw Candice's magnified dark eyes dance behind the phony glasses she wore. "Your day job is that boring? Seriously, do you work for Christmas Town Fantasies in your real job? Because I've seen the revised schedule and you've got a forty-hour week as Santa here. Most of the men who do this are retired. You're a little young."

"Seriously. Yes," Leon said with a sigh while putting on the beard and wig and double-checked the fastening of the white eyebrows pasted over his own. "CTF is part a family owned company called Christmas Town, Inc. that also owns a toy manufacturing plant called Claus Toys along with a couple of other businesses. Normally I handle the Informational Technology department, but with the flu knocking out some of our employees. Well, here I am. So, what's your regular gig?"

"Exotic dancer at an exclusive gentlemen's club."

"Oh, please. A classy lady like you?" He shrugged on the coat and buckled its wide belt and they walked out of the room.

"It's a classy club," Candice said with a smile as they left the changing room, locking the door behind them with her key to the room. She tucked it with its candy cane key fob into a pocket.

"Is this why you won't go to supper with me tonight? You'll be stripping at your other gig?" To his pleasure, she looped her hand inside the crook of the arm he bent to her.

"Of course. I have two performances tonight after I leave here."

"Now why would you want to work that hard?" Leon said with a laugh, going along with her joke. "That means you won't get home until one or two A.M. and you have to be back here by eleven tomorrow morning."

"The pay is good. It pays the medical bills for my poor sick momma."

"Yeah, and we've all got to help our parents, don't we?"

"Why else would you be here being Santa Claus?" she pointed out as they approached the Santa house again with its patiently, and some not so patiently, waiting children and parents.

"Good point. How about supper tomorrow night?"

"Already have plans for supper with my sick momma and a bunch of relatives. Smile, Santa. It's show time."

"Ho...ho...ho...."

The rest of the afternoon passed in a more normal routine of fairly well-behaved children smiling for their pictures. At one point, a boy took the sucker Candice handed him and said, "Thank you, Mrs. Craig."

Candice winked at him, "At this job, it's Mrs. Claus. Don't let on to the other kids in school, okay, Jim?"

"Sure thing, Mrs. Cra—, Mrs. Claus. See you Monday."

Mrs. Craig? Mrs.? Oh, damn, damn, damn, ran the regret in Leon's mind.

"You know, Mrs. Craig," he said when she passed his throne to fetch another child. "If you'd mentioned there was a Mr. Craig, I wouldn't have been trying to ask you out."

"He died three years ago," she said smoothly. "That's when I moved back to Chicago."

She brought the next child and waited while the picture was taken and the child submitted her request.

On Candice's next trip in front of him, Leon managed to get out, "I'm sorry for your loss." He thought that sounded pretty sincere considering he was still trying to extradite his foot from his mouth but at least he did managed something other than whooping "hot damn, still got a chance."

"Thank you. He was a good man. I still miss him, but time passes. Life continues."

Every time she passed his spot, he tried probing for a bit more information.

"You told that one boy—Jim? not to let on in school about being Mrs. Claus. Is he in your class?"

"No, he's not."

Kid, picture, request, then he had another chance. "What grade do you teach?"

Her mouth quirked with a smile. "I don't."

Once again Leon had to feign interest in a child's Christmas wish and smile for the camera before she came by his chair alone again.

"Are you one of the school secretaries?"

She shook her head, "No." Did he see a strand of brunette hair trail from underneath the white, curly wig she wore?

When she delivered the next child back to the parent, the photographer's assistant must have mentioned the hair because Leon saw Candice immediate tuck the errant strand away.

"Are you the school principal?" he asked when she came by him. Leon found himself getting a kick out the game of Twenty Questions with the mystery Mrs. Craig aka Mrs. Claus.

"No, I'm not." Her laugh made Leon want to hear it more.

He liked the pink blooming under golden brown skin covering her high cheek bones.

She left for a few minutes when the dry cleaner's rep came to pick up the soiled costumes. With relief, Leon saw the rep carried several opaque bags CTF supplied to all the dry cleaners for delivery of their cleaned costumes to help maintain children's illusions—at least those from who still had illusions about Santa. While the photographer and the assistant pitch hit adequately during the time Candice was gone with the cleaning rep, Leon missed her rosy lips lifted in a smile, missed the laughing joy of life in her voice.

Leon knew he could just wait until their shift ended to talk with her, but he didn't know how fast she'd be cutting out to go to whatever she had planned for tonight.

He broke into a cold sweat at his sudden thought.

Candice came back with the cleaning rep who hauled the bags of soiled costumes and Leon signed the authorization for the rush job. As soon as the rep left, Candice brought another child.

In the few moment after the child was finished and before the next one came, Leon asked the question that was making his stomach burn.

"Have you got a date tonight?"

"No," the rosy color Leon had been enjoying all afternoon drained away. "I told you I've got two performances tonight."

"Oh, right," he agreed. "It's your gig as an exotic dancer at the classy gentlemen's club."

"That's right."

She came back with a little boy and an even smaller girl. "This is José and his sister Marta." In Spanish, she added, "Sit on Santa Claus' lap and we'll take your picture. I'll translate so he'll know what you want for Christmas."

Leon promptly answered in Spanish, "Thank you, Mrs. Claus, but I can talk to José and Marta myself."

"Muy bueño, Señor Claus, esta bien." Candice said with a smile that lit up Leon's heart.

After returning José and Marta to their parents, Leon asked, "Are you the bi-lingual coordinator for the school?"

"No, I'm second generation. My grandparents were Mexican immigrants. I grew up speaking Spanish at home and English everywhere else. How did you learn Spanish? You don't sound like you learned it from a textbook."

"My parents are both linguists," Leon used the standard family storyline they used to cover the magic that enabled Santa to speak with anyone who believed in him, magic easily accessible by the entire family and everyone in Christmas Town when needed. "They started us kids young. I speak English, Spanish, French, German,

Portuguese, Russian, and am learning Japanese."

"Regular United Nations there."

"Just part of Christmas magic," Leon said with a chuckle, knowing the laugh would make her think he was making a joke.

After the last child for this shift had her photo taken, Leon was more than ready to head for a bar and a stiff drink. As soon as they got in the changing room, they exchanged greetings with the new Santa and Mrs. who headed out to start their shifts.

Behind his own changing screen, he heard the rustle and slither of Candice changing into street clothes and hanging up the Mrs. Claus outfit. He hung up his own costume and took off the belly and wondered what color her panties and bra were and if she wore a thong and barely there cups or something more conservative. With all her silly talk about being a stripper, he had visions of her honey-gold skin on full display while she wrapped herself around a pole as an exotic dancer. His favorite body part let him know a lap dance would be really nice. Maybe some day soon they'd be able to get together and he'd get her to pretend to be a stripper for him. In the meantime, he carried his boots, helmet, leather jacket out to the couch in the common area.

"How about one quick drink before we go our separate ways tonight?" Leon pulled on one boot while Candice walked out of the women's changing area, carrying a heavy coat and her own boots.

He knew she had a great body underneath Mrs. Claus' fat suit. Gray wool slacks caressed slim legs and a round bottom, a thick dark pink sweater covered the mounds of breasts perfectly shaped for a man's hands. Long black hair spilled over her shoulders and was pushed behind her ears.

"I really don't have time. I need to catch the El." She pulled a black boot over a small foot covered with a thick sock. "What kind of motorcycle do you ride?" She nodded at his helmet.

"A Ducati."

"Nice. Your dad give it to you for Christmas?" she said with a laugh.

"Yeah. One of the perks of being Santa's only son," he agreed. He reminded himself again to send that groveling apology to Krista and the Old Man. He'd find something a bit more selfless for his Christmas wish than the new model Ducati. "You know motorcycles?"

"I have a Harley."

"A Harley?" Definitely his kind of woman. "Belong to the local Harley club?"

"Yes, my husband and I joined when he bought me my bike. I've put it in storage for the winter. I don't have enough confidence to drive it when the weather is icy."

"I can handle ice and snow easily. It's not my skill I worry about, it's the other drivers on the roads with ice and snow.

"I'm so with you on that. That's why I take the El. Even when I had my car, I still felt safer riding it on icy days than driving."

"Well, if you won't join me for a drink, how about we get a couple of cups of coffee and I'll walk you to the El station?" Leon found his heart stuck in his throat the way it had the first time he'd asked a girl to a dance when he was a teenager.

Candice smiled at him, her eyes peeking at him from under her lashes. She wore no make-up and looked like a golden-rosy, fresh, ripe apricot ready to pick from the tree.

His mouth watered at the thought of tasting her.

"Sure, that sounds nice."

Leon managed, just barely, from jumping up and clicking his heels together in excitement. Stay cool, he reminded himself. Suave, debonair, sophisticated.

"Great," Leon stamped on his second boot. They picked up coffees, then at the exit door to the mall, bundled up in their coats, gloves, and scarves, took one last deep breath of the warm mall air, then stepped out into the biting wind.

"So what are you doing tonight?" he asked while they fought the wind.

"I keep telling you."

"Right. Exotic dancer. I give up. Keep your secret."

Sipping on the coffee while they walked through the blowing wind, Leon hunted for topics. Somehow he didn't think "How about a hotel and strip naked for me later after you finish whatever secret thing you're doing tonight?" was exactly suave, debonair, or sophisticated.

"Hey, what do you do at the school?"

"If you guess," Candice's eyes sparkled like black diamonds, "I might consider having breakfast with you in the morning."

"All right! Let me think. Not a teacher, not the bilingual coordinated, not the principal. Secretary? Custodian? Cafeteria lady?"

She laughed and shook her head at each guess. "Here comes my train. One last guess."

"Can I have a hint?"

Her lips, still rosy despite the freezing wind, smiled. "Marian."

"Marian. Marian." An old musical his mom liked to watch slid into his brain. "Marian the Librarian! You're the school librarian!"

Candice laughed while she went through the turnstyle to go to the train. He grabbed her hand.

"Hey, where I can I pick you up for breakfast in the morning?"

"A Ducati doesn't have a bitch seat, Leon. Why don't you meet me here at 9:30 and we'll find someplace nearby?" She pulled her hand from his and ran to the train doors.

He yelled, "I can borrow a car!"

"Okay. Pick me up at my apartment."

"What's your address?"

"You're Santa's only son. Santa knows where everyone lives. Figure it out."

The doors slid shut on her smiling face and the train headed down the track.

Chapter Three

Leon pulled more yarn from the skein and crocheted a few more rows on the latest blanket. There had to be a way to hack into the Old Man's private files to get Candice's address. His problem was, he realized with disgust, he was too damn good at his job. He developed the Naughty and Nice software. Surely he could figure out a damn back door without having to run a spy program to break the Old Man's password.

"You know, for someone who professes to be a bad-ass," Sarah, one of the Santa operatives said as she worked to input her data into the computer for the Naughty and Nice list, "that constant crocheting really blows the image."

"Bite me. This happens to be my one hundredth blanket for The Linus Project. There's been a lot of little kids comforted by the blankets I've made. My goal is five hundred. Did you finish your homework?" he smirked at the curly-haired toddler-appearing elf who happened to be older than he. Her current assignment had her undercover at an elementary school as a kindergarten student, not a teacher. "You don't want to have to do it all on Sunday night."

"Oh, please. Like I can't do that in my sleep, brat," she snapped back at him. "At least I managed to wrangle my way out of playing Rudolph in the kindergarten Christmas play."

"Now that I would have paid money to see," he crocheted another row, then took a swig of his beer while he studied the guts of his Naughty and Nice software program on his laptop.

"As my daddy in this scheme, you still have to be

there."

Leon groaned. "Off key kindergartens massacring Christmas songs. Oh, what fun. I thought Clay was playing your father in this scenario. Damn it, there has to be a back door." He scowled at the laptop's screen and drained his beer.

"Our other roommate has been designated to be my dad," said Barney, also an elf, looked about six years-old and had been married for Leon's entire life to Sarah. Barney at spent his weekdays at a different elementary school posing as a First Grader and, like Sarah, weekends at different malls and stores checking out the kids and the level of toys in stock.

Barney gave a bowl of ice cream to Sarah along with a juicy kiss that made Leon flat out jealous because he already wanted to kiss Candice that way and didn't even know her address. Damnation.

Barney sat down on the couch beside Leon and began scooping up his ice cream with oatmeal cookies. He propped his sock clad feet on the coffee table next to Leon's laptop. "What are you looking at, Leon?"

"Studying this damn program. Between Joseph, Lorena, and me, we made it hacker proof."

"Which program is that?"

"The Naughty and Nice list," said Sarah around a mouthful of ice cream and cookies.

"We all input data into it every evening, what's so hard about finding out some information from it?"

"Have you ever gone looking for someone's name?" Leon challenged.

"Nope, never had any need."

"Try." Leon closed the software guts and opened the Naughty and Nice regular program.

Barney logged in under his own name and password. When the Search screen came up, he asked, "Who are you looking for?"

"Candice Craig."

Barney typed it in and hit Enter. Immediately the

screen went blank. Up popped Santa Claus' frowning face and a swinging index finger.

"Uh, uh, uh. Only bad little boys and girls try to peek at someone else's information. Don't make me have to add you to the Naughty List."

Sarah came running over from the computer she'd been using and clasped Barney's hand.

Barney's face paled. "Is that linked straight to Santa along with my password and name?"

"No," Leon assured them. "It's just a warning. I programmed it. Don't worry about it. It's just a deterrent."

"Your jokes are sick, Leon," Sarah said. "Makes me wish Joshua had aimed an inch or so higher." She gave a huff, kissed Barney, and went back to her computer. "Why don't you show Barney your bruise?" she added sweetly.

Leon shifted the ice pack against his thigh. "No."

"Aw, come on, show me the bruise," Barney said with a laugh. "Poor Leon." He ducked away from the cushion Leon threw at him.

"Poor Leon what?" Clay, the fourth apartment mate, walked in from his shift as Santa at a different mall accompanied by the aroma of pizza from the box he carried with him along with a brown bag.

"Please tell me that's another six pack," Leon said. "This is the last one from the 'frig and I don't want to have to drag out into the cold again to get more."

"What else goes with pizza? So, what happened?"

"Leon got kicked by a kid," Barney said, finishing his ice cream and standing up to carry his bowl to the kitchen.

"Almost did damage to his favorite body part," Sarah added, handing her empty bowl to him to take back to the kitchen.

"I thought you had more practice at this Santa Claus job, old boy." Clay dropped down to the Barney's vacant space on the couch, popped opened a beer and handed it to Leon. "Here, you need this more than I do."

"Thanks," Leon took a swig, pulled up his software

program again, and picked up his crocheting.

"Always reminds me of that old Sylvester Stallone, Sandra Bullock movie when you do that. The one where Stallone was a cop who'd been iced—literally—and came out of it knowing how to knit while Wesley Snipes came out knowing how to make a bomb from a gum wrapper."

"Yeah, yeah, you all can just stop making fun of my hobby now or—."

"Or you'll tell your daddy on us?" snickered Clay.

"Oooh, we're gonna end up on the Naughty List."

"Right along with Leon and the kid who kicked him."

"So, how'd this kid manage to get the drop on you?" Clay asked around a mouthful of pizza.

"Blinded by love," sang Sarah, logging off the program. "All yours, lover."

"Thanks, gorgeous." They exchanged another juicy kiss while Leon exchanged an eye roll with Clay.

"Get a room, you two."

"They've got one. I don't know about you, but they keep me awake half the night."

"I'll get you both some earplugs tomorrow while I scout the stores for the Naughty and Nice list," Sarah said when she came up for air. "Hurry up, lover. I'm going to change into something more comfortable."

Leon watched her leave the room. She wore a pair of pink overalls with a Disney princess shirt under it and Disney princess tennis shoes. "You know, we're damn lucky CPS doesn't have a clue what happens in this apartment. They'd think we're a bunch of perverts."

"So, you got distracted by a woman, huh? About damn time. Want a beer, Barney?"

"Yeah, thanks, Clay."

Clay strolled across the room and handed him one while Barney continued his data input still talking, "Ain't that the truth about Leon? Between this sudden urge to look like a punk and the crocheting, I'd begun to worry about his orientation. The black leather clothes and dying his hair and eyebrows black just scream of 'I am a man!'

as if anyone might have a doubt."

"Yeah," Clay agreed, sitting back down on the couch, "kind of wondering myself if he were taking after his Aunt Noel."

"Ha, ha," Leon drank some beer and scowled at Clay and Barney laughing like a couple of loons. "I've had lots of girlfriends. And what the hell's wrong with a change of appearance?"

"You're just going overboard, Leon," Sarah stood in the doorway in quilted robe. "You've got that hotshot motorcycle, changed your name, dyed your hair. The length doesn't bother me. I know you're growing it out again for Locks of Love, but still. You didn't have to dye it."

"I like it black."

"From a female's point of view, let me tell you, you look better as a blond."

"Huh?" Just because she used to baby-sit him when he was a little kid, Leon resented Sarah always nagging him like a second mother or one of his sisters.

"Your skin coloring's not right. You look sallow and sickly as a brunet."

"Thanks a bunch."

"And Leon is a punk name," Barney added. "Sounds like someone who goes looking for trouble. Go back to Noel."

"Oh, like my Aunt Noel? This suggestion from the man who's wearing a cartoon character sweatshirt and who wears tennis shoes that flash lights when he walks and criticizes me for making blankets for traumatized children being helped by The Linus Project?"

Barney studied Leon making him feel like a squirmy worm. No, a worm had more dignity. More like the way-too-drunk who ate the tequila worm. Or, Leon wanted to squirm at the thought, a spoiled brat who threw a temper tantrum.

Leon swallowed his self-humiliation which tasted as nasty as the tequila worm from the trip to Cozumel when he was eighteen. "I'm sorry. I lost my temper. I'm tired of everyone criticizing my hair and teasing me about my hobby."

"Yeah, well, okay. I'm sorry about the teasing," Barney apologized. "You're right. The Linus Project is a really worthwhile program. You deserve admiration about contributing to it rather than being teased."

Clay cleared his throat. "I'm sorry about picking on you about the crocheting, too."

"But your black hair still sucks," Sarah added.

"Thanks a bunch. Mom put you up to this?"

"Naw, just stating the obvious."

"Sarah, stop harassing the boy," Barney said without looking up from his data while his fingers flew over the keyboard. "He has to live with his own decisions."

"Yeah, but we have to look at it."

Clay shoved the pizza carton out of his way, retrieved his own laptop from under the coffee table, and booted it up. He popped open another beer and handed it to Sarah who wedged herself on the couch between him and Leon.

"Tell me about this woman who distracted you enough that a kid kicked you," Clay said as he started putting his data into the Naughty and Nice program.

"Yeah, Leon, maybe we can help," Sarah added.

Leon stared at the guts of his software program again, trying to divine a vision to help him go into a back door. He crocheted furiously, hoping that by keeping the creative side of his mind busy, his logical side might find the solution.

He'd forgotten what an elegant program he'd created. Like studying a painting done by several artists, he saw the distinct differences in the programming where Lorena and Joseph had written their sections to mesh into his and where he had smoothed all the styles into a single purposeful operation. But with three of them working on it, they'd definitely covered their asses and plugged any possible holes. Even the contractor they'd hire specifically to hack into it had admitted defeat.

"Leon? Hello, Leon? The woman? Why are you still trying to get into the Naughty and Nice program?"

"I need a back door to hack into the Old Man's account. I need to find her address."

"Why? Are you planning to stalk Ms. Candice Craig?"

"Mrs." Leon corrected. At the sudden silence, he looked up from the laptop monitor. "Widowed several years ago. Doesn't even wear her wedding band any longer. I haven't deteriorated into that bad on the Naughty List."

Relief flashed across all three faces.

"And I'm not planning to stalk her. I'm taking her out for breakfast provided I can find her address. And borrow your car, Clay?"

"I get to drive the Ducati?"

"Natch."

"Deal."

"Pity you two aren't elves and can't use the magic traveling dust without the Transportation elf's help," Sarah gloated.

"Such are the limitation of the non-elf," Clay said, with the pop and hiss of opening the last can of beer. "Now I get to use the Ducati, if we find Mrs. Craig's address. Why didn't she give it to you anyway? Playing hard to get?"

"I guess so, in a way. She thought I was joking when I told her I was Santa's only son, so she set me the challenge of finding her. 'Since Santa knows where everyone lives.'" he quoted her response. "If I can't find her, I'm supposed to me her at the El station near the mall at 9:30 in the morning and we'll go to breakfast then."

"And, of course, she's had her personal information deleted from the easy access data bases. And you don't have authorization to get into the other data bases."

"Exactly. And the Old Man doesn't share his information either. 'Confidentially, son, confidentially.' And don't suggest I suck up to Holly because she's just as tight lipped as he is when it comes to the Old Man's business."

Clay grinned at him. "I've got a back door of my own. Let me have the Ducati for a week and I'll try my connection."

Sarah and Barney both started to laugh. Leon looked at each of them. "What is so funny?"

"Is it a deal?" Clay asked.

"Yeah, yeah. Deal. You can use my Ducati for a week and I'll drive your clunker. Who's your connection?"

Clay unsnapped his cell phone from his belt with the same pizzazz his great-grandfather, a sheriff who help civilized the Old West, whipped out his six-shooter. He hit the first speed dial button. "Hey, Joy, how are you doing, darlin'?"

"Joy? My Joy? My twin Joyeux?" Leon's head swiveled from Clay to Sarah to Barney, all of whom grinned at him. "Darlin'? he hissed at Clay who had the audacity to wink at him.

"Yeah, that's your brother. Yeah, I know he's over-protective. But he might soon get his own life, then maybe he'll leave you girls alone." Clay paused, then said, "Well, darlin'—"

"Darlin'?" Leon nearly strangled on the word. He didn't know what was worse—some man calling his sister 'darlin" while wearing a smile normally only produced by winning the entire pot at poker or Sarah and Barney snickering at him.

"Oh, darlin', that's just your twin being a pain in the ass. Yeah, that's right. Standard operating procedure with him. The only reason I'm trying to help him out is I'll get to ride the Ducati for the next week and he'll be stuck with my junker."

Leon weighed the advantage of Clay getting Joy to help find Candice's address versus getting Clay off the phone with his sister. His sister, damn it. Clay and Joy?

Reluctantly Leon faced the unpleasant fact he was out of luck trying to break the relationship up. In the first place, Joy might finish the job Joshua started this afternoon and she knew how to aim better. Leon shifted the ice pack again and hoped he didn't limp in the morning.

Plus he liked Clay. If Joy dated someone, at least she picked someone he liked. Not that she gave a damn what his feelings about the matter were—obviously. Otherwise she would have told him.

Oh, great, he realized with disgust, he was feeling sorry for himself just because his twin didn't bother to tell him she was dating a friend of his. Like he would have been happy to find out earlier? But, damn it, when they were little, he knew all her secrets and his other sisters' secrets, too. When did they stop telling him things?

Probably, his conscious smacked him across the head, it started when he beat up the boy in high school who broke Holly's heart and insisted on double-dating with Krista and Chrissy, not to mention Joy who never got to talk to a boy alone if her brother was anywhere near.

But he just wanted to take care of his sisters, he tried to justify to himself.

Almost if his sisters were all in the room with him, he heard their voices raised in chorus, "You can stop it right now. We can take care of ourselves."

"Just get the address for him. Anything else he wants to know about the lady, he can find out on his own. That's why it's called dating. Thanks, Joy, we'll be waiting for your text message. And, I'll call you later."

On the last sentence, Clay's voice dropped to a deep tone that made Leon squirm. He'd used the tone himself with former lovers. But, damn it, Clay was using it on Joy? His twin sister? Hell, he hoped they weren't having phone sex.

Oh, cripes, he wished he hadn't thought about them and sex. His stomach roiled at the thought of the two of them in bed. Together. Joy naked and doing the sweaty nasty with Clay?

He might have to kill Clay anyway and take his

chances with Joy's ire. Now to figure out how to get rid of the body. Damn shame the magic transportation dust the elves used didn't work on a human like Clay.

Surely, the Old Man would understand the necessity of killing Clay. He might have a way to dump the body. He probably had a bag of coal labeled for Joy already.

But then, if Joy came through with Candice's address, he might eventually be able to make some naked, sweaty plans of his own. Did he really have any right to judge his twin? Or the rest of his sisters? His head logically answered, "No." His gut screamed, "Kill the bastards who got his sisters naked!"

Leon took firm control of his gut reaction. He'd have time later to kill Clay and anyone else who got one of his sisters naked. For now, he wanted Candice's address. Leon forced himself to make civil conversation.

"How is Joy going to get Candice's address?"

"She figured your mom might be able to talk your dad into releasing the address."

"She's going to tell Mom and Dad!" Leon yelped.

"Gotcha!" Clay yelled. Sarah and Barney joined him in hooting with laughter.

"Sometime when you least expect it, I'm going to kill you," Leon promised.

"At least," Sarah put her empty beer can on the top of the pyramid stack on the empty pizza carton, "he's not threatening to put you on the Naughty List."

"You say that like Santa and Mary don't know all about Joy and me."

"Yeah, we've all known," Barney informed Leon. "They've been dating over a year. You're about the only one who didn't know."

"Over a year?" Was he that self-absorbed he hadn't realized his twin had been dating his friend? Yes, he had been. He'd been so concerned about changing his image from the nice geek Noel to someone who'd get more respect—or so he had thought, because it hadn't happened—he hadn't paid attention to what anyone else did. And just wait a damn minute. He narrowed his eyes at Clay. "Mary? Mary? Since when do you call my mom 'Mary?'"

"Since Joy and I became unofficially engaged at Thanksgiving," Clay said. His eyes crinkled with laughter while Sarah squealed and jumped up to hug him.

Leon glared at Clay. "She's not wearing a ring and how come no one told me?"

"Aw, poor Leon. Left all alone in dark," Barney said shaking Clay's hand. "Congratulations, Clay. She's a wonderful girl. May you have a terrific life together. Although that may be a stretch considering who your brother-in-law is going to be. You can let go of my wife any time now."

"Thanks, Barney and Sarah," Clay said releasing Sarah from his hug. She went straight into Barney's. "Joy wanted her engagement ring as her Christmas present. She wants to announce our engagement at a party after Christmas so not to interfere with the rush we're all dealing with right now. We're having a March wedding with a honeymoon in Hawaii. I was going to ask you to be my Best Man, but with that sour look on your face, I'm not sure any longer. You might slit my throat and then Joy will have to kill you."

"I'm sorry," Leon swallowed hard. He was losing his twin. Never again would she turn to him with her problems. From now on, Clay would know her secrets and he wouldn't. Just like he didn't know about this engagement. Life was going to be very strange. "It's a shock. I just found out you and Joy are dating, um, have been dating. Then you hit me with this engagement news."

"On the plus side, Leon, you're finally going to be gaining a brother," Sarah pointed out.

"Come on, gorgeous. It's getting late. Let's go to bed and leave these boys to discuss their future together privately."

"And we need some private time of our own," Sarah

agreed. Arms wrapped around each other, they headed to their bedroom.

"Yeah, Barney's right. I'm finally getting a brother. And at least I like you, Clay. Most of the time." Come to think about it, maybe Clay might be willing to take over the Santa Claus magic when the Old Man retired. He'd been doing the mall gigs for years now. This might be his chance to escape everyone's automatic assumption he'd be the next Santa Claus.

Clay looked at him solemnly. "I like you most of the time, too. Except for times like right now when you get that look on your face like you're plotting something."

"Nothing you need to worry about." At least not now, Leon added silently. But let's just see what happens when the Old Man decides to retire. "Welcome to the family. I'll keep my mouth shut until you and Joy make the official announcement. Can I at least congratulate her or do you think her feelings will be hurt that you've told me?"

It took him a minute to realize those words came out of his mouth. He actually asked for Clay's opinion about Joy's feelings. Maybe he was going to be able to accept this situation easier than he thought at first.

"She told me to go ahead and tell all my roommates," Clay said with a satisfied smile. "She knows I'm ready to shout it from the rooftops."

Leon's cell phone beeped with the text message signal. Joy's cell phone number showed. When he thumbed View, an address popped up. He hit reply.

"Thanks," he text back. "Congrats engagement. Clay good man. Luv U."

A few moments later, Joy's text popped up again. "He the Best. Luv U 2."

Despite Joy's affirmation of her love to him, jealously still galled his stomach. His memory gave him the sound of Joy's voice through the years. At four, "You're the bestest, Noel." At eight, "My brother is the best." At twelve after her first crush stamped on her heart. "I'll always love you best, Noel." At college during a companionable night watching movies and drinking in the apartment they shared, "You're always my best friend."

Now Clay was the best and he was just her twin.

But he wanted her happy, the way he wanted all his sisters to be happy.

"Alwys b happy." he text to her.

"4 evr," came back .

Leon turned to Clay, busy putting in his data and pretending to ignore Leon's and Joy's text messages to each other. "Take care of her."

"Promise."

Male bonding done, Leon busied himself with getting GPS directions to Candice's apartment house, then correlating the El routes and schedules to figure out what she had to take to get to the station by the mall at 9:30 in the morning. He wanted to be waiting outside her apartment early, just in case she decided to run errands before heading to the El.

Chapter Four

Candice pulled on her gloves and wrapped her muffler against the wind outside before she stepped out of main door of her apartment building. Then she saw her breakfast date.

Wearing a black leather coat, with a dark maroon knitted ski cap and matching muffler, Leon leaned against the front fender of an old beat-up Ford Escort. His long legs in black jeans were crossed at the ankles of his black boots. He pulled the muffler off the bottom half of his face and smiled at her.

Despite the wind, cold and sharp enough to freeze a person's eyeballs, his smile warmed her as though someone had turned on a blast furnace. This heat though started deep inside in her most intimate being and spread through her, tightening her breasts and making her melt.

"Son of a gun."

"Nope," he said with a grin, "son of Santa." He walked to her and kissed her, his mouth warm against her cheek in the cold morning wind. "Morning. Ready for breakfast?"

"Sure," she replied easily, slipping into the passenger seat after Leon opened the front door.

He shut the door, which promptly bounced open.

"I'm going to have to slam it," he warned.

"Go for it."

Leon banged it shut. It flew open and into him, making him gasp. Something hit the pavement with a metallic ping. Leon hung onto the contrary door, breathing heavily.

"Are you okay?" Candice got out of the car, prepared to catch him or call 9-1-1, whichever might be necessary.

"Yeah, just knocked my breath out. If it wasn't winter and I didn't have on this heavy coat, it might have hurt, but..." he took another deep breath. "Okay. Let me try again."

Candice started to get into the car, then glanced at the door. "The door's not going to stay shut." She stuck her finger in the empty socket where the latch was supposed to be. Leon groaned.

"I heard something hit the ground." She searched, then bent down, and retrieved the broken piece. "Yes, here it is."

"Damn."

"Why don't I run up to my apartment and get some wire? We can wire it shut temporarily and you can get it fixed later." She came back a few minutes later with what had been a thin wire clothes hanger. "I cut it with pliers while I was upstairs so I didn't have to make a second trip up to take the pliers back."

"Smart lady. Thanks." Leon had already set the door into the frame and wrapped the wire through the open window around the door frame and the column between the front door and the back door.

Candice looked at the still sagging door. "Leon, I wouldn't feel safe riding with the door like that. I'd be afraid it'll fall off."

"You can ride in the back seat."

"I'm serious. I think it's going to fall off the first time you hit a pothole and maybe cause someone else to have an accident when it falls. It needs to be fixed."

"The whole car needs to be junked."

"Let me make a call." Candice called her uncle and told him about the problem while Leon watched her. "Thanks, I'll have him leave the keys with Momma." She snapped the cell phone shut and told Leon, "I'll get in the backseat and direct you around the building to the tenant parking. You can leave it in the slot reserved for our apartment. We don't use it right now. I sold my car a few months back. Either my uncle or one of my cousins will fix the door later this afternoon and you can come back after work to pick it up and stay for supper."

"That's asking a lot of your family."

"That's what family's for. It's not a problem. They'll be here for supper tonight anyway, so they'll fix it."

"I don't want to impose on your family dinner."

"Again," she said, getting into the backseat, "this is not a problem. It's potluck so we can stop and pick up something on the way back from the El if you want to contribute. My uncle owns a car repair shop and he won't be fixing the car door for free. He'll charge you for parts and labor, although he won't charge for coming over here or Sunday rates. Now, come on. Park the car. We'll leave the keys with Momma and go have breakfast before we catch the El."

But when they stood outside her apartment, Candice took one sniff and turned to Leon. "I hope you like chorizo and eggs because it smells like Momma's started breakfast."

"Smells great, but how did she know we were coming?"

"Family grapevine. I called my uncle, he told my aunt, she called Momma. You watch." she unlocked the door.

"Ah, good, Candy, Tia Yolanda called and said your cousin Raul will be here this afternoon to fix Leon's car." Unlike Candice, her English held the intonations of the Spanish she learned to speak first. "And you must be Leon. I'm fixing your breakfast. No need to go to a restaurant."

It made Candice happy to see a sparkle in her mom's eyes and some color in her face. She'd even gone to the trouble to pop on a wig. "You didn't have to bother Momma, but thank you. Momma, this is Leon. Leon, this is my momma, Carmelita Hernandez."

"I'm pleased to meet you, Mrs. Hernandez. Thank you for making our breakfast. It smells wonderful."

"Take off your coats and come to the kitchen. Do you

want coffee? Candy, hang up the man's coat and fix him some coffee."

"The Women's Movement skipped Momma and my aunts," Candice said with a grin, watching her mom bustle back into the kitchen where the Mexican sausage sizzled and popped. No surprise, she also smelled flour tortillas cooking.

To her astonishment, Leon helped her out of her coat. "Missed my household, too. My dad taught me to hold open doors, pull out chairs, and," he hung up her coat on the rack nailed to the wall beside the door, "hang up coats." He added his jacket and muffler to the rack, stuffing his cap into a coat pocket.

"Thanks. Coffee, then while I help Momma finish breakfast?"

"Sure, thanks. Candy, is it?" he added with a grin.

"Only to Momma," she told him in the same tone she used with rambunctious children in the library.

"Yes, ma'am. This is none of my business, but is your mother ill?"

"Cancer," she answered briskly, having learned to hide her grief and worry. "We're buying time with some of the experimental drugs."

"I'm sorry," he said quietly. "I thought you were joking about needing money to help your 'poor sick momma.'"

"Unfortunately, the medical insurance only goes so far. We're getting along. With my job and two part-time jobs plus help from the family and a couple of fund-raisers they've sponsored, we're getting along. It's tight, but the medications are keeping her with us. And, as you can see, she has some really good days. Like today." Candice threaded her hand under Leon's upper arm and tugged his bicep, enjoying the warmth of his arm radiating through his sweater and the flex of the muscle. Just the little bit she'd seen of him made her aware he worked out and hid a really great body under that fat suit and now with his sweater over a shirt.

Too bad she didn't have time to pursue more than an acquaintance and pleasant working relationship with him. Besides not having the time, she didn't dare let him get close enough to her to realize what her second part-time job was—the job paid so much more than playing Mrs. Claus.

Automatically, she touched the statue of St. Jude, patron saint of lost causes, on the small altar her mom kept and then the icon of Mary Magdalene. Despite her assurance to Leon, they desperately needed all the money she earned. And she'd do anything to add days to her only remaining parent's life.

"Sit, sit, Leon. Candy, fix the man some coffee." Her mom told her while the old wooden rolling pin clunked on the cabinet as she rolled out another tortilla.

Candice poured coffee for all three of them, then she nudged her momma away from the stove. "I'll finish this up. You go sit and drink your coffee."

She flipped the cooked tortilla off the griddle and tossed on the one her mother had rolled out. Checking the pork sausage pungent with the Mexican spices that were the comfort food of her childhood, Candice decided it was cooked enough to add the already scrambled. She flipped the flour tortilla on the griddle, then added the beaten eggs into the chorizo. She added the finished tortilla to the stack and finished scrambling the eggs and sausage together. With that cooked and the pan off the burner, she rolled out and cooked a few more tortillas.

Throughout the meal preparation, she kept an ear on the idle conversation at the kitchen table, occasionally trying to redirect the conversation if she thought her mom was probing too near Leon's personal business. So far they learned he was the only son with four sisters, one of whom was his twin. His twin sister was engaged, but "It's still pretty much a secret for now. They're going to have an official announcement party after Christmas."

Then she heard, "That's a very old car you drive Leon. Is the Christmas company your family owns not making enough money that they can't afford to pay you enough for a good car?"

"Momma! That's none of your business." Plus Candice had no intention of letting her know Leon normally drove one of the most costly motorcycles around. She'd get the aunts busy with wedding plans. Heck, just having him to breakfast, getting her uncle to arrange repairs on the car he drove, and then bringing him back here for dinner with the family was going to have everyone planning the wedding. And they hadn't even had a date yet. Breakfast in the family kitchen wasn't exactly an intimate meeting.

Leon laughed. "It's a pile of junk, isn't it? It's not mine. I have a motorcycle, but it doesn't have a passenger seat. That's my sister's fiancé's car. He and I are roommates right now. Actually, he has a better car and truck at his home in Montana. The problem is for two years in a row, he had cars stolen and stripped while he was doing the mall Santa Claus job for the family company. Last year he bought that piece of junk because he figured no one would steal it."

"Steal it? It may get towed away by the city as abandoned if he's not careful," Candice told Leon who just laughed.

"That's his problem then, isn't it?"

They ate the meal in companionable conversation. After washing the few dishes, Candice and Leon caught the El.

In the relatively quiet of the Sunday morning El, Leon said again, "I really do appreciate you getting your uncle and cousin to take care of that door latch for me."

"You're welcome."

"And I will take you out to breakfast or maybe supper some night before you start your evening shift."

"Thanks. I'll look forward to it."

"So, what is your second part-time job?"

Candice clucked her tongue at him, "Tsk, tsk, Santa's only son, I keep telling you I'm an exotic dancer at a classy gentlemen's club."

"I'm a classy gentlemen. Maybe I'll catch your show some day," his pale blue eyes lit with laughter. "If I knew the name of the club."

"You discovered where I live. You can try to figure that out yourself also."

"I'll track you down. Some night when you're twisting around a pole, you'll look into the audience and see me watching you."

"In your dreams," Candice joined in his laughter at her "joke" while her mind screamed Oh, God, over my dead body you'll see me in next-to-nothing with money stuffed into my g-string and string bra while men yell nasty comments. The money, she reminded herself as she did during every performance, helped keep her momma alive and out of pain. What the money paid for made up for the humiliation.

Abruptly, she changed the conversation. "Why do you dye your hair black? What color is naturally? Blond?"

Leon stared at her. "I like it black. Why do you ask? And how do you know"

She shrugged. "I grew up with brunets. I noticed your arms when you changed costumes yesterday. What little hair you have on your arms is blond. Plus your coloring isn't right for a brunet."

"Let me guess. You think my skin looks sallow and sickly."

"I wouldn't go that far," Candice said, taken aback by his irritation. "It's just a little pale for a brunet. Usually brunets have a more ruddy complexion. Yours is as fair as a red-head's. I didn't mean to get you upset. I was just curious why you wear it black."

"I guess I just wanted a change in my life," Leon muttered, barely audible above the moving train. "I don't suppose you like my name either."

"Your name? It's not like you have a lot of choice on what your parents name you. Or did you change it also?"

"Yeah, I changed it, too. You don't like it?"

"To be truthful, Leon's never been a favorite name of mine. I grew up in a neighborhood where Leon was a pimp who drove a red El Dorado. So, no. My associated memories with the name Leon are not good." Candice had no idea where this conversation was headed. "Actually, I did wonder a bit about the way you signed N.N. Claus on the dry cleaner's paperwork yesterday. I couldn't figure out how Leon came from N.N."

"The name is actually Noel Nicholas. My sister who's engaged to the man who owns the junk pile car is my twin, Joyeux." his mouth snapped shut as though he said too much.

Candice bit back her laughter. "Joyeux Noel? Your parents are really into Christmas, aren't they?"

"You have no idea just how much. When I decided to change my life, I flipped my name backwards and Noel became Leon."

"Get teased a lot when you were a kid?"

"That has nothing to do with wanting a life change," he snapped out with a frown at her.

"Well, the teasing is why I won't allow anyone but my momma to call me Candy. I got tired of being called by every brand of candy there is in the market. Or being told how sweet I was." She frowned with her tongue out like she was gagging. To her pleasure, Leon chuckled. "And this time of year, I got called Candy Cane all the time." And still use the name at the second dreaded part-time job. The money. Keep focused on how much the money helps Momma's life, she reminded herself yet again.

"Yeah. I get tired of people singing 'No-el, No-el' at me."

"Wouldn't it be easier to just change the pronunciation rather than your entire name?"

"Huh?"

"I use my full Candice, rather than let people call me Candy. If you don't want people calling you 'No-el' then introduce yourself as 'Noll.' After all Joel isn't pronounced 'Jo-el,' but Joll with the long 'o' and the long 'ell.' The only difference between Noel and Joel is the first letter. Why shouldn't you pronounce it 'Noll?'"

"That never occurred to me." His pale blue eyes looked thoughtful, then he smiled at her and her entire body flushed with heat that had nothing to do with the inadequate heating system on the El. "Yeah, that'll work. It'll make my family happier, too. Thanks, Candice."

"Quite welcome," she tried to answer casually even though her mouth had dried completely. She watched his mouth, wondering what it would be like to kiss those smiling lips.

He touched her hair, then her cheek, and moved closer to her. His voice lowered, making it seem as though they were the only two people on the train or even in the world. "Would it leave me open to be slapped with a sexual harassment suit as your supervisor if I kissed you?"

"I think Santa kisses Mrs. Claus a lot, don't you?" she whispered

"I know they do. I'm their only son."

He moved closer, then took her lips with his. At first his mouth just pressed against hers, moving as though he weren't sure of his welcome. But she'd made it through two performances last night with the vision of him as his only audience. She'd gone to sleep hungering to kiss him. For the first time since she'd been widowed, her hot, erotic dreams had featured someone other than her late husband. And now her dream lover was kissing her as though he were nervous she was going to reject him. Not a chance.

She lightly outlined the seam of his nibbling mouth, then welcomed his invasion. He probed and twisted throughout her mouth as though he were trying to decipher all her secrets with the touch of his tongue. He invited her to into him and she took her own time finding his sweetness. His hand tunneled through her hair and he tilted her head back to delve deeper. She held him closer to her regretting the heavy jackets and thick clothing separating their bodies. Their mouths continued to enjoy the joining she knew they both wanted for their entire beings.

Even in the first flush of love for her late husband, she hadn't wanted to give everything about herself to him. She had love him tremendously, but not with the intensity she'd had for this man whom she'd met a bit more than twenty-four hours earlier. She never thought she believed in love at first sight. Lust at first sight, yes. But love, she always thought, had to grow. But with Noel—she no longer thought of him as a 'Leon,' but with the sound of Noll—she knew deep down inside her this was more than lust.

If this was love as she thought, did she have the nerve to tell him about her second part-time job? If she did, would he accept what she had to do to keep her momma alive? Or would he despise her as she detested herself for getting nearly naked in front of strange men in two shows every Friday and Saturday and playing up to their sexual fantasies? Would she hate herself more if she kept it a secret from him?

She ended the kiss, knowing the answer to the last question. She let her head rest on his shoulder. He stroked her hair and she enjoyed the thought of this closeness continuing for the rest of her life.

But truth had a nasty habit of coming out and the truth about her secret job was nastier than most truths. She needed to tell him now before they went any farther in this relationship. She cringed at the thought of trying to convince him, but knew unless they had truth between them, this tenuous connection would never blossom to its fullest possibilities but would grow twisted and be ruined.

"You're a bit quiet. Public displays of affection bother you?"

"Not with you," Candice said. She sat up and looked into his eyes. "I have a confession."

"You've already told me you're an exotic dancer. I'm cool with that." His blue eyes sparkled like a sunlight on water. He moved closer to kiss her again, but she put her hand on his chest.

"That's not a joke," she told him. "I need you to know it because I can't bring myself to let you continue to think the exotic dancer job is a joke."

"Hey," he lifted her hair off her coat and smoothed it behind her shoulder, "I'm not taking it as a joke. I think you're a hot exotic dancer. You probably pack the joint."

"Noel—"

"You know. I like that. Noll," he nodded. "I can definitely get used to my name being pronounced Noll."

She took both his hands in hers. "Listen to me, Noel. I'm very serious here. I need the money to pay for Momma's cancer. I am an exotic dancer on Friday and Saturday nights."

His eyes and face showed his puzzlement, but she continued talking.

"I do two shows. I pole dance at The Gentlemen's Hot Club. I dance under the name of 'Candy Cane.'"

She saw the growing dismay take the place of his confusion. She dropped her eyes, unable to bear the hurt disillusionment in those ice blue eyes.

"I strip my costume down to a string brassiere and a g-string. I don't lap dance and I don't go topless or bottomless."

She let go of his hands and wasn't surprised he didn't take hers in his or that he moved slightly away from her.

"I make several hundred dollars each night. The money all goes to Momma's care. I have to help her. I have to." She searched his face, praying he understood.

Instead, his face looked like it was carved from stone.

"I'm sorry you're disappointed in me, but I'm not going to continue to lie to you. I don't want to quit the job as Mrs. Claus, but I will if you want me to. I'm begging you here. Please don't tell my family or the school district. My family won't understand. The school district will fire me. Please promise you won't tell."

"I promise," he said, his voice no longer lifting with

warmth and humor. "I won't tell anyone that might affect your main job or your family. You don't have to quit the Mrs. Claus job. But you will understand if I don't join your family for dinner tonight? I need some time to think about this. If you'll have your uncle or your cousin take the car to the repair shop, I'll pick it up there tomorrow."

Candice nodded. She didn't know how she was going to be able to continue to work with Noel, but she brought this on herself. She had to live with her actions and her decisions.

Chapter Five

"Hi, Dad."

"Hi, Leon."

"Noll, Dad. I've gone back to my own name, but pronouncing it Noll instead of No-el."

"Works for me, Noel," his dad promptly said, using the new pronunciation. "Frankly, just between the two of us, the No-el bit was your mom's idea. I've always like your Uncle Noel and think he and Charlie are a great couple, but—and don't tell your mom—I've always thought No-el is a little girly sounding for a boy."

For the first time in nearly a week, Noel laughed. "That's what I tried to tell Mom. She said I almost ended up a Junior."

"So you would have, but your mom had her heart set on Joyeux Noel for you two."

"I can deal with Noll a lot better than No-el."

"I'll pass the word around here, Noel. How are things? I'm getting some great data for the Naughty and Nice list. Thanks for doing such a good job setting the computer program up and running and for helping fill in there in Chicago to release some of our operatives. I've also gotten reports people are feeling better from the flu, although it's still pretty bad here in Christmas Town. You'll be able to come home soon. That'll make your mom happy. She's worried I'm working too hard and am going to catch that flu myself. She's such a worry wart."

"Okay, just let me know when you need me back there. If they're still having problems down here, I can ask the Transportation elf to make arrangements for me to commute," Noel said. He hesitated, but his dad had always been there to help him in the past. This was a bit more complicated than learning how to throw a football properly or confronting a teacher who graded unjustly. "Dad, I've got a problem. Personal, not having to do with work."

"Hang on, son. Let me go to my office."

While he waited for his dad to come back to the phone, he endorsed the back of the check for the sale of the Ducati over to the "Carmelita Hernandez Medical Fund" and added the bank account number Candice's uncle provided. He put it and the deposit slip her uncle gave him into the bank envelope and stuck on a stamp. Before he dropped it in the mail box, he rubbed his thumb over the artist's rendering of his dad making the Christmas Eve run. Considering how as old as he was, he found it a little weird to be missing his folks the way he had the first year he went to the all boys summer camp.

As his dad moved through the main workshop to his office, Noel heard the background chatter of elves and human workers prepping for the coming Christmas. Finally, he heard the wooden chunk of his dad's office door shut, then the creak of his leather chair conforming to his dad's body.

"Still there?"

"Yes."

"I probably should have just called you back, but I was afraid if I hung up, I'd get distracted by everyone else's issues and forget to call."

Noel heard the hiss and then the sucking, puffing sound of his dad starting his pipe.

"I've always regretted that this time of year, you children always get the short end of my time."

"You always made time for us. Even if it was just a quick hug at night before bed. You and Mom are the best."

"You're a good boy. Your mother and I are proud of you. Now, what can your old dad help with? You still want that new Ducati for Christmas?"

"No. In fact, I just sold mine. Dad, I need advice."

"What's the problem, son?"

"I've met a really great woman."

"And why is this a problem?"

"There's a problem."

"Apologize to her."

"Wait just a minute. What do you mean apologize? You don't even know what the problem is."

"I've been married to your mom for a lot of years. In all my years of Santa, I've met a lot of people. Sure, I don't know what the problem is, but with the female of the species—be it human, elf, or those purple critters from out Andromeda way—if there's a problem, the male caused it. So, say you're sorry and make amends. Fast. Diamonds are usually your mother's favorite way for me to make amends."

"Dad, she's a stripper."

Noel heard his dad blow out smoke and knew by the exasperated sound he was in trouble.

"I was afraid that was going to bother you when you found out."

"You knew?"

"About Candice Hernandez Craig being an exotic dancer? Of course, I knew. There's not much about a person in the database of the Naughty and Nice list that I don't know. I didn't tell Holly, of course, when she came snooping through my computer trying to figure out my password to get Candice's address for Joy to give to you. Joy said Clay told you about their engagement, by the way."

"Yeah, he did. I'm going to be his Best Man. But, how can I bring a stripper home to meet you and Mom?" Noel's mouth blurted out before his brain had a chance to stop it.

"Ho, ho, ho," his dad laughed. "It's come to 'meet the parents' already, son? Your mom's going to be so happy. She thought you were never going to settle down. Bring Candice up here. Even if you tell your mother about this part-time job, she won't care what Candice does any more than I do. We just want you to be happy. You do know why she's an exotic dancer?"

"Yeah. That's why I sold my Ducati. I just mailed the check to be deposited into the account to help pay for her mom's treatments."

"You're growing up. Now you need to decide why Candice's part-time job bothers you so much. Once you've figured that out, you'll know how to fix things with her."

"I just wish she didn't do it. Dad, I know you don't have enough magic to heal Candice's mom, but can I have my Christmas wish be a fund to cover her medical expenses? I don't know how much it's going to be or how long."

"Sure, I'll be happy to arrange it. Now, I'd like you to fulfill a Christmas wish for me."

"You? A Christmas wish for you?" Noel swallowed, totally stunned at his dad's request. "Dad, you've never asked for anything for Christmas."

"First time for everything." This time when his dad puffed out smoke, he sounded contented and pleased. "Here's my wish from you. Once you figure out why Candice being an exotic dancer bothers you, I want you to figure out if you're trying to rescue Candice the way you've always done for your sisters or if you have other reasons to want to see to her mom's comfort. It's an admirable Christmas wish you've made and I'm happy to grant it. I just want you to know why you want to do it. In the years I've been Santa, I've learned I can't rescue everyone, as much as I want to. So, for my Christmas gift from you, I want you to do some soul-searching and decide why you want to do this."

"Can't I just give you a kidney or a lung or something?" Noel did his imitation of the whiney kids who begged at the mall. "It would be easier."

"Ho, ho, ho."

His dad's laughter warmed him the way it had since he'd been little.

"Dad?"

"Yes, Noel?" his dad answered between chuckles. It amazed Noel that never once did his dad slipped from

'Noll' back to the old 'No-el.'

"I love you."

"I love you, too. Take care of yourself. And fix that problem with Candice. Your mom wants another daughter to love."

****

Candice stepped from the club's back door and pulled on her gloves, ready to make the walk to the El. The money belt she wore under her clothes was stuffed tonight. Someone had even tossed her some hundred dollar bills. It always made her a bit sad to take the money men threw on the stage at her or tucked under the strings of her brassiere or thong. As much as she needed the money for her momma, it worried her some of these men might be giving her money that their own wives and children needed.

"Hi, Candice. Can I give you a ride home?"

Candice looked at Noel, holding his knitted cap in his hands. The long black hair was gone. In the streetlight, short blond—almost white-blond—hair gleamed.

"When did you cut your hair?"

"This afternoon after I left the Santa gig. I'm sending eleven inches to Locks of Love."

"That's kind of you. Is this your natural color?"

"Kind of. The stylist stripped out the black, then colored it match my natural color so it won't look weird when it grows in. Matched the eyebrows, too."

"That's nice." Candice stepped around him and started down the street. She needed to hurry to make her train.

"Candice, please. Let me take you home."

"I think it best we keep things work related. I'll see you on Monday night."

Noel put an hand on her arm. "I'm sorry for my attitude this past week. I'm sorry we've been nothing but polite to each other."

"I rather expected it." She shook off his arm and continued on her way, her boots ringing on the sidewalk and echoing off buildings.

"I'm sorry I confirmed your low opinion of me."

That stopped Candice. "I actually didn't have a low opinion of you. I thought you would understand. I'm disappointed in myself for getting my hopes up."

"Candice, please. I need to talk to you. If you won't let me drive you, I'll ride the El with you. I'd rather not leave the car here, because as junky as Clay's car is, I really don't want it stolen and stripped. If he loses this car because of me, he might choose someone else to be his Best Man when he marries my twin sister."

At the rumble of a train passing overhead, Candice checked her watch by the street light. "That's my train getting into the station. You've delayed me so long, I'll never make it now. I'll have to wait a half hour for the next one and it's too cold. I guess I'll have to go home with you."

Candice huddled into her coat in the inadequately heated car. She finally tucked her feet under her body as opposed to leaving them on the floor where cold air blew on them from the so-called heater.

"Hold the wheel for me, please?"

"Why?"

"I'm going to take off my coat for you to wrap around yourself. I should have asked your uncle to repair the heater, too."

"I don't need your coat."

"I'm taking it off anyway." Noel stuck a knee against the underside of the steering wheel while putting his right elbow against the top of the wheel.

In disgust at men and their single mindedness and Noel's in particular and, she had to admit, a bit in fear for her life, Candice leaned over and steadied the steering wheel while Noel pulled his left arm from the coat sleeve. She resisted the magnetic pull to lean against his warm body but concentrated on keeping them straight on the road.

He took the steering wheel again and stuck his right

arm out. “Pull my sleeve off for me, please?”

She got it off, then pulled the entire coat from behind his back. Still heated from his body and smelling of his clean, fresh scent, Candice found herself wrapping it around herself the way she wanted Noel’s arms around her.

“I talked to my dad—.”

“Oh, you called Santa Claus?”

“Yes. He granted me my Christmas Wish. Every year, he gives all of us a chance to wish for the one thing we want with all our hearts.”

“How nice for you. Are you getting a new Ducati?”

“No, I’m not. I’ll explain in a minute.”

“You know,” Candice watched the glow of the passing street lights on the grubby snow. “This is another thing I’m annoyed with you about. I told you my darkest secret and you walked away from me. But you don’t bother even telling me your parents’ names—”

“Mary and Nicholas Claus,” Noel interrupted.

“Of course. The perfect names for Santa and his wife. Why do you still keep pretending you’re Santa’s only son? I don’t give a damn you won’t ever introduce me to your parents, but this Santa stuff is ridiculous.”

“I’d like to take you tomorrow to meet my parents. I can get substitutes for our Sunday afternoon mall jobs, if you’ll come with me.”

“Oh, joy, I get to meet the real Santa Claus and his wife? What fun! Are they in town or are we going to the North Pole and back in one day?”

“With Christmas coming soon, it’s hard for Dad to leave the workshop right now and Mom’s busy in the kitchens. Besides, I think you’ll believe us easier if you actually see our place at the North Pole. I just need to let the Transportation elf know when we’re ready to leave.”

“Gee, gosh. A Transportation elf. Why don’t we get magicked there right now?”

Noel ignored her sarcasm and quietly asked, “Will your mom be okay if you don’t come home tonight? Do you need to get one of your aunts or cousins to stay with her?"

"Are you crazy? I'm not calling anyone and telling them I'm staying with you. They'll think we're sleeping together."

"Then," Noel continued calmly, "how about if I spend the night on the couch in your apartment and we'll leave for my parents' place first thing in the morning?"

"Why don't you go back to your own place and leave me alone?"

Noel swung the car behind the apartment building and drove into the parking slot she'd directed him to when the car door had fallen off. "Because I love you and I want to make amends for my behavior."

"You—?"

"I love you. I figured out the reason I was mad about you being an exotic dancer was mainly because I didn't want other men to see your body. I don't want to share you." He paused, then said, "I was at your shows tonight."

Candice thought of the money in her belt. "Were you the one tossing the hundred dollar bills? Because you felt sorry for me and Momma?"

"No. I tossed a couple of twenties, but not any hundreds. I can tell you why you earn more money than any of the other girls dancing."

"Speak, oh wise one."

"Not wise, just observant. When the other girls danced, they looked like they were disassociating themselves from their bodies. They just went through the motions. But when you danced, you shared your joy in life with everyone. And yet there was something in your eyes that made every man there want to take care of you and help you be happy just for the privilege of sharing your happiness with him."

He stroked her hair and laid his palm against her cheek. "I knew the sadness came from worry over your mom. I realized I'd had the chance all of them wanted and blew it. I want to take care of you and your mom and help you be happy, just for the privilege of sharing your happiness with you."

Candice blinked back tears at the sincerity in Noel's voice.

"My Christmas wish from my dad was a fund to pay for your mom's medical costs."

"Your dad's going to pay for my mom's medical expenses?"

"Not by himself. But he has a lot of influence. He'll make the arrangements. I'm not sure how he's going to do it, but very soon you won't have any medical bills to worry about."

"Your dad may not be the real Santa Claus, but he's definitely close enough to the real one for me." This time Candice didn't bother to blink away the tears. Noel put his arms around her and she laid her head against his sweater while she cried with gratitude. She finally got herself under control and dug a packet of tissues from her coat pocket. Noel took the tissues from her and wiped her face.

"You do that so well," she said with a sniffle, "like you've had lots of practice mopping up sobbing women. I got your sweater all soggy. I'm sorry."

"Hush." He put a finger over her lips. "With four sisters, I've had soggy sweaters before and definitely have cleaned up many a teary face."

She laid her head back on his shoulder, happy to have Noel hold her.

"I need to tell you about the rest of the conversation I had with Dad. His Christmas wish from me was for me to figure out why I wanted him to take care of your financial burdens to take care of your mom.

"I've got a habit through the years of rescuing my sisters. Actually, they consider me extremely over-protective."

"They're lucky to have you." Candice felt his lips brush the top of her forehead.

"I'm the lucky one. Anyway, I realized I wasn't asking him to take care of the money situation because I wanted to rescue you. I just want you to be happy. You're happiest when you're with your momma. I wanted to give you the opportunity to quit these extra jobs so you can spend as much time as you can with her. That's why I asked Dad for the funds. So you can have quality time with her to build the memories to keep her alive for you for the rest of your life. I love you. I really do. And I'd be honored if you'll let me spend the rest of your life with you sharing your happiness with me. Will you marry me?"

Candice answered him with a kiss.

When they came up for air, Noel dug in the pocket of his coat still wrapped around Candice. "I hope this fits." He slid a princess cut diamond ring on the third finger of her left hand. "Not that I want to pressure you or anything, but will you be comfortable getting married soon? I'd really like to be married to you."

Candice looked at the ring sparkling in the parking lot's security light, then lifted her face to Noel's again. "My momma's not going to live much longer. I'd like her to be at our wedding."

"We can see my parents tomorrow and tell them, then Monday get the license and get married Tuesday. If you don't mind a Justice of the Peace wedding."

"I don't care as long as you're there and my momma's watching. Will your parents be able to come?"

"Christmas is important, but their children are more important. They wouldn't miss it. Invite your whole family. If I know my mom, she's been planning a guest list for my wedding and my sisters' weddings for years. Plus she's a whiz at organizing. She'll come up with a great reception even if it is on the spur of the moment."

"I bet if she and my aunts can get together on Monday, even the Queen of England will be envious she's not invited to the party."

"As long as you're happy."

"I'm always going to be happy with you."

"I promise I'll do my best to help you stay happy."

About the author...

Betty Hanawa writes paranormal erotic romances, filled with snarky humor that frequently slips into the ironic. Her books are receiving high praise and are eagerly anticipated. Her aunts are delighted with her success. Her children are embarrassed to discover their mother knows about sex. And she really enjoys being the scandal of her small town.

The Christmas Star

Roni Adams

Chapter One

"Chrissy? Chrissy Star?"

Chrissy looked up and frowned. She didn't recognize the man standing at her table. His brown eyes, jet-black hair, and olive skin didn't ring any bells. Neither did the broad shoulders and muscular chest hidden beneath the deep green polo shirt. Nope, definitely not a guy she would have forgotten. So how did he know her name?

"I'm sorry, have we met?" she asked.

The stranger smiled. "You don't remember me?"

Feeling her cheeks warm, she looked at him even harder, but still nothing. "No, I'm afraid I don't."

"It's ok. It was at least five years ago." He held out his hand, "Nick Christopoulus. We met at the CPA convention in New York."

Furrowing her brow, Chrissy thought back to the boring conference and the stuffy people she'd met. Suddenly a vivid image of a man with dark heavy glasses and a pocket protector materialized. Her mouth fell open as she stared back at him. The Nick she'd met was at least fifty pounds heavier, and considerably nerdier than this man. "Wow," was all she could manage to get out.

He laughed and slipped into the chair across from her. "Lasik eye surgery, and a nasty illness." He shrugged. "I was sick for a long time, but I lost a lot of weight so I guess I can't complain too much."

Chrissy couldn't stop staring. She was looking at a real life before and after photo. "You look fantastic. I mean, not that you looked bad before, but..."

Nick laughed. "Its okay, I know how bad I looked before. Getting sick was a good wake-up call."

"And the Lasik?"

He shrugged. "Once I changed all that fat to muscle I

figured I might as well keep going and ditch the glasses too."

Chrissy took a drink of her cocktail still unable to get her head around the two men being the same guy. "So what brings you here? Vacation?"

"Sort of, I bought property on one of these islands two years ago and have been trying to spend as much time here as I can. Especially in the winter."

Chrissy thought about the white sands and warn sunshine she'd enjoyed since arriving. "It's a wonderful place to escape the snow and cold."

As Nick took a long swallow of his drink, she watched him. His mouth could only be described as inviting and she wondered how he kissed. His bronzed hands were large and rough, definitely not like the usual pasty white accountant type she normally met. His jet black hair and olive coloring, and, of course his last name, told her he was of Greek heritage. He was exotic. Yes, that was the word, exotic.

A zing of instant attraction tightened her tummy and her toes curled in her flimsy sandals.

"You must be from up north too then." He placed his drink on the table. "The winters are just too long aren't they?"

If he only knew just how far up north! She tossed her hair. When his gaze fell to the open v of her neckline, she felt herself blush under his scrutiny. The look of interest when he looked into her eyes, she knew was reflected in her own.

"Yes, winters are very long," she mimicked.

The waiter appeared and set her salad in front of her. Nick stood up and she felt a pang of disappointment. Of course he was leaving, why wouldn't he? He was probably here with a girlfriend or a bunch of friends. He most likely wasn't here alone like she was.

"Listen, I've already had dinner, but if you aren't too tired, would you be interested in joining me for a nightcap at the restaurant bar, say around eleven?"

"You're staying at the hotel? I thought you said you had a place around here?"

"I bought property, but there's no house yet. So what do you say, eleven?"

Having a drink with Nick sounded like a nice way to spend the evening. "I'll be there," she promised.

"I'll see you then." He smiled and turned away.

Chrissy watched him walk past the other diners and down the steps to the boardwalk along the beach. She dug into her salad and watched the ocean waves crashing on the shore. It was the kind of night made for lovers. The stars overhead were huge, and the full moon hung over the ocean like someone had painted it there. Several couples walked hand-in-hand stopping every once in a while to embrace. She sighed as she watched them. It must be wonderful to be in love and committed to another person. Was she ever going to find that? What difference did it make if she did? She shook her head in disgust and finished her drink. It wasn't as if she could even consider anything serious. Her family wasn't exactly the kind you took someone home to meet.

She always felt guilty when she thought that way. It wasn't her parents' fault. They'd given her a life most could only dream of having. The fact that she could never marry or consider having a family was a small price to pay for all they'd given her. Once more, she watched the silhouette of lovers on the beach, maybe, just maybe this year her Christmas wish could have something to do with her own loneliness. That would be pretty selfish, though. Her annual wish should be used for important things like ensuring all the children in the world have enough food to eat and clothes to wear. Asking for something only for herself would be wrong and completely against the way she was brought up.

So she couldn't ask for forever love, maybe she should just take matters into her own hands. Maybe meeting Nick for drinks could be the start of a temporary romance. Just because she could never have a future with someone didn't mean she had to live her whole live celibate did it?

She could have the time of her life, and then go home to the family business like always. Maybe if it worked out she could do this every year. Setting down her fork, she made a decision. Every December she'd enjoy herself, completely and thoroughly.

***

Nick was at the bar by ten thirty. He wasn't much of a drinker. Even now he was conscious of not taking in too many calories so he sipped club soda and lime. Chrissy had certainly been surprised to see him. A few days ago, he'd overheard the hotel staff talking about a woman with an unusual name. Since there weren't that many women named Christmas Star in the world he figured it had to be the beautiful woman he'd met in New York. He'd never forgotten her. A beautiful brunette with sparkling green eyes, she'd always worn sweaters that hugged her curves close enough to make him forget whether he was debiting or crediting.

She'd been polite to him; but he knew she was out of his league. But tonight he hadn't gotten that impression at all. He could waste time being annoyed that five years ago she wouldn't have accepted an invitation for drinks, but what was the point? Five years ago he couldn't get a date with anyone. He was a very large, very introverted bean counter back then. If it hadn't been for getting sick and meeting Dr. Cronin, who had introduced him to the world of fitness and taking care of himself, he probably would still be living his life the same way. Alone, night after night with his computer and potato chips for company. But now with at least his physical appearance changed, he was on equal footing. Unless he completely read her wrong, the look in her eyes earlier had been interest.

Running into her in the restaurant and acting as if he didn't know she was staying at the hotel had seemed like a great idea at the time. But now he wondered what he'd been thinking. Chrissy Star was the most beautiful woman he'd ever met and he had no clue what they'd talk about. Under this new muscled body he was still the same geeky accountant.

It wasn't as if he hadn't been dating the past few years. He'd had several relationships with some very good-looking women. But they all left him cold after a while. They were materialistic and immature. What he longed for was someone who enjoyed the same things he did. He wanted a down-to-earth girl that he could laugh with and share a future with.

As if sensing she'd come into the room he looked up. He watched as she scanned the bar, and he lifted his hand to catch her eye. She smiled and made her way gracefully through the crowded lounge. She wore the same black dress from earlier, but she'd slipped a lacy shawl over her shoulders. She looked amazing.

"Hi," she said with a warm smile.

"How was your dinner?" Taking her arm, he helped her climb up onto the bar stool next to him and signaled to the bartender. He watched as she crossed her shapely legs. They were toned and firm. Maybe she worked out on her lunch hour like he did.

"It was very good." She turned to the bartender. "May I have a peppermint schnapps on the rocks, please?"

He grinned at her drink choice. He knew she was unique, even her choice of drink was refreshing. No white wine or Chablis for her. She was like a breath of fresh air. For a few seconds neither said anything and then both started to speak at once.

She laughed and ducked her head. "You first."

"I was just going to ask if you were still with the family business. I remember something about you working for your father?"

She sipped her drink and nodded. "I've helped him with his books since I was a teenager. When I decided to go into accounting he pretty much handed the whole thing over to me."

"I'm impressed. Even if it's a small company that's a

huge responsibility."

He watched her slim fingers with short pink nails trace the rim of her glass. "It's much easier now that I handle it and he stays out of it." She grinned, and he could see she didn't mean it in a bad way. He had this feeling she adored her father.

"Working for family sometimes can be tough."

"Mmm, that's for sure. How about you? You were with a really large international firm right? Are you still there?"

He was thrilled she remembered. He would have sworn she barely remembered his name. "Yeah, for the moment I'm still there."

The music in the bar was suddenly much louder and he saw her lips move, but couldn't make out what she was saying. He leaned closer and the scent of her light perfume filled his nostrils. It was a blend of something sweet like cookies but with a spicy undertone. It was like nothing he'd ever smelled before and yet it seemed completely familiar. She stiffened and he realized he was too close. He cupped his ear to let her know he couldn't hear her.

She nodded and tipped her face to speak directly into his ear. "Where is the office located?"

Her body pressed into his and the warmth of her breath on his ear revved up all his senses. He hardened and had to step back so she wouldn't notice. She'd probably think he was a complete pervert if she knew something that simple had aroused him. Then again, if it affected him that way, maybe it worked on her the same. He leaned down and purposely let his breath out slowly as he spoke into her ear. "I'm working in New York."

She turned her head, and he saw desire flash in her green eyes. She nodded and took another sip of her drink. The loud music had been annoying before, but now it turned to a familiar Christmas tune and that was even worse. He couldn't carry on a conversation like this. Once more he leaned towards her. At the same time she must have been going to lean towards him to speak, and their heads bumped and her breasts pressed into his arm. He saw her lips form, "Oww." She rubbed her head.

That was enough, he took her hand and tugged. "Come on," he mouthed and jerked his head towards the door.

She smiled and picked her glass up off the bar and slipped daintily off the stool. Her hand still in his, he led her through the crowd to the back patio. The evening was still warm but not uncomfortable. He breathed a sigh of relief as the music receded. She pulled her hand free and he let her go, not wanting to seem too pushy.

"Why does everyone think loud music is enjoyable?" he asked.

"I have no idea."

"The fact that it was Christmas music made it even worse."

"You don't like Christmas music?" she asked tucking a strand of hair behind her ear as she looked up at him.

"No. Definitely not. In fact, that's one of the reasons I'm here. I try to escape the craziness of this season every year. Here in Greece, and especially on the island, Christmas isn't the commercial craziness it is at home."

"I see. So it isn't Christmas you detest, but the commercial aspect of it?"

"Well, I'm not a big fan of it either way. I don't like racing around looking for the right present, spending way too much money on things people will only return anyway. I especially hate it when they lie to kids and tell them a big fat old man in a red suit is going to come to their house at night and leave them gifts. It's just weird."

"Did you always think that way or only after you grew up?"

He had no idea. Nothing major ever happened to make him hate Christmas. He wasn't a deprived child. There were always presents from Santa as far back as he could remember and his whole family still loved the holidays. Nothing traumatic had ever occurred to make him hate the season, but as the years went by he grew more and more cynical about the holiday. It wasn't even that he was overly religious and felt the holiday needed to get back to some true meaning, he just didn't like Christmas.

"I don't know," he shrugged and gave a self-deprecating laugh. "I guess I'm just like old Ebenezer Scrooge. I'd rather be counting my gold than worrying about what gifts to get my nieces that they will only return anyway."

"I like Christmas," she said quietly and set her empty drink glass on a small table as they walked by.

"Most folks do," he said. Up ahead of them it was dark, the lighting from the hotel was fading away. He wondered if she'd be nervous walking with him alone. He glanced at her, but she didn't appear to be uncomfortable.

"Will you stay here through the holidays?" she asked.

"Are you kidding? My parents would have my head on a platter if I missed Christmas. No, I'll head home the afternoon of the twenty-fourth, and pretend to enjoy all the merriment and craziness. Trust me, I'd much rather be here."

"All alone? On Christmas?" She furrowed her brow and looked at him as if he'd just grown horns.

"You know what my idea of a perfect Christmas would be?" He stopped walking to lean up against a post. "To be with someone I love, all alone, at my house on the island. Away from the snow and the cold and the millions of family members all talking at once and fighting for the bathroom."

"But those are some of the best parts about Christmas. The family all together, fighting, laughing, loving. At least that's what mine does and I love it."

"So you come from a pretty large family?"

She nodded and looked out over the ocean. "Bigger than you could imagine."

The moon was high and full and he watched it with her. "Then why are you here all alone a few days before wonderful holiday?"

"Oh, I'll be home before Christmas morning. I wouldn't miss it for the world. But my father's business gets really crazy this time of year, so I tend to take my vacation and stay out of the way. There's not a lot I can do to help anyway."

"This is the company's busiest time of year so you go on vacation? Isn't that a bit like taking the week of April fifteenth off?"

She shook her head. "It's hard to explain."

"Where did you say home was again?"

She turned to face him. He looked at her full mouth, her lipstick had faded leaving her lips a light wine pink. How soft would they feel under his?

"I didn't," she answered and lifted her chin slightly. Was that an invitation? Was she lifting her head so he would kiss her in the moonlight? He wasn't sure, so he better not. Sometimes he hated how insecure he still was at certain times.

Once more she brushed her hair back and tilted her head as she stared back at him. "Your eyes are an amazing shade of brown."

He lifted his eyebrows. "They are?"

"Hmm. They remind me of gingerbread men fresh from the oven."

"I can assure you they aren't made of ginger. I'm allergic to it."

Her mouth fell open in shock. "You're allergic to gingerbread men?"

He nodded. "The ginger. Can't eat it, I get hives, and my throat closes up." He made a face and put his hands around his neck as if he was gagging.

She laughed, but then covered her mouth with her hand. "I'm sorry. It's just so odd; I mean you hear of folks being allergic to strawberries or peanuts but gingerbread?" She shook her head. "That's one of my favorite smells. I love gingerbread baking in the oven."

"My mother used to feel bad and would always make

me a sugar cookie shaped like a gingerbread man, but somehow I always felt deprived."

"I should say so. What's Christmas without gingerbread men?"

"Maybe that's what started my dislike of the holiday? Maybe deep down inside my allergy to ginger somehow scarred me so deeply that I can't enjoy anything about it."

She laughed but then looked at him as if maybe he was serious.

"I'm kidding. I don't know what it is about the holiday, its just not enjoyable to me."

All of a sudden she pushed away from the rail. Had he insulted her?

She touched his arm. "It sounds like you've never found the true meaning of Christmas in here." She placed her hand over his heart and he felt it leap beneath her palm. Before he could react, however, she was walking back the way they'd come.

He followed her and together they walked in silence to the hotel. What should he do now? Had he completely blown it with her? Was she going to hold it against him for not liking Christmas? Then he remembered her name, Christmas Star. Of course! What an idiot he was. Anyone born on Christmas would have to love the holiday.

They reached the front door of the lobby. "Chrissy?"

She looked at him.

"I hope my hang-up with the holiday isn't going to stop you from seeing me again."

She quirked one eyebrow. "Did we have a second date planned?"

He took her little smile to be a good sign. "I hadn't gotten to it yet, but yes; I'd like to ask you out again. I'd love to show you the piece of property I bought."

For what seemed like the longest moment of his life, he waited.

"I think I'd like that. Should we go late morning?"

He held open the door for her to walk through. "Want to meet me in the lobby around eleven?"

She nodded and waved and he watched her walk towards the bank of elevators.

Chapter Two

Chrissy had just bitten into the flakey, buttery scone with homemade jam when her phone rang. Setting her napkin aside, she moved across her room to answer. "Hello?" She swallowed the rest of her breakfast, hoping it wasn't Nick hearing her chewing.

"How's it going?" The warm lyrical voice of her younger sister, Krista, was surprisingly clear considering where the call was coming from.

"Fine. It's going fine. How about there?"

"You know crazy as always, but in a good way."

She sank to the edge of the bed and twisted the phone cord around her finger. She easily imagined her family scurrying around the workshops, checking lists, and making sure everything was in place. "I feel bad I'm not there."

"Why? So you could be under foot and asking 'what can I do?' twenty times an hour?"

She heard the smile in her sister's voice. What she said was true; there was no point arguing. "Sometimes I wish I was like you, Joy, and Noel, and could feel like I pulled my own weight this time of year."

Her sister laughed. "Well I wouldn't want to be you for all the snowflakes in the North. We only have to bust our butts six weeks a year. You have to work hard the whole year."

It was pointless to tell her fun loving sister that most folks worked all year long. "Have you seen Jack lately?"

Krista had a crush on the long time family friend, Jackson Frost, for as long as Chrissy could remember. As far as she could see, Jack didn't even know her poor sister existed.

"Yes, but as always he kept a good six feet away from me. I swear the man thinks if he gets too close he'll melt."

"Maybe he's afraid some of your warmth will rub off on him and he'll be out of work." Chrissy teased.

"Now stop that, Jack's not cold. He's got a good heart."

"Hmm. Yes, he does, but I still don't see why you want a man with ice literally running through his veins." A bit of jam had fallen on her leg and she wiped it with her finger and then licked it off. She eyed her breakfast across the room.

"Enough about me. Tell me about your vacation. Is it hot? Tell me the sun shines all the time, and there are gorgeous men in swim trunks and bare chests playing volleyball on the sand."

Chrissy thought instantly about Nick and couldn't wait to see him bare-chested, running on the beach. "Wow you've got quite the imagination, but I did meet someone last night." She felt funny even telling her sister about it. Maybe it was guilt for knowing what she was planning on doing with Nick that caused her embarrassment.

"Tell!"

She shouldn't have said anything. It was bound to be all over Christmas Town as soon as she got off the phone. Krista was a notorious gossiper. "He's someone I met a long time ago at a CPA convention. His name is Nick."

"Ohh poo, a boring accountant? Couldn't you meet someone exciting? An actor? Or a doctor?

"He's very nice, and very good looking. He has property here on the island and he's going to show it to me today."

"All alone? Chrissy, be careful. I mean, you don't know this guy and you're all alone there."

"I'm fine. Don't worry. I wouldn't do anything that was dangerous. Now don't you have some more dolls to finish accessorizing?"

"Yes, actually I do. I don't know how I'll ever be ready by the twenty-fourth."

"You will; you always are. I gotta get ready for my date."

"Did you tell him yet?" Krista asked lowering her voice.

Chrissy frowned, "Tell him what?"

"Does he have any idea that you are Santa Claus' daughter?"

"Yeah, well, that's not exactly something you share over drinks. I'm probably not going to tell him."

"You're not?"

"No. I'll only be here for two weeks and then I'm back home. It's not like he's going to be able to come see me at the North Pole."

"It could be arranged."

Chrissy closed her eyes and let out a sigh. "No. You don't understand how mortal men are. It's better to just not bring something like that up."

"Well, what happens at the end of two weeks? That's it, thanks for the memories, see you around?"

"Yeah, what's wrong with that? I'm going to have the time of my life, maybe with Nick, maybe not, but I'm not going to think about what happens after that. Whatever happens here stays here."

"I think you're crazy. What if he's someone, you know, special?"

Chrissy stood up ready to end the conversation. "Look I know this is hard for you to understand, but I can't bring a guy home to meet my parents. It's different for you. You're an elf; you date other elves. Elves know about flying reindeer and penguins for pets, but mortal men," she closed her eyes as the hopelessness of her love life closed around her again, "Let's just say most mortal men barely believe in love, they certainly aren't going to believe in Santa or his daughter."

"Honey,"

"No Krista, I can't. Don't worry about it. Look I gotta go. Miss you."

"Miss you too, can't wait until you're back home."

"I'll be home before Dad leaves on Christmas Eve. Give Mama and Daddy a big hug for the others and me. And check on Dasher for me, he gets so depressed when I'm gone."

"I saw him yesterday afternoon and he seemed fine. He was out practicing jumps with the others. Hey, Chrissy?"

"Yeah?"

"Have a good time. Who knows, maybe the accountant has a wild side."

"Good bye, Krista."

Krista laughed. "Bye."

She was still smiling as she stepped into the shower a few minutes later. Her sister's words rang in her ear. If Nick was interested, she was going to have a good time. She'd already made up her mind. For the next two weeks she was going to soak up some sun and some fun.

***

"The only way to get to your property is by boat?" Chrissy was surprised when Nick led her to a private dock later that morning.

"I should have told you last night."

Chrissy looked down at her sundress and sandals. "Will this be ok? Should I have worn sneakers?"

"I'll help you, you won't slip." Nick jumped down into the boat and reached his arms up to her.

Gingerly, she set one foot onto the seat of the boat and it swayed with her weight. Nick's hands spanned her waist as hers rested on his shoulders. He swung her down into the boat. Chrissy clung a bit more than necessary pretending she was off balance.

"Ohh, I guess it rocks more than I thought."

Nick's hands were still on her waist. She could have sworn he started to lower his head and then checked himself.

"Have you been on a boat before?" he asked settling her into the seat next to his.

"I guess I haven't, no." Chrissy brushed her hair

back. Nick walked to the back of the boat and leaned over pulling in ropes and some plastic looking items. Were they to protect it from hitting the docks? She didn't want to sound like a real idiot and ask.

The boat shifted as he sat in the driver's side and turned the key. "Ready?"

His brown eyes twinkled; she smiled back at him and nodded.

He pushed a lever down and the boat moved backward out of the dock. Before long they were flying across the turquoise ocean. Chrissy raked her hands through her hair trying without success to keep it from whipping her face. Finally, she gave up and just let it fly as the sun warmed her skin and the wind kissed it.

What an amazing feeling! It was almost as good as flying with her father in his sleigh. It was so freeing. The boat's engine roared making conversation impossible, but as she watched Nick he turned to look at her and words weren't necessary. He leisurely swept her body with his gaze and the smoldering look in his eyes made her temperature rise even higher. He was thinking about the same thing she was! They were alone and there was definitely a powerful physical attraction between them.

It might have been only a few minutes or half an hour, but soon they were pulling up to a small cove. Several houses dotted the landscape spaced far apart. There was no one around and Chrissy watched as Nick expertly maneuvered the boat into a small dock slip and cut the engine.

"Obviously you've been boating a long time," she said, as he tied up the boat and tossed the protective plastic things over the sides.

Nick nodded. "My grandfather had a place on the water. I grew up working with him on his fishing boats in the summer." He walked back over to where she sat and held out his hand. "Be careful when you stand up, don't slip."

She clung to his hand, stood up, and followed him to

the side.

"Hang on to the back of this seat while I get out. The boat will lurch a bit, and then I'll help you out."

She nodded, and as he predicted, the boat swayed with his shifting. He reached down. Chrissy took his hands, stepped up onto the seat, and then onto the solid dock. Nick didn't release her hand as they walked up towards land. She reveled in the feel of his palm against hers and the natural way their two hands snuggled together. She hadn't held hands with a man in a very long time. With her other hand she tried to smooth her hair and Nick looked down at her. "You're beautiful."

Chrissy felt color rise in her cheeks and found that she did feel beautiful. Nick looked at her in a way that made her feel as if she was the sexiest woman in the world. She pulled her gaze from his rich brown eyes. The property was definitely secluded and she could see where some land had been cleared. "Is that where your house will sit?"

Nick dropped her hand and moved ahead. Standing in the middle of the clearing, he described where the front porch would be and the back deck. "And I want windows. Huge floor to ceiling windows that overlook the ocean."

Chrissy crossed her arms over her chest and watched his face. He was so passionate about it. What would that feel like? To own something like this. Something you built yourself and could make it anyway you wanted to. Back home she had her own private quarters, but it never felt like her own place. Her rooms were like a small apartment, and she liked it, but she wasn't passionate about it the way Nick was about this piece of land and his dream.

Nick came back over to stand in front of her. He reached out, brushed a strand of her hair back. "What do you think?"

Chrissy felt as if she'd known him a lot longer than she had. There was no awkwardness with him. She cupped his face with the palm of her hand. "Amazing," she said softly, looking into his eyes.

When his gaze fell to her lips, it was natural for her to part them. He lowered his head, looking once more into her face as if expecting her to stop him. She closed her eyes and leaned in to him. His lips were firm and she sighed as they covered hers. His arms slipped around her waist and pulled her close and she rested her hand on his shoulder. In his arms, she felt incredibly feminine and delicate.

His lips lightly brushed hers, once, twice, teasing them with feather light strokes. She opened her mouth, inviting him to kiss her more intimately. He obliged and Chrissy's head spun. The sensation was much the same as flying across the ocean in his boat. Her insides dipped and swelled and she lost her breath which made her head spin. Nick tasted so good. Nothing in her life before could compare to the headiness of this kiss; it was a connection she didn't understand and wasn't about to question. His lips tenderly kissed her even as he seemed to be pulling away, but he went back for more as if unable to completely stop. Finally, when he lifted his head, her knees buckled.

He caught her up against him. "Sometimes once you get off the boat it's hard to walk on land again."

It was nice of him to give her an excuse, but she had to be honest. "I don't think my legs feeling like rubber has anything to do with the boat." She looked up at him from under her lashes and saw the surprise in his eyes at her statement. But, as if he was trying to keep himself in control, he turned away.

He led her through the clearing by the hand all the while talking about the house and how it would look. "It's going to take years, but there's no way to speed that up. I have to do what I can when I get here."

"'How often do you think you'll get here? After it's done, I mean. It seems such a waste to have a beautiful vacation home you only see once a year."

He sucked in a deep gulp of air and dropped her

hand. "I haven't told anyone else this."

They stopped walking and Chrissy hoisted herself up on to a large boulder that seemed as if nature had put it there just for that purpose.

"I'm quitting my job." Nick squared his shoulders and a hint of fear crossed his face. "I don't want to answer to anyone else again. I don't want to get two weeks vacation and some benefits. I want freedom. I want to have a life."

"You don't have a life now?" The idea sounded crazy. Not work? How would he support himself? Was he going to become a permanent beach bum? He didn't seem like the kind of guy who would be like that. Maybe he wasn't what he seemed after all.

"Not the life I want. I want to work when I want to work. I want to be free of rules and order. If I wake up and it's a gorgeous day," he threw his arms out wide gesturing to the beach, "I want to be able to go boating or lay on the beach or even just turn over and go back to sleep. People work their whole lives to do that when they retire. I want it now."

"How will you support yourself? I mean it's a lovely plan but the reality is that you'll need to eat." Oh God, he wasn't planning on waiting tables or something was he? What a waste. From the conversations she'd had with him several years ago, he was a brilliant accountant. Still the passion in his voice was contagious and she found herself hoping that he had a good solid plan and could make it work.

"I think I can make a go of a virtual accounting firm. It's a thought I've had for a while now and I think it can work. I'll get satellite out here. That way I can work when I want to, not between eight and five."

"You know most small businesses take years to become solvent. Are you going to have enough money?" I shouldn't even ask him that. Chrissy chewed her bottom lip thinking he'd tell her to mind her own business.

He ran his hand around the back of his neck. "My grandfather left me some money that I invested wisely. I think I can make it two years if I'm careful."

"And you'll live here the whole time? You won't mind being alone here on this island for years?" That would be a nightmare. She was used to having people around all the time. Even dinner at her house with the immediate family made up close to twenty. This vacation was nice, but she found she missed her brother and sisters not to mention the hundred or more others that lived there.

Nick ducked his head and looked chagrined. "I'm not much of a people person, to be honest. I like my solitude." He shrugged and looked out across the water. "Besides, its not like I'm stranded on a deserted island. Anytime I crave company I can head into the mainland. Who knows maybe I'll meet someone who wants the same thing and we'll live here in our own paradise."

An immediate image of Nick and some stranger wrapped in each other's arms floated before her eyes. She could imagine him whisking some other woman out here and making love to her on the secluded beach.

Nick loomed over her all of a sudden. "You think I'm nuts. You think why would anyone leave a high paying successful job to take a chance like this?"

His comment was pretty true to what she thought, but she didn't want to discourage him. Who was she to approve or disapprove of his dreams? His gingerbread colored eyes showed his misgivings. He'd just shared with her his plans and she was honored he'd opened up like that.

She reached for his hand. "I think if you put your mind to it you'll make it work. I can see how passionate you are about it and you can do it, Nick, I know you can."

He smiled and bent over to press his lips against hers. Chrissy framed his face in her hands and her heart raced. They were all alone on this island, and her sister's teasing about having fun rang in her ears.

When he lifted his head and rested his forehead against hers he seemed to be trying to catch his breath. "I'm trying really hard to be a gentleman."

Chrissy pulled back until he lifted his head to look at her again. "What happens in Greece stays in Greece?"

He raised his eyebrow. "Lady, those are some dangerous words. Don't say them if you don't mean them." His voice was deep and she shivered in reaction.

Feeling flirty and desirable she slid her hands up to rest flat on his chest. "I never say something I don't mean," she whispered.

Nick crushed her to him so hard she slipped on the rock. A sharp pain shot through her where her upper leg scraped on the hard surface.

"Ohh," she cried out, clinging to him to keep from falling.

Nick helped her down. "Are you ok?"

Her printed sundress covered her upper leg, but she could feel the burning sting. Turning away she lifted her skirt to inspect the damage. High up on her thigh, an ugly red welt had formed and three spurts of blood trickled down.

The blood was staining her new dress, but she couldn't hold her skirt up from it as the cut was up way too high. Nick handed her a tissue and she slipped it under her dress to press against the cut. "Thanks," she muttered.

"Does it hurt?"

She nodded.

"I can't believe what an idiot I am."

She glanced at him. "You didn't do anything. It's no big deal."

"Sure it is. Here we are, all alone, romantic as all get out. We share this kiss that rocks my world, and what do I do? Scrape you against a rock. That's me, Mr. Romance."

The tissue seemed to have stemmed the bleeding, but to be sure Chrissy ripped off a piece of it and left it pressed to the wound. Poor Nick, he looked so embarrassed. "It was a very romantic moment, and a wonderful kiss." She took his hand and squeezed it.

The romantic moment was gone, but she didn't want

him to think she was upset. “Tell me again about your house. You never said what you envisioned for the front yard. Will you have grass here? Or leave it natural like it is?”

Nick searched her eyes before turning back toward the clearing. He slid his arm around her shoulders and she nestled against him as he told her more about his plans for his island retreat.

Chapter Three

Nick felt all kinds of a fool for ruining the kiss earlier. From the amount of blood that stained her skirt, he imagined the cut was pretty deep. It had to hurt. Once back in the boat, he watched as she inched her skirt up to inspect the damage. The sight of her milk-white skin caused his pants to tighten. He couldn't help it; she was so damn beautiful. When she looked up he darted his eyes away.

"Did the bleeding stop?" He pretended a nonchalance he was far from feeling. It could be his imagination but he could swear he saw the hint of lace under her hand where she had bunched the material of her dress.

He looked back at her.

She pulled the tissue away and winced. "Yes."

If only he knew her better, a lot better. He longed to get down on his knees in front of her and kiss it better. Actually he'd like to kiss everything until she felt better. Forcing his thoughts away from what that would be like, he focused on getting the boat ready to head back to shore.

The sun was incredibly hot by now and he yanked his t-shirt off, and tossed it aside. The look in Chrissy's eyes as she stared at his bared chest was enough to make him hard again. He held her gaze and smiled letting her know without a doubt that he loved that she found him attractive. The wind whipped her hair, and her eyes glowed. It was obvious that she enjoyed the rush of the boat ride. It took every amount of effort he had to concentrate on speeding across the water. He'd much rather drop anchor and pull her into his arms.

****

As Nick tied up the boat, Chrissy wasn't sure what to do next. How did she go about letting him know that she didn't want to go back to her room? Not alone anyway. She bit her bottom lip. Living where she did, at the North Pole, she was fairly secluded from mortals of the opposite sex. She'd dated some in college and she wasn't a complete innocent, although she was still technically a virgin. She'd even dated a few elf males, but her status at the North Pole as Santa's only mortal daughter always kept even the wildest elves from doing anything with her. It hadn't mattered much before, she'd never met a man, mortal or not, who made her want the things Nick made her want just by looking at her.

The thought of his hard body, that bronzed chest and those muscular legs made her insides quiver. Watching his powerful forearms bulge as he dealt with the boat was making her half crazy. What was wrong with her? She never felt this wanton before. Ever.

She didn't dare look at him when he joined her and handed her the tote bag she'd left on the boat. "Thanks," she mumbled, and tucked her hair behind her ear.

"So," he started.

But when he didn't finish she was forced to look up at him. Her heart palpitated and her mouth went dry at the fire in his eyes. He was thinking the same thing she was! She swallowed hard.

"Thank you for a lovely day, Nick. I enjoyed the boat ride and seeing your island."

He reached out and cupped her cheek in his hand, caressing her skin with his fingertips. "Is this a brush-off?"

"What? No, I'm not brushing you off. I was thanking you. It was lovely and I did enjoy myself."

His thumb traced her bottom lip and she parted her lips tasting the sale on his skin. "I'd love to invite you to see the sketches of the house but they're on my laptop in my room. I'd be worried that you'd think I'm trying to lure you to my room if I asked you to come see them." He looked insecure, afraid of what she'd say.

She swallowed hard and smiled up at him. "I'd like to see them. Maybe I could come by your room in an hour or so? I'd like to clean up." She waved her hand at her skirt.

He stepped back from her. "I'd almost forgotten about that. You should use some ointment on it. I'll get you some if you don't have it."

She shook her head. "I'm sure there's some in the first aid kit I have in my suitcase."

"Listen, why don't you stay in your room?"

Her heart plummeted. Stay in her room? Didn't he want her to come to him?

"I was going to say, how about I get my laptop and bring it to your room with some snacks in about an hour? It's too early for dinner, but I'm starving."

Chrissy smiled and tugged her tote bag higher on her shoulder. She was starving too, but not for cheese and crackers. "That sounds good. I'll see you in an hour."

With a small wave she started to turn to leave, but he caught her hand. She frowned until he pulled it to his mouth. It would have been a cheesy gesture from anyone else, but from Nick it warmed her all the way to her toes. He pressed his moist mouth to her palm and then closed her fingers over it. "Thanks for not laughing at my dreams today," he said hoarsely.

She knew her cheeks had gone red, and she didn't know how to respond. She nodded and he released her hand. Walking quickly away she kept facing forward, if she looked back, she might have thrown herself into his arms.

All the way to her room her imagination worked overtime. Images of her and Nick falling into her room, her back up against the wall, him hot and heavy and impatiently tearing at her dress, her ripping his shirt over his head. She could hardly think clearly enough to get her card in the door lock and had to swipe it three times before it opened.

Once inside, she was grateful that housekeeping had cleaned up the mess she'd left earlier. She tossed down her bag and stripped, hitting the shower. She reached for her favorite body wash letting the familiar scent of peppermint fill her senses and calm her. As her hands moved over her body, she realized every nerve ending seemed to be resting right below the surface. She couldn't remember another time when she anticipated something as much as whatever was going to happen with Nick this afternoon.

Blowing her shoulder length dark hair dry and fluffing it, she frowned at her reflection in the bathroom mirror. Why couldn't she have been blessed with more 'on top' like her sisters. Her mother always told her it was the elf blood that gave them their 'little extra.' "You'd think with Santa for a father he could work a little bit of magic," she muttered, as she tore through her wardrobe trying desperately to figure out what someone wore to do this. Bathrobe? Nope, too obvious. Shorts and a halter-top? Hmm, maybe. She wished her sisters were around to advise her, every one of them had fantastic taste in clothes and knew exactly what to wear for every occasion.

She chewed her bottom lip and settled her hand on a short black skirt her sister Joy had tossed to her a few weeks ago. "Its too tight on my hips," her younger sister had complained.

Chrissy eyed it speculatively. Not having the curves of her younger sister, she knew it would fit. It wasn't her usual style, it was very short, not mini length short, but several inches about her knee. Everyone told her she had gorgeous legs. Looking down she hated how white they were. Here in Greece all the women were bronzed and beautiful, she felt like she'd been indoors way too long. She held the skirt up to her; it had tiny snowflakes on it. She fumbled in her drawer for a pair of black lace panties, after stepping into them she dropped her robe and slipped into the skirt. Now for a top.

She searched her closet again, but nothing seemed

right. Returning to her dresser she pulled out a couple of t-shirts before snapping up a candy-cane red knit top. The front scooped low, but not too low, just revealing the swell of her breasts. She yanked it on over her head and turned to the mirror. Hmm. Cute. She turned this way and that deciding it didn't look bad without a bra, you could hardly notice anyway. A quick glance at the clock had her rushing back to the bathroom for make up and a quick spray of perfume.

She hung up her robe and opened the door to the patio. Stepping out she inhaled the fragrant smell of flowers mixed with the ocean breeze. Leaning against the railing she closed her eyes picturing Nick coming in and wrapping her in his arms from behind. He'd press his hardness against her and fill his hands with her breasts.

"Hardly filling them," she muttered, walking back into her room.

As she paced restlessly doubt began to creep in. Nick was sexy as all get out and remembering the passion that exploded when he'd kissed her, she had no doubt that if they did make love things it would be fantastic. But was it wrong to even think about doing this when it can only be a vacation fling? Absolutely no way for commitment or a future?

"So what?" she asked her reflection. She lifted her head as if to convince herself that what she was doing wasn't wrong. Life isn't a fairy tale no matter where you live. It's not like Nick is the man for me anyway. He hates Christmas, family, and I'm even beginning to think he doesn't like to work for a living. No, definitely not husband material.

"Am I looking for a husband?" she stopped in her tracks. She'd already convinced herself she couldn't ever be married, so where had that idea come from? Nick was sexy and fun to be with. The boat ride, the island, the kiss! She'd had a great time and whatever happened the rest of the day, she was going to stop worrying and simply enjoy herself. She inspected her outfit once more and decided she didn't look as if she was expecting anything. She could easily wear this skirt and t-shirt out for a walk or down to the café for an Espresso.

The knock at the door made her breath stop. Pressing a hand to her stomach to calm the butterflies she walked barefoot across the carpeted floor. She opened the door to a scowling Nick.

"Shouldn't you have asked who's there?"

"I knew it was you," she held the door open and he came in holding his laptop.

"You shouldn't take chances like that. A beautiful woman all alone in a hotel is vulnerable." He scanned her from head to toe and then back up again.

Chrissy's nipples hardened under his gaze. Damn. Could her body be more obvious? Look Nick, no bra! I'm easy, come and get me. She turned around and shut the door.

Nick walked out onto the patio and set the laptop on the small table. He pushed a few buttons and she frowned. Was he really going to show me drawings? She sighed and joined him, taking a seat in front of the computer. Nick stepped behind the chair, framing her body with his arms as he clicked keys. She felt completely surrounded by him. Hmm this isn't that bad. On the screen a three-dimensional drawing, much like a blueprint, popped up.

He raised his hand to indicate a spot on the screen and his arm brushed against her shoulder. "See right here, this is where we were standing in the clearing."

He pointed out various places on the screen and with each movement the muscles in his arms would shift and bulge. Chrissy watched the screen, but she wasn't listening to a word he said. All she could do was feel. His body heat warmed her; his breath smelled minty fresh as if he'd recently brushed his teeth. Maybe because he was going to be doing some kissing?

She shifted in her chair, casually leaning back until her head was pressed against his chest. He stopped talking and turned his head towards her. "I think I could bury the generator, um, over here."

I could think of something to bury. Chrissy nodded and tipped her head hoping he might decide to kiss her neck. But Nick was back to talking about his drawings. She reached up to rest her hand on his arm, but at the same time he began to straighten and his hand came in contact with her breast.

"Uh, well what do you think?" he asked as if he hadn't touched her.

I'm thinking I want you to do that again only mean it this time. She laid her hand against his bronzed forearm. "I think it's wonderful," she hoped her voice was breathy and sexy.

For a moment she thought he'd ignore the way she looked at him, all but begging him to kiss her. Then he lowered his head and claimed her lips.

Chapter Four

Chrissy's lips were so soft and warm and he couldn't stop the groan that bubbled into his throat as they parted. Her scent, that unique Chrissy scent of peppermint and spice and something else he couldn't name surrounded him. He felt as if he had been given a taste of the sweetest candy on earth and he couldn't get enough. She made tiny noises of pleasure in the back of her throat, and he shifted them until the chair was facing him. He took her face in his hands kissing her harder. She bent her head back so far he was worried it would snap. He cupped her scalp in his hand and let her thick hair tangle in his fingers.

Her hands slid up his chest and he kissed his way down her neck to the middle of her throat. Her pulse beat rapidly and he dragged his mouth across it knowing his own matched it in tempo. It was awkward leaning over her like this, he couldn't kiss her properly. He hauled her to her feet and looked into her eyes. The hunger he saw reflected spurred him on and he bent to scoop her up into his arms.

He felt like a romantic hero from a movie when he swept through the patio doors. He really hoped someone on the beach below them had seen his moves and knew where he was taking this sexy woman.

Chrissy's open mouth on his neck tortured him. She nibbled lightly, her breath hot and moist and making him nuts. He shuddered and tried to focus on walking without dropping her. An oversized chair was just inside the door and he sank into it, cradling her in his lap. No matter how eagerly she was kissing him, he had no idea if she meant for this to go further than kisses and he wasn't going to be so bold as to drop her on the bed. That would have been a quick way for this romantic interlude to end if she wasn't thinking like he was.

Her arms looped around his neck as she settled herself comfortably in his lap and kissed him. Her t-shirt had ridden up and his hand encountered the soft bare skin above the waistband of her skirt. He flattened his hand and slid it under her shirt to caress her back. Encountering no bra made him groan and eager to feel those perky breasts bare in his hands. Chrissy pressed into him and he kissed her with all the passion he felt. He devoured her tongue, suckling it into his mouth and soothing it with a stroke. Chrissy mimicked his action and his head soared above the clouds at what she was doing to him. She twisted, and he slipped his hand around to her rib cage then upward. Her breast sat in his hand like a small ball and he traced his thumb across her already hardened nipple. Chrissy kissed his neck and he heard her breath catch as he molded her breast in his palm. She was as eager to touch him as he was her, and she shoved his shirt up and splayed her hands across his chest.

Nick pulled her t-shirt up higher until her breasts were exposed. He wanted to see her—taste her. Chrissy arched her back and closed her eyes as he lifted her until he could take one cherry red nipple in his mouth.

Ahhh, more peppermint and a sweetness that he couldn't even describe filled his mouth. She must wear a specially made perfume that made her taste this good. It was like licking the finest candy cane he'd ever eaten. He loved it and couldn't get enough, which was very strange since he normally hated Christmas candy. His hand molded one breast while his mouth devoured the other. Chrissy's fingers were in his hair and she pressed closer to him as he feasted. Nick slid his hand to the hem of her skirt sliding his finger underneath and reveling in the silkiness of her bare thigh.

He lifted his head and looked at her breasts. They were swollen from his attention, and so perfectly formed he was surprised they were real. He swallowed hard. Chrissy opened her eyes and for a long second he just stared at her, loving how she looked with a flush on her cheeks and her eyes dark with desire. All for him, all because of him. He couldn't quite get his head around it. Chrissy Star, the cool accountant beauty was half naked in his arms and didn't look as if she wanted to be anywhere else.

"You're beautiful," he said.

She smiled back at him and shrugged her slim shoulders. "I'm too small," she whispered looking embarrassed.

"You are absolutely perfect." He lifted one small breast and pressed his lips to her nipple. She cried out and he suckled until she was writhing in his arms. He molded his hand to her bare thigh hoping he was going to find out about those lace panties when she winced. He immediately froze and looked up at her. Damn. He forgot about her cut. Strike two, Christopoulos. First your fumbling gets her the cut and then your fumbling hurts her again. What an idiot. He lifted the hem of her skirt to inspect it her leg.

"Did you put something on it?" he asked not touching the spot, but caressing the soft skin around it. The bruise was nasty looking with a skinny red line through the center.

"It's ok," she said hoarsely.

His gaze took in snow-white thighs, and black lace that covered or sort of covered a patch of darkness. Chrissy wasn't slapping his hand away so he edged her skirt up higher and looked at her. With her red t-shirt pushed up, he had a beautiful view of her bared breasts and her black lace panties. She lounged in his arms and he began to shake. He couldn't help it. She was so sexy. It was all he could do not to explode. What more could any man want? Especially a man like him. He was a nerd. He shouldn't even have a chance with a woman like this. But she was here, and unless he was very mistaken, she was warm and willing.

Still, he wasn't going to seduce her and have her regret it later. With a huge amount of willpower he settled her skirt back into place and pulled her t-shirt down covering the delectable cherry points.

Chrissy's face revealed her confusion. Nick gently set her away from him and stood up. His Khaki pants bulged and her eyes caught and hung there. He wasn't embarrassed for her to know how much he wanted her, but he wanted to make sure she knew they didn't have to go any further.

"I really did come here to show you the drawings of my house. I didn't plan this." He raked his hands through his hair.

She scooted to the edge of the chair. Her head was even with his pants and he started to take a step back but she reached out and traced one finger along the ridge of his zipper. She lifted her face to look at him. "Nick."

Her tongue snaked out to wet her lips and she seemed unsure what else to say. Her fingers reached for his belt and slipped it open. He couldn't move as she lowered his zipper.

"I want you," she said spreading his pants open until his erection peeked out from behind his boxers.

Before she could reach for him he caught her face in his hands and kissed her hard. He pulled her to her feet and still kissing her walked with her to the bed. Chrissy shoved his pants down until they pooled at his feet and took hold of him through his cotton boxers. Clenching his teeth, he filled his hands with her breasts. He pressed them together through her t-shirt and lowered his mouth to the cleavage he'd formed.

He sat down on the edge of the bed and lifted her shirt. He took her in his mouth and she wrapped her arms around his head pressing him to her. He licked one ripe nipple and then the other, back and forth. Chrissy pulled her shirt off. He pressed his face against her stomach inhaling the sweet wonderful scent of her skin.

"Nicky," she moaned.

He drew his hand up her leg and under her skirt, this time cupping her wetness and loving the way she shuddered. He dragged his finger back and forth across the lace covering until she whimpered and then he pulled her panties down. It was pure male ego, but he loved the fact that she was hot and ready for him.

Five years ago, he'd worshipped her from afar never even daring to dream about holding her in his arms, now he was about to make love with her. He had no idea what would happen when her vacation ended, if she'd ever see him again, but he knew one thing. She'd never think of Greece without thinking about him. He unzipped her skirt and it fell to the floor. The sight of her standing in front of him naked except for those black panties was like a fantasy come true. He stood up, took her hand, and led her to bed.

****

Chrissy's head spun, her body was on fire! Nick kept starting and stopping. He touched her until she almost came apart in his arms and then he stopped. It was like the sweetest form of torture on the planet, but it left her all but begging him for more. She followed him to the side of the bed and watched as he drew back the white coverlet. He plumped the pillows and she wanted to scream for him to stop wasting time. But when he turned and looked at her, promising without words all that he was going to do to her, she shivered. Nick pushed his boxers down and climbed onto the bed and pulled her with him. His body was toned and hard without an ounce of spare flesh. He drew her up beside him and slid one strong thigh between her legs and kissed her. Chrissy kissed him back, prepared to give him everything she had to give. Finally she was going to make love and be made love to, by a real man. And Nick was sure a man. She reached down to find him hot and throbbing. She smoothed her hand up and down, exploring, touching the tip of his penis, and stroking him until he shuddered.

Nick kissed her harder, groaning as he pulled her even closer to him. He inched his thigh upward until it was between her legs and pleasure coursed through her making her want more of what he was promising.

She thrilled to the feel of the unleashed power in his embrace. His muscles were bunched and he seemed to be trying to hold himself in check, but was rapidly losing control. Chrissy slid to her back and Nick followed her. He moved over her and settled between her legs. She wrapped her arms around his waist and arched up toward him. He kissed her with a passion she'd only read about in books. Her body was a mess of tingling nerve endings when he nibbled at her neck. Shivers of desire danced up her spine when he kissed her lower, closing over one nipple. It felt so good! She loved it when he feasted on her breasts, she could lie like this forever and let him do whatever he wanted as long as he didn't stop.

When his hand explored the flat planes of her stomach and moved lower her legs seemed to spread open for him on their own. His fingers stroked her moist center and the nerve endings that were already overly sensitive exploded. She jerked against him.

"Ohhh," she whimpered. Her voice wasn't one she recognized. "Mmm, Nicky."

She arched up again trying to kiss him or touch him. Her hand reached to touch him once more, but he moved away from her. Before she realized his intent, his warm breath was between her legs and sensations she'd never felt before rocked through her. A burst of adrenalin mixed with incredible pleasure washed over here and she felt as high as when she flew on the back of a reindeer. Stopping him never entered her mind, and she bucked against his mouth as he kissed her, lavished her, and drove her wild.

"Oh Nicky, oh my, oh don't, ohhhhhhh," she cried out. Chrissy's head thrashed on the pillow and she was unable to focus on anything except what was happening to her. As the pressure climbed, she grabbed hold of the sheets, bunching them in her fists. Nick lifted her hips higher against him. The sensations coursing through her body were too much and then she felt her entire being tense and coil as if she were a spring. Nick slid one finger inside her as his mouth continued its magic. With a sharp cry, she exploded in a lightshow of sensations so powerful her body jerked and bucked all on its own. The world tipped and turned and she felt as if she was free falling through space.

Nick caressed her. He soothed her with his hands, and murmured gently against her. When the tremors slowed, he kissed his way up her body, pausing to nuzzle her breast. He reached her lips, but it was too much of an effort to open her eyes and look at him. This was what she'd been missing out on all this time?

Nick brushed the damp hair off her forehead. "You ok?"

She was fine, more than fine, but she was also embarrassed at how loudly she'd expressed her pleasure. Cautiously she lifted her eyelids to look at him. Nick looked incredibly pleased with himself. She knew he felt some type of male pleasure at her responses. She slipped her arms around his back and then lower to cup his bare butt cheeks. "Yes."

It was time for his pleasure to be as vocal as hers. She placed her hand on his bare hip and shoved him to the side of her so she could reach between them.

He closed his eyes and moaned when she wrapped her hand around him. As she stroked him, he lowered his head and took her breast in his mouth, teasing the hard peak. She shivered at the sensations zipping through her once more, but was intent on turning the tables on him. He'd been way too proud of himself. This time it was going to be her with the cat that ate the canary look on her face. She went completely on instinct, letting his body's response lead her in the right direction. Pushing him down until he lay on his back, she loomed over him. Her aching breasts brushed his chest and it felt good. She did it again and he reached for her taking both breasts in his hands. He stroked her with his thumbs making her head spin.

"Mmmm," she moaned looking down at his hands on her body.

She loved watching him touch her. His dark skin against hers was a turn-on. He lifted both breasts and buried his face in them. When his mouth closed over her nipple again, she gave in and let the sensations wash over her. He pulled her closer so he could feast on first one and then the other, and she forgot she had been going to make him crazy.

"I don't know why, but I can't stop tasting you," he said pulling her nipple into his mouth again. "They're like gum drops."

Gum drops! They weren't that small. Chrissy pulled away, before the pleasure pulled her under.

"It's my turn to see how you taste," she said, kissing his chest and working her way down his body until she his erection come into view. "Can I lick your candy cane?" she asked, all wide-eyed and innocent. Before he could answer she lowered her mouth.

He groaned harshly and bucked his hips up against her. It was more than obvious he was enjoying this as much as she had. She ran her hands up and down him, suckled, licked and thrilled to the sounds he made as she explored every inch of his hardness. His fingers tangled in her hair as she focused on her task.

"Hmmmm," she murmured and drew her tongue along the length of him as if he truly were a candy cane. The image of the peppermint treat in her head guided her movements and she was so caught up in what she was doing, she was stunned when he suddenly pulled her away. Before she realized his intent he had her underneath him once more.

Nick's breath came in short quick gasps, and she watched him struggle to open a tiny square package. Of course, a condom! She'd never even given that a thought.

Did he bring one with him? Was he that sure of her? Should she feel bad about that? As he spread her thighs and looked down at her, it really didn't matter why he brought it, she was just relieved one of them had protection with them. His eyes held the question and she smiled her answer. Nick bent and kissed her hard as he entered her. She tried to stop the wince at the burning sensation, but couldn't quite hold it in. He jerked his head up and stared at her in shock.

"Ahh Chrissy," his eyes looked at her with...was that pity? Damn it. He wasn't going to stop now when she was this close to knowing everything. He slipped out of her.

"No. Don't stop." She reached for him and pulled his face back to hers, kissing him hard. She smoothed her hands down his back and urged his hips back into position.

"Damn," he murmured harshly against her mouth. His fingers found her once more and manipulated and toyed until she was half crazy, but Chrissy didn't want another orgasm like that, she wanted him inside her.

"Please, Nick."

He began to enter her, slowly, but she wanted more and she lifted her hips in invitation and pressed him harder against her. She didn't think anything could feel as good as what he'd done to her earlier, but somehow the weight of him on her, him filling her took everything to another level of pleasure. Her hips danced against him in a rhythm she didn't even know she knew.

He kissed her and pumped faster. When her world started to explode again, she clung to his back, digging her fingers into his skin. She cried out her climax hoarsely as her body shook and shuddered. Nick thrust deep and hard and his body tensed and then jerked as he growled against her throat. Chrissy felt as if she were on an out of control sled heading for the bottom of the hill. It went faster and faster until she hit a large soft snow bank that stopped her fall.

Long moments passed before Nick whispered. "I can't

believe you didn't tell me you never did that before." He lifted his head.

She put her fingers over his lips. "I'm glad it was with you."

He kissed her gently and then edged off her. She watched him wrap the used condom in a tissue from her nightstand. Then he pulled the coverlet over both of them and pulled her back into his arms. Draped across his chest, Chrissy looked out the patio where her door still stood open. How many people had walked by on the beach below and heard them? She giggled.

"What are you laughing about?" he asked.

She splayed her hands across his chest, weaving her fingers in the fine hairs. "I was thinking we should have shut the patio door."

Nick kissed her temple, smoothed his hand over her hair and chuckled. "Next time, let's spread a blanket right out there on the floor."

"Hmm, that sounds nice. In the dark, with the stars overhead, wouldn't that be nice?"

Nick didn't answer, but his hand continued to stroke her bare back. More long moments passed and he didn't say anything else. What should she do next? Did they take a nap? Or should she get up and take a shower and be casual about what just happened? What was the protocol for afternoon sex with someone you only knew a short while? Finally, when he didn't seem inclined to be making any type of move, she sat up and brushed back her hair. Nick's eyes clung to her bare breasts and she wished again she were more voluptuous like her sisters.

"It's just about dinner time, how about I go to my room, take a shower, get changed and we'll go out?" he asked.

Her face must have showed how disappointed she was at the idea of him leaving. He cupped her cheek and sat up and kissed her. "Or I could shower here."

Chapter Five

The waves crashed into the beach sounding like the sounds from a nature CD. Chrissy couldn't believe that she was walking along the sand hand-in-hand with Nick when only two days ago, she'd been envious of the lovers she'd seen strolling by. She looked up into his face lit by the full moon. He was her lover. She had a lover! She grinned remembering all over again their afternoon and the shower they took together. As if they'd reached some predetermined spot, Nick stopped and took her in his arms. As she tipped her face up for his kiss, her heart thundered and she wondered if another moment in her life would ever again be this perfect. She knew it wouldn't. This was what she had. Tonight, tomorrow and the rest of her vacation, but that was it.

The idea of never kissing Nick again, never making love with him again, made her cling to him. He groaned in his throat and wrapped her tighter in his arms, his hands cupping her rear end through her sundress and lifting her up against him. When neither could catch their breath, she broke away and raked her fingers through her wind blown hair.

Nick caught her hand again, and pulled her down to sit with him on the beach. Chrissy drew her knees up and wrapped her arms around her legs, tucking her dress around her. Her bare feet dug into the still warm sand.

"What's wrong?" he asked.

Chrissy turned to look at him. Her heart leapt as she studied his strong angular features, his dark hair and even though the moon shadowed them she knew how brown his eyes were. He was so good looking. "Why do you hate Christmas as much as you do?"

Nick furrowed his brow and leaned back on his elbows. “Does it matter?”

She chewed her lip, wondering the exact same thing. Why was she pushing an issue that she knew was going to drive a wedge between them? Was that what she was trying to do? Push him away because she knew in a few days she’d have to let him go anyway?

“I was just curious. I love the holiday so much; it just seems odd to me that someone would hate it as much as you do.”

Nick picked up a stone and tossed it in front of him. “I guess if I had to pinpoint it, I’d say I started hating it when I discovered that Santa was simply a myth that adults tell children to explain the abundance of gifts they get. I think some parents give their kids huge Christmas’ because they feel guilty for not giving their kids what they really need. Their time.”

He seemed to struggle with the words, and Chrissy kept quiet, not wanting to interrupt him.

“I believed in Santa, like all kids, and when I found out he wasn’t real, that it was a big lie, I felt like an idiot. I mean if you can’t trust your parents not to lie to you, who can you trust? To this day I can’t stand people who aren’t honest and upfront about things.”

He looked at her and she hoped he couldn’t see how red her face was. She could feel the warmth in her cheeks. Her stomach flipped over. “Do you really think it hurts kids to believe in Santa and all he stands for?”

Once again he tossed a stone. She could tell by the rigid way he held himself that he wasn’t comfortable with the conversation. He had no idea how important it was to her and she couldn’t seem to stop pushing the issue.

“Kids should know that their parents love them and believe in them. I don’t think they need to have a pile of gifts under a tree to know they’re loved.”

“Ok gifts aside though, don’t you think it’s great for kids to have something to believe in?”

“The most important thing that kids can believe in is

themselves. We need to teach kids that there is no magical figure out there that's going to make their dreams come true. They have to do that themselves through hard work. Give them self-confidence and the skills to get ahead. That's what we should be teaching them instead of 'eat your peas or Santa's not coming.'"

Chrissy wanted to reach out and touch him. It was becoming very obvious that Nick had, at some point, been deeply disappointed by Santa and he'd never gotten over it. It wasn't unusual, her family had run into this before. Sometimes they were able to make childhood dreams come true even decades later.

Softly she asked, "Was there ever something you asked Santa for that he didn't bring you?"

Nick jerked his head around and she knew by the look in his eyes she'd hit her mark, but he wasn't ready to admit it. "That's ridiculous. My parents bought me everything I asked for every year and then some. There's no big psychological reason behind my dislike of the Santa story, it's just something I personally think is ridiculous."

She'd pushed enough. If she didn't want tonight to end badly she'd better back off. Smiling, she scooted closer to him and slipped her hand to his thigh. She leaned in towards his ear and heard his breathing hitch. "Do you believe in mistletoe?"

He chuckled and she kissed his ear, running her tongue around the outer shell and down to the sensitive place below his neck. Her hand slid higher on his thigh. Nick moved quick and had her on her back before she realized his intent. She let out a brief cry of surprise as she hit the sand. He leaned over her. "I love everything about the mistletoe legend. But there isn't any for miles around." He darted his eyes up and down the beach.

Chrissy grinned. "There's lots of seaweed that might do as a substitute."

Nick shook his head. "No, someone who is such an ardent believer in Christmas and all things Christmas needs the real thing."

"So what should we do?"

Nick leaned down and brushed his lips over hers. "I just happen to have some in my room."

Chrissy wrapped her arms around his neck and leaned up for another kiss. "Thank goodness you came prepared."

Nick kissed her hard and she opened her mouth under his. His hand slid down to cup her breast through the cotton of her dress. Chrissy's nipple hardened at his touch. The fire that blazed to life was like nothing she could ever have imagined. Restlessly, she wiggled under him wanting more, knowing they couldn't out here, but not ready to get up and break the spell that surrounded the moment.

"Nick," she breathed, as one hand slid up her skirt and caressed her inner thigh.

"I know. But I can't help it. I've thought about this for a long time."

She frowned. A long time? They'd only just met again day before yesterday. She opened her eyes to look at him. "What do you mean?"

Nick's hand stilled. "What?"

Chrissy pushed at him and he moved off her. She sat up, brushing at the sand. "You said you've thought about this for a long time."

A red flush crept into his face. "Chrissy, when we met at that convention, I was blown away by you."

She frowned. "We barely spoke; I can't believe I made much of an impression on you."

"Well you did and even though I knew back then you were way out of my league, I was determined if I ever had the chance to meet you again, you'd remember me."

Chrissy tipped her head and studied him. "You're not saying that you lost the weight and did the big makeover for me?" There was no way someone would do something like that. It was crazy. Was he crazy? She took a step back wondering if she should be worried that he was a stalker type of guy. That would be her luck, some crazed lunatic that was good in bed. "I mean you had no way of even knowing where I was or worked or anything."

Nick reached out for her, but she took another step back. "I tried to find you. Tried to find any information on you and the best I could find was where you'd graduated, but then it was like you disappeared off the earth. I had no idea what your father's company was called, so, no I didn't track you down or anything like that."

"So what are you saying?"

Nick shoved his hands into his pants and stared out across the ocean before responding. "All I'm saying is that you were this beautiful sexy woman and I knew that the way I looked back then, I didn't have a snowball's chance in hell of ever being with someone like you. When I started losing the weight, I started working out. I didn't love it at first, but I kept seeing your face in my mind and it pushed me to keep going. When I finally was physically fit, I decided if I ever ran into you again I wouldn't pass up the opportunity."

"The opportunity? What? The opportunity to sleep with me? This was all pre-planned?" Her illusions of this wonderfully romantic and spontaneous meeting suddenly seemed dirty and illicit to her. She crossed her arms over her chest feeling trampy in the sundress that an hour ago had seemed so sexy.

"No! Not like you think. I saw you when you checked in. I managed to 'run into' you in the restaurant and invite you for a drink. But I didn't plan the rest. How was I to know if we'd even hit it off? I just wanted the opportunity to get to know you."

Chrissy tilted her head. It still sounded like a set up to her. Nick wasn't the man she thought he was even an hour ago. What had he said to her about not liking people who lie or aren't what they seem? She studied him as he stared at her and she realized that he was waiting for her decision. Whatever she did next would set the course for the rest of their vacation. Did she really want to be alone the next week and a half? Wasn't it kind of flattering that he had been so infatuated with her, that he never forgot her? The images of their afternoon in bed swam before her eyes. Was she willing to toss away the rest of her holiday over this?

She lowered her arms and took a step towards him. "I'm being silly. What difference does it make?"

Nick grinned and hauled himself at her as if he were a linebacker. He scooped her up and she laughed, wrapping her legs around his waist and her arms around his neck as he swung her around. "You had me scared to death, angel."

"Oh Nick, do not ever mistake me for an angel. I'm nowhere near that good."

"Is that so? How about we go inside and you can show me just how good you are and I can decide?"

Chrissy dropped her legs from his waist and slid down his body, thrilled by the hard protrusion she rubbed past. "Are you asking to play hide the candy cane with me?"

"That sounds like a Christmas game I can really relate to."

Laughing they ran up the beach hand in hand and out of breath they burst into the lobby of the hotel. They tried to be quiet as they ran past the front desk but laughter exploded from them. They'd just reached the elevators when the desk clerk caught up to them. "Miss Starr, you have had several urgent messages. We were just going out to look for you."

Chrissy took the pink note slips from the young man. Her heart plummeted as she scanned one from her sister asking her to call home as soon as she could, another one from another sister, but finally the last one from her brother Noel. "Where the hell are you? Call home now. Noel."

"Is everything ok?" Nick asked.

Chrissy shook her head and with a frantic glance at the crawling elevator lights, she ran for the door to the stairs. "I'm sorry, I have to call home. I'll call you when I know what's going on." She yanked open the door and ran up the four flights. In minutes she was in he room and dialing home. She glanced at the clock on her nightstand while she waited for someone to answer. "Joy? What's going on? Ok, slow down, just tell me."

Chapter Six

Nick stood where she'd left him at the elevator, unsure what to do. The sheer panic on her face had told him something was seriously wrong. As the elevator doors opened he stepped inside and headed to his room. He'd give her some privacy to make her call, but if he didn't hear from her in twenty minutes he'd go to her room.

Stepping out onto his balcony he marveled at how perfect a night it was. The stars were bright and the moon full. Just a few minutes ago he'd been holding her in his arms on the beach, anticipating a night of her in his bed and another day of starting all over again. He knew it was foolish to think Chrissy might care for him as much as he did her, but he hoped. Their discussion about Christmas and his dislike for it nagged at him. Would she hold that against him? She'd seemed pretty annoyed at his attitude. It wasn't like he would ever ask her to turn her back on the holiday. As long as she didn't expect him to help her trim any Christmas trees.

Stop it. He had to stop thinking of a future with her. For all he knew she was only with him for a vacation fling, not thinking beyond the end of the week. It was only in his mind that he had already hoped they'd have something more. He glanced at his watch, knowing before he did that it was only a few minutes since he'd left her. He hoped everything was ok. What if it wasn't? Would she leave? He couldn't stand it any longer; he walked back into his room and headed up one floor to hers.

He knocked at her door and heard her call out to hang on. She pulled the door open with one hand, the other holding her cell phone to her ear as she spoke. Tears were streaming down her face and she took several deep breaths. “I’ll be there. Yes, I know. Tell him to hang on and tell him I love him.”

Nick frowned. Who was she talking about? A boyfriend back home? Chrissy folded her cell phone and raced across the room. He watched as she yanked her suitcase up onto the bed and frantically began tossing clothes into it.

He shoved his hands in his pockets and disappointment settled in his gut. “You’re leaving?”

She nodded and sniffed. “I have to. There’s a flu epidemic at home, everyone has it.” She glanced up at him and her lower lip trembled. “My father is really sick; he’s never sick. This is horrible.”

“Your mother’s with him isn’t she? And didn’t you say you have like three sisters and your brother at home?”

She nodded and raced into the bathroom returning with an armful of toiletries that she tossed into her bag. “Yes, but some of them are sick too and some of them are already out filling in for those that are down with this bug. You don’t understand. My brother says that three quarters of the production department is in bed with this thing. I have to get home and help or it could spell disaster for this holiday season.”

Nick had no idea what she was talking about. Most companies were already done with their holiday manufacturing. It was only a few days to Christmas. “What kind of business is your family in again?”

Chrissy yanked open all the drawers in the dresser and grabbed her shoes off the floor tossing them into another bag. “Toys. We manufacture toys.”

Nick frowned. “Wouldn’t all the toys have to be made and shipped to the stores already? I mean even Amazon.com only lets you order until midnight tonight to ensure Christmas delivery.”

She gave him a strange twisted look and snorted. “Yeah, well we ensure delivery on Christmas morning so it is imperative it happens. You have no idea the magnitude of this right now. You have no idea what this could mean." She waved her hand as if attempting to find the words she needed and she couldn't.

"I think maybe your family has set themselves up for disaster trying to deliver on Christmas."

She sniffed and closed her suitcase. "Never mind, Nick. I can't explain it and I don't have time to try. I have to go."

"I'll take you to the airport." He walked over and helped her zip her bags closed, not sure what to say or do. She was racing out of his life and he didn't know how to stop her.

"No. Its fine. My, um, father is sending private transportation. It's on the way."

"Where will this private transportation pick you up?"

Chrissy stopped at that and looked at him. "Don't worry about that, I can get there. If you could make sure these bags get to the hotel manager, he has my address and will ship them for me." She hesitated for a second before she walked over to him. With a sad look she wrapped her arms around his neck and pressed her mouth to his in a quick but solid kiss. He tried to hang on to her, but she jerked away and walked to the door.

"Nicky, I'm sorry. Thank you for everything and I know that you'll make it all work out with your dream house and your work situation and well, everything." She started out the door. "Damn it," she came back in and yanked her purse and cell phone off the bed.

Nick grabbed her hand. "I can't let you go like this. I need to know you're ok. How can I reach you; I don't even have your cell number?"

She shook her head and grabbed her upper arms. "Please, Chrissy, don't walk out of my life. I can't stand it. I-I know its nuts, but I love you."

"Ohhhh, Nicky, don't say that." Her shoulders drooped, but she lifted up on tiptoe and kissed him. A hungry kiss that was full of desperation. His hands went to her hair to keep her close and he practically bent her over backwards with his need to show her how much he wanted her. But when she pulled away, he let her go.

She pressed a card into his hand. "You can email me, but I'm warning you from now until the day after Christmas I'm going to be a bit nuts. You're going to be here until the twenty-fourth, right? I'll try to call, I promise."

And she was gone. He watched her head down the hall and back through to the stairs. He glanced at the card in his hand.

"Christmas Star, CFO, Claus Toys, Inc." No other information except her email address. CStarr@northpole.com"

"North Pole?" What the heck? Then it dawned on him. She lived in North Pole, New York. No wonder she loved Christmas so much. He'd read about that little town. It dedicated itself to making children's dreams come true; it made them believe they really were in Santa's North Pole. He knew nothing about Claus Toys though, never heard of them. He'd have to Google them later on. But North Pole, New York wasn't all that far from where he lived. He could easily visit her. Granted she was going to be busy now, but maybe by the New Year. Yeah. That was a great idea. He'd surprise her for New Year's Eve. Feeling better, he picked up her suitcase and bent to get her smaller bag. He spied a photo lying on the floor. He picked it up, ignored the writing on it and turned it over.

A couple dressed like Santa and Mrs. Claus sat in a very realistic looking sleigh with reindeer. In front of them sat several people including Chrissy. She looked so happy, her eyes glowed out at him from the picture. The others could only be her brothers and sisters. Although they didn't look anything like her; in fact, she was definitely the odd one in the bunch. But the one thing they all shared was the obvious glow that came from being happy. He looked again at the couple playing Santa and Mrs. Claus; they certainly looked the part. They were both round, and the suit was great. And the sleigh, it had to have cost a fortune, was outlaid in gold unless he was mistaken. He turned the picture over. "Mom and Dad, in the new sleigh. Joy, Noel, Krista, Holly, me and the reindeer."

He tucked the picture in his pocket. It was the only one he had of her and while he knew he couldn't keep it forever, he as going to keep it until she got in touch with him to get it back.

Nick reached the lobby and saw a flash of her as she disappeared through the front doors. He didn't stop to think, he followed her at a flat-out run. He watched her jog to the corner of the hotel and glance back. She stumbled when she saw him. "Nick, please. I can't do this right now. I have to go. Please go inside."

"Why can't I wait with you? It's late, Chrissy. I don't want you out here all alone."

She glanced behind her at the empty parking lot and then back at him. "Please Nick, don't. You won't understand. Please just go."

As he reached her side, he heard a loud swoosh. Her face paled in the moonlight. "I have to go."

She turned on her heel and ran to the far back corner of the parking lot. He chased after her, wondering if there was a car back there she was taking somewhere or a cab. But what he saw dropped his jaw.

Chrissy climbed into a one-person sleigh, very much like the one he'd seen in her family photo only much smaller. In front of her were two enormous animals that looked every bit like reindeer. She settled herself, grabbed the reins, and looked out at him once more shaking her head. She was obviously mad that he saw her, but right before she slapped the reins together she pressed her hand to her mouth and blew him a kiss.

Then, right before his eyes she literally took off into the air, soaring high above him, above the hotel, and up into the clouds.

Nick just stood there stunned. Shocked. What the hell had just happened? Was he in a dream? Was he going to wake up and find Chrissy still next to him that it was only this afternoon and none of this had happened?

He looked around hoping someone else saw what he'd just seen. But there was no one else there. Numbly, he walked back into the hotel. The clerks at the desk were doing what they normally did and seemed unconcerned that a woman had just climbed into a sleigh with flying reindeer and flown off. There had to be an explanation. He fingered her business card again. North Pole. Weird. This is just too weird.

"Um, Miss Starr asked me to get her bags to you. She said you would ship them to her home."

The manager punched some keys on the computer. "Yes sir, I have her information right here. We'll take care of that immediately. I do hope her family is ok, she said it was a family emergency."

"Yes, her father I guess has come down with a bad flu. Would it be possible for me to get that address? I'd like to send her my condolences."

"I'm sorry sir, that's against policy. I would be happy to include your note with her luggage if you'd like. It'll go out tomorrow morning."

Nick pushed away from the counter. "She gave me her email; I guess I'll just send it that way.""

"Yes sir, that's a good idea. Anything else we can do?"

Nick gave a harsh laugh. "No, I can't think of anything. Good night."

Chapter Seven

Chrissy pushed through the enormous wooden doors of Santa's castle. Kicking her sandals off, she raced barefoot up the sweeping staircase and down several long winding halls to her parents' suite. The doors were open and she burst through looking around frantically. Voices from the bedroom carried her over the thick emerald green carpet and into the next room.

Her parents turned as she appeared. "Oh no, who called you home?" Her father scowled.

Chrissy walked across the room to stand in front of both of them, inspecting her father's pale cheeks and listless eyes. His nose was as red as the famous reindeer's and her mother looked worn out and worried. "It doesn't matter who called me, they should have called sooner. Why aren't you in bed?"

Her mother, Mary, shook her head. "He won't listen. He won't go see the healer and he won't rest. He still insists he's going out on Christmas Eve."

"Of course I'm going out." Her father bellowed. "I work one night a year, Mary! It's not going to kill me."

"It just might. You know, even your powers might not be enough for whatever this bug is everyone has." Turning to her daughter she said, "Go see the healer and get some medicine right away. We've had some good luck with those that have taken the healing powders before getting any symptoms."

"How many are down with this?"

Her father started coughing, his belly shook beneath his undershirt, and his eyes slammed shut. He coughed and coughed and her mother guided him to sit on the bed, but he brushed her off as soon as he sat down. "Stop fussing," he gasped.

Chrissy bit her lip. This wasn't good; she had to do something. "I'm going to go find the others. Then I'll go into the shop and see where we stand."

She reached for her mother and hugged her, feeling her shoulders beneath her hands. It was unusual for her mother to be this thin and this upset. She glanced at her father once more.

"I'm sorry your vacation got cut short, honey, did you have a nice time?"

Chrissy couldn't stop thinking about Nick and how he looked as she flew—literally—away from him. Her heart squeezed, but she didn't have time to deal with those feelings right now. "Yes, it was nice, but I'm glad I'm here. You should have called sooner!"

"Don't need you here, nothing you can do to help." Her father wheezed as he collapsed against the pillows.

"Jeez, thanks Dad, nothing like knowing I'm good for something." She shook her head and tried not to let his words upset her. He didn't mean them the way he said them, but it was bad enough that she felt inept compared to her siblings who had elf powers.

Her mother walked with her across the room and pulled the heavy double doors to the bedroom closed behind her. "I don't know what we can do if he insists he's going. Holly has already said she's going to ride with him, but I don't think he can do this."

"Why can't he freeze time, you know, hold things off a week or so or until he's better?"

Mary smiled and rested her warm hand against her daughter's cheek. "It's admirable that you think your father can do something that amazing, but even Santa can only freeze time for twenty-four hours. Only long enough to make sure the deliveries are made."

Chrissy nodded. "Where are Joy and Krista?"

"I think they're in the parlor, they were going over

the lists once more. Your father finally gave them the password to the computer program so they could pull them down."

"I'll go find them," as her mother started to say something she nodded. "Yes, Mama, I'll go see the healer first."

Her sisters were engrossed in a meeting with the Naughty and Nice lists and after talking to them for a brief minute she hurried up to her room to change. Twenty minutes later she walked out of the medical center, rubbing her arm from the shot he'd insisted on. She also had a handful of packets of powder with instructions to take them at bedtime every night.

The factory was strangely quiet with only a third of the normally thousands of elves at their benches. In her office she pushed aside all the papers, opened the small refrigerator, and popped open a diet soda. Flying literally across the world last night had only allowed her a few hours sleep and she was trying hard to figure out where to start when her phone lit up.

"Yes?"

"I'm sorry to bother you Ms. Starr, but your brother has called a meeting in the large conference room with everyone."

"That's fine, Missy, one of us needs to get this organized." Chrissy set the phone back down and took a second to close her eyes and prepare for whatever lay ahead over the next several days. Grabbing a stack of files that she didn't know if she'd need or not, she took her diet pop and headed upstairs to the main conference room.

****

Nick dropped his suitcase inside the door of his apartment and flipped on the lights. Tossing his keys on the table, he moved through to the kitchen and grabbed a beer out of the refrigerator. His apartment was as quiet as when he'd left three weeks earlier, but somehow now it seemed lonely and cold too. There'd been a time he'd imagined coming home and having Chrissy with him. It had been a crazy thought, but he pictured them in his living room sitting on the leather couch, talking about their vacation in Greece and making plans for when they'd go back again.

"Stupid."

For at least the hundredth time he took her business card out of his shirt pocket and fingered the letters. The sight of her flying away in that contraption and her email address had given him some very odd dreams. He knew there was a logical explanation, everything in life had a logical explanation, but he'd yet to come up with one. He'd already emailed her the night she left. But he'd heard nothing back.

After unpacking his laptop and firing it up he checked emails. Nothing. It had been two days and no word from her. Even though he'd already Googled it several times already and turned up nothing. He still couldn't stop himself from trying once more. He keyed in Claus Toys. Same as before a long list appeared, but this time there was a completely new entry at the very top. He clicked on the link.

Photos and text appeared and he glanced at the bar that was still loading, surprised by the amount of content. The first photo was one you could see in holiday advertisement. Elves sat around long workbenches making toys. They looked similar to what he'd seen on TV over the years, although he had to admit some of the female elves were pretty attractive. Another photo showed some of the female elves posing for the camera and his eyes bugged out. These elves were quite well endowed. He never noticed that in the cartoons when he was a kid.

The next photo showed Mrs. Santa Claus in the kitchen baking gingerbread men. He shuddered and was just about to click to the next one when he noticed the woman in the scene. It was Chrissy! His Chrissy!

He frantically tried to zoom in, but the web site wouldn't allow him to look any closer. Frustrated, he clicked through picture after picture on the site. Another picture showed the outside of what apparently was Santa's factory and there on the sign was the name, "Claus Toys, a division of Christmas Town, Inc." He stared at it. Obviously Chrissy's family company was completely devoted to making children believe there really was such a place and that Santa was completely real.

He read the text anxious to learn everything he could about this strange role-playing company. "Santa's five children." There was another picture and there was Chrissy in the middle of her brother and sisters. The description named them as Holly, Krista, and twins Joy and Noel. The son sat astride the most spectacular motorcycle he'd ever seen. Obviously, this weird family had some serious money.

How had he missed this web site earlier? He must have Googled five times over the past two days looking for anything and now today there it was at the very top of the Search Engine list. Something was not right about that. He rubbed his hands over his eyes. Jetlag had set in with a vengeance. Leaving the laptop open to the photo of Chrissy and her siblings, he set it on the coffee table. After finishing off his beer he headed to his bedroom.

Lying in the dark, it was no surprise that all he could see was Chrissy. He missed her laughter, her smile when he showed her his island, her tenderness as they made love. He wasn't sure which hurt more the ache in his heart or the ache lower. Flopping over he tried to block his mind from the thought that he might never see her again. He still planned to go to North Pole in New York right after Christmas, but in his heart he knew she wasn't going to be there. She was somewhere else and he had a feeling it was somewhere he could never hope to find on his own.

It was so hot in here. Why was his furnace up so high? He could have sworn when he came home he hadn't turned it up. He shoved at the blankets with his feet. He'd have to get up and turn the thermostat down; he couldn't sleep like this. He swung his legs over the side of the bed and dropped his head into his hands. He was so tired. What the heck time was it? He opened his eyes to look at the bedside clock.

"What the hell..." he blinked and looked around. He was no longer in his bedroom, but the room looked familiar. He knew he'd never been here before, and yet he knew where everything was. The bed was an enormous four-poster monstrosity that took up half of what could only be called a suite of a room. At one end, a small couch and comfortable chair made up a small sitting area in front of a fireplace. Turning towards the sound of water hitting the shore, his eyes widened at the sight of the floor to ceiling curtains. He stood up and slowly crossed the room, half afraid, half knowing exactly what he would see outside the large picture window

"Oh God, oh my God." His knees buckled as he yanked the sheer fabric back and saw the view of the Sea. The windows opened with a push and he stuck his head out. "What the hell is going on?" The view out the window was the view he had shown Chrissy last week. He'd stood here and told her, "This is where the bedroom window will be and when I wake up this will be the view out my window."

He turned back to the room, walked across the floor and out the bedroom door. In the large hallway he looked down, once again knowing what he'd see. He was in his house. His dream house on his island. The house that hadn't been built yet. Obviously, he was dreaming. He'd dreamed of being hot and he dreamed of getting out of bed, and he was dreaming up this whole thing. Jetlag had made him a bit crazy that's all.

If he really were dreaming, then Chrissy would be there too. Maybe in the kitchen. He sprinted through the house. What a dumb dream. She should have been next to him in bed and he could be having a really good dream right now. Still, she had to be here somewhere.

As eager as he was to get to Chrissy, he couldn't help

admire how beautifully the house was designed. The whole back wall gave a view of the sea that couldn't be measured; it was even landscaped perfectly.

"Chrissy," he called out. "Chrissy!" Anxious to see her, if only in his dreams, he raced through the door to the kitchen and stopped cold. She wasn't there, but the stainless steel appliances, the tiled floor and the granite counter tops were everything he ever could have dreamed. It was spectacular.

But no Chrissy. He frowned. What kind of dream was this if he didn't get to see her? He slid open the glass doors that led to the outside patio. In his flannel pajama bottoms he was immediately overheated. The sun was brutal and the sand under his feet was hot. It all felt so real.

Maybe Chrissy was here, lying on their private beach in that tiny little bikini he loved so much. He ran down the path and around the winding curve as if he'd done it a hundred times before, and he had, only on paper. He knew where each plant was and where the beach shack would be. He scanned the white sand, but found no sign of the woman he loved. The beach furniture he'd placed on his drawing was there, but not the beautiful woman he imagined lounging on it.

Dejected, he sank to the sand and dropped his head into his hands. This had to mean something. Did it mean that he needed to forget about his dream of having her here with him on his island? Or was his dream trying to tell him how empty his life would be even if he had all this but not her? He swallowed hard. When was he going to wake up? Then again, maybe he didn't want to wake up. If he couldn't have Chrissy in real life, maybe he could stay here in this dream.

No, he had to wake up. He had to get back to his mission of finding her. And he would find her. Tomorrow morning he'd Mapquest that silly little town and go there. If she wasn't there, he'd keep looking. If she didn't want him to find her, she'd have to tell him to his face. He wasn't willing to let her disappear from his life a second time.

He stood up and walked back along the path to the winding front porch. On the side of the stoop he saw a small plaque and leaned forward to read it. Claus Construction—erected December 24. The year was now and he frowned. "I can't even dream realistically." It was as if the house was just built today. Things were getting weirder and weirder.

"Maybe I'll just go back to bed and close my eyes. Maybe I can't wake up because I'm not in bed." With one more look around at his house, he climbed the stairs and crawled back into bed.

Chapter Eight

"Daddy, please don't do this." Chrissy added her pleas to her sisters' and mother's as Santa continued to don the famous suit. It had taken him an inordinately long time, as he had to stop and sit down when his coughing spells worsened. He had a fever, he was weak, but he still insisted on going. Chrissy glanced at her sister Holly, who picked at her fingernails.

"You're going to freeze in that outfit," she said, scanning the scantily clad elf.

Holly glanced down. "We don't feel the same cold you do, remember? Besides, I'm cute."

Chrissy rolled her eyes. "Yeah, if you're working an adult holiday party. I hope you don't run into any sleepy fifteen year old boys in that suit."

Holly shrugged. "I just might make some older boys dreams come true."

Santa began to cough again and both sisters turned to their father again. "I want all of you out, I need to talk to Chrissy," he demanded.

"Oh but Papa, you need to get ready. We need to leave in under an hour."

"Holly, don't lecture me, I know my schedule. Now go, I need to talk to your sister."

Chrissy turned to her sister and mother. "I'll get him ready. I promise. Maybe put together some more hot chocolate and pack up those cookies for the trip."

Her mother touched her shoulder as she walked by with Holly. Chrissy turned to her father. He sat in his overstuffed chair catching his breath.

"Come here," he called and patted the footstool in front of him. "We haven't talked yet about your

Christmas wish and here it is time for me to go."

"Its ok Papa, we can talk about it later."

"Nonsense, you know I'll have a late night and I'm afraid this time I'll have to freeze time as long as possible. I have a feeling it's going to be a slow go."

"I wish you'd let Noel do this and Holly..."

"They're not ready, you know that."

"They're about 300 years old, when do you think they'll be ready?" Chrissy smiled to soften her arguing.

"I'll know when they're ready, but back to you. What is it your heart desires this year, my precious child?"

Santa's large hand reached out to cup her cheek, and she tried to hide her thoughts from him but she knew it was no use. Her father could see them whenever he wanted and he saw them now. "Ahh, Nick Christopolous. Is that who you wish for?"

Chrissy thought of Nick and their times together but quickly switched her thoughts, not wanting her father to see all her memories. "It's not him, Papa, or rather it's for him. Nick hates Christmas. He's lost the holiday spirit and thinks it's a huge waste of time."

Santa chuckled. "Yes I've heard something along those lines about him. You know my policy on that."

She nodded. "I know, once they don't believe in you anymore, you cross them off the list, but I think Nick has a good heart. I know he does. He has this thing about people lying to him, and he felt as if you were a big story his parents made up."

"Most adults do. It takes a very special adult to still believe in Santa Claus."

Chrissy's eyes filled with tears thinking of all the years Nick hadn't received gifts from Santa. No special packages dropped down his chimney, no candy canes in his stocking, no gingerbread. "I was hoping, I guess, maybe if you could somehow make him believe again."

"Sweetheart, you know that I can't do that. I can't make someone believe in me."

She knew that. Even as sadness settled around her

heart she knew that it was the only small chance she had of a future with Nick. If he believed in Santa once more, she might be able to help him believe that she was Santa's daughter. It had been a foolish wish.

"There has to be something else I can get you this year, some other wish that's within my power."

Chrissy shrugged. "I suppose peace on earth would be nice."

Santa began to cough again and his chest heaved. Chrissy's eyes flew to her father's. "I know what I want. I want you not to go tonight. Please Daddy, I couldn't bear it if something happened to you. Think of the children. What would life be like with no Santa?"

She threw herself into his arms and he held her against him. She could hear the wheezing in his chest. His large hand stroked her hair and patted her back before he pushed her away. "Don't you fret about that. I'm going to be fine. It is only twenty-four hours. I'll come back and I promise I'll go to bed for a week if that's what it takes." As she started to say something more he set her away and stood up. "I promise you, little girl, I'll be back and I'll take care of myself. Now I'm counting on you to help your mother here tonight and tomorrow."

Chrissy sank to the footstool once more and bowed her head. There was nothing she could do. Her father was going out sick. He couldn't give Nick the Christmas spirit and if Nick had no Christmas spirit, well it wasn't too far fetched a notion to recognize that he couldn't believe in Santa's daughter if he didn't believe in Santa. Obviously she couldn't think about a relationship with someone like that. She needed a believer. Maybe next year she'd ask her father to help her find a nice elf. She stood up and walked slowly out of the room. Elves were nice. Some of them. She could make a good life with an elf man. Besides, her sisters had whispered to her about how good elves were in bed. Something about magical powers that mortals could never hope to achieve.

She brushed the tears away. She didn't want an elf,

she wanted Nick. Nope she didn't want an elf; she wanted a scrooge. A Greek non-believing scrooge! With a soft cry she ran to her room, not ready to face her family until she'd gotten herself under control.

****

"Open your eyes, Scrooge!"

Nick's eyes flew open. He was still in this weird dream. But now he had company.

"Christopolous! Over here."

Fingers snapped and Nick sat up. His eyes widened, and he knew a moment of fear when he saw the very odd looking character across the room.

He was dressed all in black leather. He had white-blonde hair and a nasty scowl on his face. In his hands he held a very large scroll like you'd see in an old movie.

"Who are you?"' Nick asked.

"It doesn't matter who I am, what matters is why I'm here." He moved across the room. "You need to get up and get dressed."

"Why?" Nick asked, but found himself climbing out of bed. He forgot how high off the ground the bed was and he landed in a heap on the floor.

The weird character rolled his eyes. "Oh boy, my sisters sure know how to pick 'em."

"Your sister? Do I know her?"

The elf scowled deeper. "Yeah, you sure do. In more ways than one too, from what I could see."

Nick spied a pair of khaki pants and a shirt lying on the settee at the end of the bed and he picked them up. The weird looking character turned to face the window. "How do you like the house?"

Nick pulled the pants on and tucked in the shirt. "Considering I designed it, I love it."

The weird man tuned back around. "You designed it, but you didn't build it."

Nick yanked a polo shirt on and studied him. "Who did you say your sister was?"

"I didn't."

"Do you know why I'm having this dream?"

The blond guy looked at him again, this time with one eyebrow raised. "You think you're dreaming this? HAH! You are quite the sap, but hey, if this is what Chrissy wants."

Nick's eyes widened, and he fumbled as he slipped his shoes into the loafers sitting by the edge of the bed. "Chrissy? You know Chrissy?"

The elf rolled his eyes again. "Yeah, she's one of my sisters. and I'm not real keen on what you were doing with her in Greece, but we won't go there right now."

"So you're Noel?"

"Noll, it's pronounced Noll. Let's go, we're late."

"Go? Where are we going?"

"To the big house, moron. Come on, it's the twenty-fourth and I'm buried up to my icicles in stuff to do."

Nick followed Chrissy's brother down the stairs and out the front door. There on the driveway sat a big Harley. Remembering the web site, he realized that his subconscious mind must have conjured up the motorcycle. This was some kind of dream.

"It's not a dream, quit saying that. The one on the website was my Ducati. My wife gave me her late husband's Harley for a wedding present. She hadn't been able to bring herself to sell it after he died. When she found out I sold my Ducati to help her with some financial problems, she gave me the Harley."

"I didn't say anything."

"You're thinking it. It's not a dream; this is reality, buddy. Unfortunately."

Noel climbed onto the bike and tossed a helmet to Nick. "Put that on and hang on."

Nick strapped on the helmet and climbed on the back of the bike. "There's no way off this island except by boat."

Noel gave a snort and kick-started the bike. The Harley roared to life and headed down the path that ran along the beach. Nick hesitated a moment and feeling incredibly uncomfortable placed his hands on the back of the leather jacket, not wanting to wrap his arms around the other man. The bike went faster and faster. They were headed straight for the water.

"It's a dream, it's a dream," he muttered to himself. Maybe the bike would turn into some type of Jet Ski or something. It wasn't his concern, he wasn't running this dream, Noel was.

As the bike's tires hit the water, Nick suddenly felt weightless. Looking around, he realized they were flying in the air. "Holy Shit!" Not caring about how it looked, he wrapped his arms around the other man's waist and hung on tight. "What the hell are you doing?"

"Just shut up and ride, Scrooge."

It could have been seconds or hours. Nick had no idea how much time passed by before the bike was on solid ground again. All around him, the scenery was white. Everything was covered in snow and ice but strangely enough he was completely comfortable without a coat until Noel jerked his arms from around his waist and he all but fell off the bike. "Hey man, I said hang on, not climb up the back of me."

"Sorry, I've never, uh flown on a motorcycle before."

Noel let his breath out in a disgusted sigh and jerked the helmet from him. "Come on, this way."

Nick shivered. "It's freezing up here."

The blond man glanced at him in disgust. "It is the North Pole."

"Th-the-the North Pole?"

But Noel kept on walking until they reached the front doors of the castle. They opened without him touching them and a rush of warmth greeted Nick as he stepped inside. It was eerily quiet.

"Everyone's out at the barn getting the sleigh ready." Noel snapped his fingers and two very cute elves appeared. "Take him to the guest wing and keep him there until we call for him." He pointed his finger at them. "Do not do anything, got it?"

The two elves glanced at him and giggled. Nick

couldn't help but notice that just like on the web site these elves were very well proportioned.

"And you, Scrooge, keep your thoughts pure. You're in Santa's castle now."

Then he turned on his heel and headed down the hall. His black leather books thumping purposely until he was out of view. Was Chrissy here? Nick looked around amazed at the sheer magnitude of the foyer. The ceiling had to be...he couldn't even judge how high up it was. The two elves motioned for him to follow and climbed the stairs that seemed to go on forever. Finally, at the top they walked down a very long hallway and unlocked the door at the end. They giggled once more and motioned him to enter.

Chapter Nine

"You want to run this by me one more time?" Chrissy glared at her brother. Her hands were on her hips and she didn't know how she was holding back from strangling him.

"I brought lover boy here; he's in the south wing." Noel tossed a few more provisions into the sleigh. Walking to the front, he tightened the reins again.

"Why is he here? How the heck did you explain to him who you were?" Chrissy marched around the front of the reindeer, pushing their heads aside as she glared at her brother.

"He thinks he's dreaming. He's not the brightest bulb on the Christmas tree, is he?"

"Of course he thinks he's dreaming. He doesn't believe in any of this. How could you do this to me? How could you have brought him here? How am I going to explain it all to him?" Her brother ignored her ranting and she followed him around the back of the massive sleigh. "Put him back. Put him back right now and he'll think it really was a dream."

"In case you hadn't noticed, sister dear, I'm a bit busy tonight." He dodged a nip from one of the reindeer and he turned to point his finger at the huge animal in warning. "First you want him, now you don't. I wish you'd make up your mind."

Chrissy pressed her fingers to her temples to try and stop the pounding. Was she coming down with the same flu the rest of Christmas Town had? No, she felt fine, it was her brother giving her a headache, not a virus. "Noel, he's a mortal. You can't just pluck him from his apartment and zap him here."

"He wasn't in his apartment."

"What?"

Noel handed her a small snow globe. "Have a look."

She was almost afraid to, but slowly she shook the globe and looked inside. Her eyes widened as the view of Nick's island cleared. There was the house just as he showed her on the blueprints. She turned the globe slowly and the interior of the house came into view. "This is Nick's dream house. Why are you showing me this?"

"That's where he was when I brought him here."

Chrissy looked up. "You built it?"

"I never said that. Look, mortals aren't normally that smart anyway, well except for my wife of course, but this one, he keeps muttering about this being a dream. He doesn't get it. Why don't you let me fix you up with this new elf friend I have. "

"Cut it out. I have to go see him. Poor Nick, he probably thinks he lost his mind." She paced the floor restlessly, unable to imagine what he must be thinking "You took him directly to the South Wing? He didn't run into anyone else did he?"

Noel climbed up into the large sleigh and she could hear him rearranging things in the seat. "Where the heck are they? If Holly doesn't get out here soon..."

"I'm coming, I'm coming." Holly came running through the door. "Papa's putting his boots on right now. Everyone at their posts." She hit a buzzer on the wall and those that weren't in bed with the flu came running. It was time for the big event. The reindeer pranced in place and excitement mounted.

"Go on, we've got this covered." Noel yelled to Chrissy from the top of the sleigh.

She hesitated. No one had convinced her father not to go, but Holly would be with him. Chrissy had supervised the installation of the new GPS tracking system just that morning so if anything should happen they'd be able to locate him in an instant. They'd taken every precaution. There was nothing more for her to do.

She hurried from the barn to the castle. Her shoes echoed in the hollow halls and on the wooden stairs as she raced up them. Suddenly nervous she paused and instead of going all the way to the top, she headed to her room to freshen up. Nick was here. If he thought it was a dream, she better make it a good one.

****

Nick paced the sumptuous suite of rooms restlessly. He'd already tried to leave but there was some type of barrier that stopped him. He couldn't see it, but as soon as he reached the door there was a feeling, a strange unpleasant feeling that pushed him backward and kept him from going any further. Then he'd hear the giggling, and he knew that even though he couldn't see them the elves were there, watching him. He sighed and turned back towards the center of the room. The furnishings were what could only be described as the very finest. No expense had been spared to keep the guests of this suite completely comfortable.

"Hmm, guest or prisoner?" He had to wonder if he wasn't the first person taken hostage and held in this strange place. He'd even started doubting whether this drama he was in was really a dream. Until he tried to explain the house on the island and the flying motorcycle and oh yeah, the little details about being in Santa Claus' castle.

A sound on the other side of the door drew his attention. He expected to see the goofy blond biker when the door opened, but it was Chrissy who walked in. She looked different. In Greece she was beautiful, magnificent but here she looked almost regal. She walked across the carpet softly, as if she were gliding. Her long dress flowed with her and he thought she looked like the angel from the top of a Christmas tree.

"Hello, Nick," she said softly.

"Chrissy." Nick walked across the room to stand in front of her. After she'd left the island all he wanted to do was find her and take her in his arms and never let her go. Now here she was, right in front of him and he was as shy as the first time he'd met her.

"I hope things haven't been too unpleasant so far. My brother can be pretty intimidating at times."

Nick searched her face, eager to see anything in her eyes that would encourage him to touch her. "He is, uh, different."

She laughed softly and glanced towards the door. "And the elves? I trust they were polite."

He nodded and not knowing what else to do he shoved his hands in his pockets. "Yeah, they were great. I didn't really talk to them. This is some place."

She smiled and looked around. "It's one of our guest suites. Actually if I'm not mistaken you're the first one to use it since we redecorated."

"Chrissy?"

"Hmm?"

Nick leaned in closer. "This is a dream, right?"

She looked disappointed at him. She reached for his hand and he struggled to get it out of his pocket. Their fingers linked, she tugged him to follow her to the small settee across the room.

He sat down, but wouldn't release her hand even when she tried to pull away. After a moment, she stopped and he lifted their joined hands to his lips. "If I'm dreaming, I don't care, I need to hold you again. To kiss you." He stared at her, not bothering to hide the pain and longing he felt inside. When she left him that night, she'd taken his heart with her. "I have nothing to lose. Tomorrow I'll wake up and you'll be gone again."

"Oh, Nicky." Her eyes welled up.

He started to pull her into his arms, but she stiffened and he stopped. "I miss you so much. I love you. I do, I know it's too soon and too fast but I know I love you."

"Nick, listen to me. This isn't a dream. Don't you remember that night I left the hotel? You watched me climb into a sleigh pulled by reindeer and I flew. You remember, right?"

Nick stared into her eyes trying hard to find some logic in all of this. He knew he had been wide-awake that night. He knew she'd done exactly what she'd said but the logical part of his brain still wouldn't accept it. "I saw you leave in some type of...something."

"I flew Nick. I flew in a sleigh. Up into the night. Those weren't just ordinary reindeer; they were part of my father's magic fleet. We breed them special and it takes years for the magic to set in."

"Magic? Santa?"

Nick's head was whirling. Maybe he should try to wake up. This was crazy. She was making him crazy. "Yep and I'm here in Santa's castle at the North Pole and those are real live elves out there and your brother drives a magic motorcycle and you are…?"

"His daughter."

"Whose daughter?"

"Santa Claus."

Nick jumped to his feet and couldn't stop laughing. "This is the weirdest dream I've ever had. First the house and the flying motorcycle, and now you're Santa's daughter."

He knew he was babbling but he couldn't seem to stop. It had to be a reaction to something. What did he have to eat last night? Nothing. Maybe that was it. He hadn't had much of an appetite since he lost her. Chrissy. He whirled back around. She sat watching him and a tear slid down her cheek. He came back to her side and grabbed her hands.

"Don't cry. Please. Not in my dreams. I can't stand it. What did I do? Tell me and I'll fix it." He pressed her fingers to his lips and kissed them over and over.

"Its nothing you can fix, Nick. Don't you see?"

"What, I don't see what?"

"I'm Santa Claus' daughter and you're a non-believer."

"A non-believer?"

"Yes, you don't believe in Christmas, you don't

believe in Santa or reindeer or anything."

"Most adults don't."

She nodded her head. "I know, and I knew that when we...when this all—" She let her breath out on a long sigh. "I can't be with you, Nick. I can't be involved with you."

She pulled her hands free, but when she went to walk away from him again he couldn't bear it. He grabbed her arm, desperate to make her stop. "If you're telling me that the only way to have you is to believe in elves and fairies and Santa Claus then that's fine, I'll believe. I swear I'll believe."

She knew he was lying, he could tell by the look on her face. She pulled her arm free. "I'll talk to my brother about getting you back to your apartment sometime tomorrow afternoon. We're all a bit busy right now, but I'll get you back in one piece, I swear." She reached the door, looked back and her eyes were full of hurt and disappointment. "Then I'll have my father take care of your memory so that you really will think this was all a dream. All of it."

She pulled the door open and he panicked.

"Wait!"

He strode across the room. "Convince me! If what we shared in Greece meant anything to you, make me a believer."

She whirled around, her eyes wide as if he amazed her. "You can't make someone a believer, Nick. It has to be inside. In here." She put her hand over her heart.

Nick walked up to her not letting any space come between them. He laid his hand over the top of hers where it rested on her breast. "You know what I believe? I believe that there's a reason why we met five years ago. I believe there's a reason why we were both in Greece this month. I believe that we were meant to be."

Without giving her time to break free he slid one hand around the back of her head and pulled her to him. He put everything into the kiss; he had to make her believe. Believe in him and how much he loved her. He couldn't let her go again. He wasn't going to let her go again. Dream or no dream he was going to hear her say she loved him and wasn't going to leave him.

He felt her relax in his arms with a small moan of surrender and returned his kiss. Fire coursed through him as their tongues reunited and their mouths meshed together. Chrissy's hand slipped out from under his so that his rested on her breast. She twisted around to wrap her arms around his neck.

"Good thing Dad just took off."

Chrissy tore her mouth from Nick's and felt her face go bright red under her sister's stare. "Joy!" she hissed in disgust.

Her sister lounged against the upstairs railing, watching without looking a bit ashamed. "Mama was wondering where you were and I offered to come find you. Figured this would be the best place to start looking. Yum, yum," she said, raking Nick from head to toe.

Chrissy glanced at Nick, who seemed amused by her little sister's antics.

"Where is she?"

"In the kitchen. She said you were supposed to help get those gingerbread men packed up for tomorrow."

Chrissy was conscious of Nick's arm snaking around her waist. "It looks like you get to meet my mother. Are you ready for that?"

He smiled. "Would that be the infamous Mrs. Claus?"

Chrissy reached behind her and took his hand again. "The one and only. I hope you're up to it."

She pulled him along behind her, ignoring her sister who smirked as she watched them descend the large staircase. Nick didn't say a word but she watched his eyes bug out as they walked down the long corridors to the back of the castle. The noise level increased as they went. "With my father gone..."

"Gone?"

Was he kidding? "Its Christmas Eve. He's gone out on deliveries."

"Oh yeah, right, sorry. I've lost track of time."

"Anyway, my mother will spend the better part of the night in the kitchen with her crew putting the finishing touches on candies and cookies that will be part of our own celebration day after tomorrow."

"Tomorrow?"

Chrissy nodded once more and pushed through the large swinging door that led to the main kitchen. It was noisy and warm; with a blur of activity. "Because Santa will be exhausted when he returns, we let him sleep until the twenty-sixth and then we all come together to talk about his trip and open gifts and eat. Mostly we eat," she laughed.

In the center of the room, sat the large snow globe. Chrissy pressed the button on the side and the snow inside the glass began to swirl as if she'd shaken it upside down. "Watch this," she instructed Nick.

He came to stand close to her side and together they waited for the snow to clear. "There. See him?" Chrissy pointed to her father's sleigh as it landed easily on a rooftop. She glanced at the text print out that appeared above it. "He's just reached Ireland." She smiled, watching her father as he grabbed a sack. "He must be arguing with Holly cause she's pouting, see." Chrissy watched her sister cross her arms over her chest and toss her hair. "Yeah, she's miffed." The picture went away and Chrissy looked up and met Nick's smile. "What do you think of that?"

"Pretty fancy."

"Chrissy!"

She turned to face the woman bustling down the long corridor of the kitchen. "Yes, Mama?"

Mary Claus joined them at the counter and smiled up at Nick. "Hi Nick, welcome to Christmas Town. Sorry for the craziness around here, but—" She shrugged and brushed her hair back. "Chrissy, I've just taken the last tray out. Can you be a dear and get me some more cinnamon candies?"

"Ok, I'll be right back," she told Nick and walked away.

Nick looked at Chrissy's mother and couldn't help but smile. She was the spitting image of every storybook picture of Mrs. Claus from her white hair to her glasses to her dress, complete with apron. She smiled back at him and he felt a rush of warmth wash over him, as if someone had draped a large blanket about his shoulders. He glanced around but couldn't see anywhere that heat would be coming from. Mary gestured to the table nestled in the corner. "Come sit down here and talk to me. It's going to take my Chrissy a while to find those candies."

"Why is that?" he asked, but obediently settled into one of the overstuffed armchairs.

Mary's eyes twinkled. "Because they're actually up here. I wanted to get you a alone for a moment."

"I see."

"Do you?"

Nick shook his head. "No, not really. When I wake up I'm going to find out what it was I ate that's caused this wild dream."

"You still don't believe, do you?" Mary shook her head and then sighed. "Nick Christopoulos, you know, when you stopped believing Santa was very disappointed. He really thought you would be one of the ones."

"One of the ones?"

"Yes, the ones who believe in him even when all logic says not to. When everyone around you tells you otherwise, Santa had this feeling you'd be one who believed."

"I see."

"You don't believe me?"

"What's not to believe? I can't help that I grew up, kids do that you know, or is Peter Pan around here somewhere too and the lost boys?"

Mary's eyes lost their twinkle for a second and then she pulled a folded list from her apron pocket. "Maybe this will help you."

She handed him the folded paper and Nick hesitated a moment before touching it. When his fingers brushed hers he could swear the taste of vanilla flooded his mouth. Weird. But then he was almost starting to get used to things being weird. He unfolded the paper and read the tidy handwriting.

Nicky Christopoulos age 9, wants water skies, a toy train, and Leggos, but most of all he wants a puppy. Parents completely against the idea. Nick swears if he gets a puppy he'll believe.

"That was it, wasn't it? That was the year you stopped believing." Mary Claus took the paper from Nick's hands.

Nick remembered that year as vividly as if it was only yesterday. All his friends had dogs. All of them, but he never was allowed to have one. His little brother was allergic and his mother said she was sorry but she couldn't risk his health. But Nick had been certain Santa would have heard him and brought him the puppy he so desperately wanted. As an adult he understood, but the nine-year-old boy hadn't. He crossed Santa off his list from that time on.

"I didn't stop believing in Santa simply because I didn't get a dog. I stopped believing because I grew up."

"I see, then how do you explain all this?" Mary waved her arm around the kitchen but then shook her head. "That's right, I forgot it's a dream. Tell me Nick, have you ever dreamed this vividly before? Ever dreamed this long before?"

Chrissy came back up the aisle and once again Nick was enchanted with her beauty. Had she been this incredibly gorgeous in Greece? It was as if there was some type of glow about her that hadn't been there before. She smiled at her mother. "I couldn't find them. Are you sure they aren't up here?"

Mary rose from her chair and gestured to one of the several elves scurrying about. "I'll get them. Give Nick one of those fresh cookies. They're always best right out of the oven."

At her word another elf came running over with a plate of cookies. Nick reached for one and then realized they were all gingerbread. He drew back his hand.

"It's ok, Nick," Chrissy said, picking up one of the gingerbread men. She took a large bite. Nick cringed. Now he couldn't even kiss her. Even one taste of it and he would break out in hives. The last time he ate something with ginger in it, he almost died when his throat closed up.

"These are fantastic. I think it's the best they've ever made." Chrissy took another bite and then offered it to him, holding it to his mouth. "You have to try these."

Nick pushed it away. "You know I can't. I told you about the ginger."

But Chrissy persisted. "Nick, trust me, you aren't allergic to these. You're in Christmas Town."

"That's ok, I'll pass."

Chrissy lowered her hand with the cookie. "If you believed, you'd eat the cookie."

"If I eat the cookie, I could die."

"Do you honestly think I'd give you something that would hurt you?"

Nick stared at the cookie and then at her again. The activity in the kitchen seemed to fade away and it was as if the two of them were standing alone.

"You can't keep thinking this is a dream. It's not. Think Nick. I flew away from you in a sleigh pulled by reindeer. You showed me your drawings of your dream house and you woke up in it on the island. My brother picked you up on a motorcycle and flew you here to the North Pole. The North Pole, Nick. My father is Santa Claus. My sisters are elves and my brother is an elf."

"Are you an elf?"

"No, my father found me on Christmas morning. I was lying in a basket under a Christmas tree with a note asking him to take me and raise me."

"What happened to your parents? Your mother?"

"My mother was dead. Apparently after giving birth to me by herself, she knew she was dying and asked Santa to take her baby." Chrissy brushed away a tear. "She was a believer and she knew Santa wouldn't let her down."

"You believe that if I bite that cookie, nothing will happen. My lifetime allergy to ginger is gone?"

Chrissy shook her head. "You can't eat ginger anywhere but here at Christmas Town."

Nick looked into her eyes and remembered the first time she'd told him his eyes reminded her of fresh gingerbread. This was the gingerbread she was talking about. Her mother's gingerbread. Mrs. Claus. He held her gaze, unable to look away. The woman he loved was Santa Claus's daughter? It defied all logic, all intelligent thought. A rationale man would know that this was a dream and just accept it instead of wondering if maybe it was really true.

"Oh no! Chrissy, come quick!"

Chrissy spun around at the sound of Joy's voice. Her sister was watching the snow globe intently. "Look." She pointed to the activity happening on a small roof. Nick ran to join them and watched as the sisters frantically pushed the button, but the globe wouldn't reveal more information.

"What did you see?"

Just then a commotion outside had everyone racing from the kitchen.

"What's happening?" Nick asked, racing along the halls along with Chrissy and her mother and Joy.

"The sleigh is coming back. Something's wrong. It's way too soon." Joy yelled and then ran so far ahead of him that all he saw was a blur. Chrissy looked worried and he reached for her hand. He was glad she clung to him instead of letting go.

"He was sick. When he left this evening, he was sick and wouldn't stay behind."

"How could he? If he didn't go, who would make the

deliveries?" Nick was shocked to hear himself talking about Santa Claus and his deliveries as if he was real. But then he was. Wasn't he? When did he realize he was real? When did he begin to believe?

Noel met them at the door to the barn and they all watched the sky. "Oh no, not you, lover boy. No one gets to see Santa." He held up his hands and Chrissy looked ready to argue, but instead she turned to Nick.

"I'm sorry Nick, he's right. I can't let you come in here with us." She snapped her fingers and an elf appeared at her side. "Take Mr. Christopoulous back to the guest suite and bring him something to eat."

"Why can't I come in there? Let me help. You might need me."

Chrissy looked at him sadly. "You're a mortal, and you're a non-believer. I can't let you in. I'm sorry." She turned to her brother. "You couldn't just leave it alone, could you? You couldn't just leave him in his apartment."

"Hey, if you think I wanted to fly all the way to Greece today…"

"Stop it! Both of you. Quit the arguing." Mary Claus admonished as she opened the doors. "He can't come in and that's settled. Nick, please go quietly and don't give the elves any trouble. We'll get you back home as soon as we can."

Chrissy was leaving him again. He watched as she joined her brother at the large door and then turned back to look at him. The look in her eyes was all he needed. He could see it. She was done trying.

"Did you bring a cookie with you?" He asked.

Chrissy glanced down at her hand where she still held half a gingerbread man. She looked back up at him. "Why?"

He reached out his hand for it. She was too far from him and instead of bringing it to him she handed it to the elf at her side. The elf in turn handed it to another and then another until it reached Nick. He took it. He didn't feel any fear. He didn't feel any concern about what would happen. He broke off the arm and popped it into his mouth. The flavors exploded on his tongue, ginger and spices and he chewed and swallowed. Then he took another bite and another until it was all gone. He smiled as nothing happened. Absolutely nothing. But the best part was that he knew nothing would happen. He didn't even expect a reaction.

"Chrissy, I'll be waiting for you."

She smiled and started to say something but her brother hustled her along and she was gone. Dutifully, he followed the elves to the suite once more but this time as he went the things around him had a different meaning. The ornate surroundings, the photos on the wall, everything. It was amazing. He was in Santa Claus's castle.

The Santa Claus. He really did exist. Children all over the world were right and adults were wrong. He'd yet to figure out why so many adults didn't believe in him, but he knew there had to be an explanation. Maybe something to do with growing up or maybe something to do with the hearts of only the innocent, who knew?

Then it really dawned on him who Chrissy was. She was Santa Claus's daughter. Did that make her a princess or something? Probably. He was in love with the Princess of Santa Claus. How wild was that? No wonder Chrissy had such a problem with his dislike of Christmas. He chuckled as the elves left him once more in his sumptuous room. He had to have driven her crazy with all his anti-Christmas talk.

Ten o'clock on Christmas Eve. He wondered when Chrissy would come back. He wondered what his family was doing right now. He'd told them he'd be over first thing on Christmas morning. Did cell phones work from the North Pole? Didn't much matter, he hadn't thought to grab his when her brother whisked him away on his motorcycle. Picking up a well-worn copy of "The Night Before Christmas" he settled back into the overstuffed chair and began to read the famous poem with a renewed appreciation for it.

****

"Ok, Papa, try to remember, where do you think the cabin was? Was it in the United States? Were you still in Europe? When I checked the globe about an hour and a half ago you were in Ireland." Chrissy tried desperately not to show her father how concerned they all were for Holly. Tucked back into his bed with healing powders in his hot cocoa, he mumbled incoherently about the reindeer and a guy from TV and something about hiding from weddings. None of them knew what he was talking about. All they knew was that when the sleigh returned an hour or so ago, he was in it alone without the sacks of toys and without Holly.

Joy raced back into the room. "Still nothing on the globe."

With their father asleep, Chrissy walked out of the room to consult with her sister while her mother stayed by his bedside.

"What are we going to do?" Chrissy forced back the panic. It wasn't as if Holly was out in the elements. They knew she was in a heated log cabin—somewhere. Her magical powers would keep her safe from whoever owned the cabin if necessary. Chrissy cringed remembering the skimpy little outfit her sister wore when she went out. "Idiot," she muttered.

"We can't do much of anything until tomorrow or the next day. Noel's out taking care of deliveries and he's going to take a long time. He's not used to this."

"Where's Krista?"

"She's gone to find Jackson. She wants to see if he has any ideas."

Chrissy narrowed her eyes. Krista only went to find Jackson because it was a good excuse for her to talk to the Prince of Popsicles. "Well, there's not much more we can do. I'm going to go back to see Nick, you keep checking the globe. Come get me if you find anything."

"Should I knock first?" Joy smirked and Chrissy shot

her a glare, but then nodded and grinned. As worried as she was about Holly and her father, it didn't overshadow the fact that Nick ate the cookie. He trusted her when she told him he didn't have an allergy to Christmas Town gingerbread men. He believed her. He believed!

She ran up the stairs towards the guest suite. The doors were closed tight and the two elves that had been appointed guards stood on either side. "Thank you, you can go now," she shooed them away and without knocking entered the dark suite.

Nick was asleep in the overstuffed chair. She crossed the room and slipped the book from his hands. She slid into his lap and nestled up against him. He stirred and she smiled up. "Hi."

"Hmm, Hi." He lowered his head and brushed her lips with his. Chrissy shifted until she could reach up to wrap one arm around his neck and pull him even closer to her. She put everything she felt in her kiss to him. Nick tangled his fingers in her hair and cradled the back of her head. His mouth was warm and tasted of hot cocoa and candy canes.

His hand slid down the side of her face to rest against the pulse at her neck and she pressed against him, longing for him to touch her and make love to her again. "Nick," she pleaded, nipping his lower lip with her teeth and then soothing it over with her tongue. "I've missed you."

"Not half as much as I've missed you." Nick pulled away from her lips.

She took the opportunity to kiss his neck, then slipped two buttons of his polo shirt free and kissed his upper chest. Chrissy's hand ventured lower down over the planes of his stomach to rest against the hardness behind his zipper. "Do you have a candy cane in there or are you just happy to see me?" she teased, kissing the side of his mouth once more before working her way towards his ear.

Nick growled and pressed her hand harder against his groin. "If we weren't in your father's house, I'd show you."

Chrissy leaned back. "You're not going to tell me you're afraid of my father, are you?"

Nick's hand covered her breast through the dress she still wore and teased her nipple until it pebbled. She moaned and wiggled in his lap.

"Your brother is a pretty scary character even if your father wasn't who he is."

Chrissy's head came up and she looked into his eyes. "Who's my father?"

Nick lowered his head and kissed her neck. "You know who he is."

She placed both hands on his head and tilted it up to look at her. "Tell me who he is."

"Your father is Santa Claus. The real Santa Claus and your mother is Mrs. Claus and she bakes one hell of a gingerbread cookie."

Chrissy smiled from ear to ear. "Tell me where we are right now."

"We're at the North Pole, I have no idea where on the globe that is, but it's pretty damn cold out."

"What else?"

"Well let's see, I flew here on a motorcycle, I watched you fly here using magic reindeer and you have elves for sisters."

Chrissy nodded. "What else?"

Nick frowned and she could see he was thinking. "You have this amazing thing you do with your tongue on my..."

Chrissy gasped and slapped her hand over his lips. "Not that! What about what you said to me when I left you in Greece."

Nick stood up cradling her in his arms. He strode across the room to the large bed and pulled back the curtains that surrounded it. "I hope you locked that door, Ms. Claus because I am about to show you just how much I love you and I do love you, in spite of you being the Princess of Christmas. Something tells me that my years of avoiding the holiday have ended."

Chrissy held out her arms to him as she lay on the bed. "Do you mind terribly if we spend the holiday with my family every year? I promise we can do Thanksgiving with yours."

Nick laughed as he wrapped her in his arms. "I suppose, but only if we get to keep the house on the island. It would be a shame to have to build it again, your brother did such a fantastic job."

"Noel didn't do that. I did."

Nick pulled back. "I thought you weren't an elf? I thought you didn't have magic powers?"

"I don't. I have something far better than magic."

"Oh?"

"I have connections, lots and lots of connections."

Nick laughed and Chrissy pulled him down to her for a kiss that left him with no question what she wanted for Christmas.

About the author...

Roni Adams currently resides in a tiny hamlet in Upstate New York. Nestled along the Erie Canal , she feels she leads a pretty blessed life. She's been married for 21 years and has three sons, ages 10-18. Although, she's been writing since she was 7 and has the "wonderful" short stories to prove it, she admits that she took a long leave of absence after getting married.

While she's not busy camping with her boys, caring for the house and pets she enjoys and sharing her stories with her readers.

Jack's Christmas Spirit

Allie Standifer

Chapter One

Should she do it?

Could she do it?

Christmas Spirit looked over the expanse of the large room with its cheery fire and felt her stomach heave. Swallowing hard against the nausea, she wished once again she had the nerve to ask for her heart's desire.

The tradition in her family was alive and well. Every Christmas Eve, her father would sit all the kids down and ask them the wish of their hearts. Then he'd do his best to grant it, if he felt the wish and the person deserved each other.

Every year since Krista could remember, she'd wished happiness for the world, peace to all humans and every child to have a perfect Christmas.

And every year, her father would look at her with those twinkling blue eyes and ask, "Is that all you wish for, Krista? Are you sure that is the only wish in your heart?"

The answer was the same. "Yes, Father, I truly wish these things from my heart."

A pat on the head and kiss to her cheek would follow and he'd be off asking her brother or sisters for their wishes.

This year would be different. Krista would make a stand for herself. She would tell her father exactly what was in her heart.

If she didn't throw up first.

****

The window showed a clear view of the happy family inside. But Jackson Frost wasn't interested in anyone but Krista. She shone brighter than the lights sparkling in the tree behind her.

Intently, he watched her face, mesmerized by the myriad of expressions flashing across her lovely features. Happiness, hope, and anxiety flicked through her evergreen eyes.

Nerves twisted his gut and made him wish he could break down the door and protect Krista from whatever distressed her. He'd hold her in his arms, kiss her sweet lips gently and whisper all the things stored inside his heart.

Unfortunately for him, it would never happen.

One touch of his frosty cold hand and she'd turn to ice in a matter of seconds. No matter how badly he ached to touch her, learn the taste of her skin and flavor of her mouth, Jack would never come within ten feet of her.

If it hadn't been for his old friend Nick, Jack wouldn't be here at all. But friendships were invaluable when you're immortal and a walking dry ice machine. He'd stick with what he had and be grateful for it.

"Jack, my old friend, what are doing standing out in the snow? Come on in." A cheery voice boomed from his left.

Nicholas Claus stood in the open doorway. One arm tucked behind him and the other held out to welcome Jack in.

Contrary to popular belief, Nick didn't always dress in red velvet pants or a spiffy red hat. The hero of all children's fantasies wore worn blue jeans, a neatly trimmed beard, a faded flannel shirt, and a beaming smile.

Watching his oldest friend, Jack moved slowly to the open door. "Thanks, Nick, but you know the cold doesn't bother me. I just came by to see what you needed before the big night."

A devilish glint sharpened the blue in the other man's eyes. "Ho, now Jack, and what would my better half say if I left you out here?"

A smile broke through the gloom of Jacks' thoughts.

"She'd skin you alive and make you sleep with Donner."

"Darn right!" Nick agreed with a hearty laugh. "Get in here or else I'll find myself sleeping in the hay pile."

Both men laughed in companionable humor. Mrs. Claus was known to one and all as the softest touch in town. Her threats were as substantial as one of Jack's snowflakes.

Even with the warmth of Nick's friendship, Jack had to make sure his friend understood this visit would be brief. "I haven't much time. There's a boat off the coast of Alaska trying to make its way to the States. Damn thing got caught up in the ice drift. If I don't get there soon, nothing will be left of it."

Nick being Nick patted Jack's shoulder and smiled indulgently. "Not tonight, son. I've already sent a 'head's up' to the Coast Guard. The rescue will come off without a hitch and you'll not be needed."

Jack looked at the other man stunned. "How could you?" he barked, frustration had him raking hands through his long thick black hair. "I'll have to leave right this minute to ensure nothing goes wrong with either ship now."

And there went any time he could have used to stare at Krista. To store and build up memories for the time when she wasn't there anymore.

Nick looked shocked at Jack's reaction. "Don't be in such an all fire hurry, boy. I told you Noel would take care of it."

Jack turned furious frost blue eyes to Nick. "When is the last time Noel did something you asked? Correctly?"

Nick had the sense to look sheepish. "He promised me this time, Jack. Said he'd do it for you."

The admission made the old man's eyes dim and Jack felt bad for pushing the issue, but he couldn't leave some poor mortals in Noel's hand. Not without checking on the situation with his own eyes.

Noel had good intentions, but in his desire to grab his father's attention, things might slip past his notice.

"It's all good, Nick. I'll just check to see if your boy needs a hand. We'll go out for some holly beer after. I'm sure everything is fine and under control," he assured the other man. He tried to make his voice light, but frost coated his words the minute they left the relative warmth of his mouth.

With a wave and half-hearted smile, Nick backed away to the door and walked inside.

Jack's heart sank. He knew Nick was worried about his only son. And he was sorry to add more worry to those broad shoulders, but Jack couldn't let someone else take over his calling.

With a heavy spirit, Jack called the cold wind to carry him south where the fishing vessel waited.

As the frozen land flew by beneath him, Jack let his thoughts drift back to Krista. His one perfect thing in a world he no longer understood.

Someday, Krista would no longer be content to spread her vitality and warmth only through the holiday season. She would want to spread her wings and spirit all over the world. Unlike her other sister, Chrissy, the CPA, who only spread around IRS reports and audits. Not much on cheer, that one.

Yep, sooner or later Jack would lose Krista to the world outside the frozen north, but until that time he'd capture every memory he could.

With the eye of an eagle, Jack saw Noel sitting on the edge of an ice burg and dove down to greet him.

Chapter Two

"So Krista, it's time for your wish."

Her father's cheery voice came from behind and startled Krista into spilling her eggnog.

"Sorry, Dad, guess I was lost in the dreaming." She explained away her nerves.

With a shrewd look and outstretched hand, Nick Claus guided his youngest daughter to the large leather chair snuggly positioned by the roaring fireplace.

Sitting against his leg, with her head rested on her dad's bent knee, Krista looked up at the man she'd admired and loved her whole life.

"Have you ever made a mistake, Dad?"

If her question surprised him, Nick didn't show it. "I'm breathing aren't I?" he answered.

She gave a little laugh. "Yeah, that you are, but what if you can't correct what you've done wrong?" She pushed desperately wanting some guidance without having to come straight out and ask for it.

A large calloused hand stroked gently over her long mink colored hair. "Well, now Krista, I can't say I understand exactly what you're getting at."

Those blue eyes that always saw more than she was comfortable with pierced her now.

She forced a laugh. "It's nothing, really. I'm just playing a game with myself is all."

He humphed and sat back in his chair. "So you ready to tell me this year's heart wish?"

Courage, she whispered to herself. She could do this. She would ask for the very thing her heart begged for. Oh and she'd make another pass at the whole world peace thing but that never seemed to work out.

With a steadying breath, Krista turned her face up. "I know what I'd really like this year." She was surprised at her moderate tone and kept going. "I'd like the world to have peace."

Her father crinkled bushy white eyebrows at her. "And that's the extent of your wish?"

This was it.

"No," her voice dropped, "I'd also like...well if it wouldn't be too much trouble..." Darn it, why couldn't she get the words out?

Gentle hands nudged her chin back up. "Out with it, Princess. I'd like to share your dreams, if you'd let me."

Seeing the caring and concern in his eyes, Krista blurted it out.

"I want love, Father. I want a man to love me beyond my perky nature and glass half full outlook. I want to be seen as a normal woman. I want to be able to curse and laugh and drink from the carton." Getting caught up in the moment, Krista pushed to her feet and paced in front of the warm fire.

"I need someone to see me not as you do. But as the woman I am. A woman with desires, needs and dreams of a family. I want what you and Mom have." Her voice dropped to pleading at the end and she hated herself for it.

Wishes from the heart were supposed to be made with conviction and certainty. Instead hers came out like a toddler begging for the last cookie.

This would never convince her father.

Again, rough fingers gently tilted her chin up and Krista was shocked by the emotions swimming in her father's face. Joy, sorrow and pride glowed from his bright blue eyes.

He dropped his hand from her face to tightly grasp both her hands in his. "I knew this day would come, Christmas. I just never expected it to be so soon. First Chrissy coming to me and now my baby girl."

Nick pulled her into a tight hug and pressed a kiss on

her temple.

Krista was stunned. "How did you know?" she asked, pulling back enough to see his face.

He gave a small shrug. "The way a father always knows, I guess. I've had you to myself for well over two hundred years. It's about time you wanted a home and family of your own."

She could only nod her head as tears gathered in her eyes.

Nick pushed Krista back to clasp her shoulders. "Now then." He cleared his throat. "You've made a heart wish that's strong and true. I'll be granting it for you."

His words caused her heart overflow with happiness and nerves. She was ecstatic her father believed in her enough to grant the wish but nervous because it was something she'd only dreamed about.

"Just remember your dear old dad every now and again," he whispered, pulling her close once more.

Krista flung her arms around his waist and held on tight. "How could I forget the first man I ever loved?" she whispered back.

And they both held tight to each other knowing things would never be the same once Krista's wish came true.

Chapter Three

Bright blond hair pulled Jack away from his thoughts. It shouldn't have been this easy to find Santa's only son, but maybe Noel had been expecting him.

The cold north currents set him gently down a few feet away. His feet made no sound when they landed on the packed snow. Jack made his way quickly to where Noel sat looking over the American's rescue.

"No hot date tonight?" he teased the other man while taking a chilly seat next to him.

The other man shrugged. "The hottest date of all…my wife

The words coming out of the other man's mouth surprised, pleased and angered Jack. He was truly happy Noel had found happiness and pleased with the things he'd heard of the woman so far. But his stomach clenched in green envy that Noel had found someone to share his heart and life with.

He hated to ask. It made him uncomfortable to pry in other's lives. On the other hand Noel had done him a favor. "Something on your mind?"

Noel shook his head, opened his mouth, closed it then shook his head again. "Nah, I'm good." He finally managed.

Letting out a quiet breath of relief, Jack turned his attention to the scampering men below. "Thanks for catching this for me."

"Not a problem."

Damn, it was awkward sitting here trying to make conversation without the benefit of beer involved.

"So," he started again. "Who's your favorite in the reindeer games this year?"

Noel glanced at him in surprise before answering. "My gold is on Donner. Mom's been babying the others and over feeding them thanks to that winter bug. Ole Donner will win by sheer speed alone over the rest of the fat bellies."

Okay, so he could do this. It wasn't a total loss. "Yeah, I noticed Dasher looked a bit hefty there in the barn."

"You went to the barn?"

At the question, Jack pulled back. Damn polite conversation and double damn him for trying to make it.

"I was wandering that way as I walked to the house."

Ice blue eyes pinned him to the ground. "That's kind of the long way to the house."

Jack refused to blush, assuming he could. It had been a number of years since his body had made the attempt. "Not like I'm in a hurry." He finally responded.

With a final knowing look in his shrewd blue eyes, Noel turned away. "Yeah," he agreed. "You've got nothing to rush for, right."

Then a smile broke through his reserve. "Although Candice said she had a special surprise for me if I'd hurry home."

The light of contentment, love and happiness in Noel's eyes caused a lightening bolt of pain to slice through Jack's heart. He shrugged it off and offered his congratulations to the other man.

"I heard about your marriage, man. I think it's great." His voice was steady, no hint of the green demon showing through.

If possible the blond's smile got wider. "Yeah, ain't love grand?"

Jack wanted to kick and curse; instead he forced himself to nod. "I'm sure it is."

He wouldn't know a thing about being in love. That implied two people sharing the same emotion, together at the same time.

Jack had never even touched a woman let alone

persuaded her to fall in love with him. But that didn't stop his heart from reaching out. That organ was held securely in the dainty white palms of Christmas Spirit. Nick's daughter and Noel's sister.

"You know something?" Noel broke through Jack's thoughts. "I learned something when I fell in love with Candy."

Oh, please, do not let Noel be about to give him lessons on love.

"I'm sure you did." Jack tried to cut him off but the other man ignored his words.

"Love is all about taking chances. If you want something bad enough, you've got to be willing to sacrifice for it. That includes your pride and ego, unfortunately." A rueful smile crossed his face.

Jack wasn't sure how to reply. Did he thank the man for his unwanted and unasked for opinion? Or merely nod his head and get the hell out of there?

He settled for a bit of both. "Oh thanks, Noel. I'd better get going."

"She loves you, you know."

The immortal heart within Jack's chest stopped beating. "I beg your pardon?"

"Christmas, my sister? She's in love with you." Noel repeated before adding. "And call me Noll, my family does." And a satisfied smile curved his mouth.

For the second time in as many minutes Jack didn't know what to do. "Noel-Noll, I'm not sure what you're talking about. I do know your sister wouldn't appreciate you talking about her with a stranger."

Noel, Noll gave him a stunned look. "Stranger?" he questioned. "Jack, we've known you our whole lives. You've been to our home for dinners, lunches and everything in between. Hell, man, you were invited to my wedding. Not that you showed up."

The thought of being included in that big noisy loving family made Jack's heart speed up. It was a nice thought but a false one. "It's kind of you to say so, Noll, but..."

But what? But he'd love to be a true part of the family? Earning his place at the table and tree by marrying the Clauses youngest child? A woman he'd never touch, never give her the children he knew she yearned for?

No, that was a silly snowflake dream. The dreams kept him company on cold nights but melted in the reality of the morning's harsh light.

Surprisingly Noll dropped it. "Like I said, love is all about taking risks."

Jack rose to his feet. "Yeah...uh...I'll be around then."

Great mistletoe, he wouldn't try this again anytime soon. Men and bonding didn't mix without sports and alcohol.

Still Noel was sharper than Jack had given him credit for. If he hadn't opened his big mouth about Krista and love, Jack would have stayed and tried to cement a friendship with the young man.

Instead he was flying over the vast frozen land of the north trying to beat down the small kernel of hope that had lodged in his heart.

Chapter Four

"Are you sure about this, Christmas?"

Her mother's worried voice was muffled by the trunk's lid. Surely her long coat had been stored in this trunk? With a sigh of regret, Krista lifted her head and the rest of her body out. Maybe it was in the downstairs closet?

"Krista?" her mother's voice called out to her again.

"Sorry, Mama, what did you say?"

Mary Claus propped her tiny hands on her small waist and glared at her youngest child. Uh oh, Krista knew that look well. She wasn't going to like what came next.

"I asked if you were sure about this scheme you and your father cooked up?"

Krista gave her mother a sunny smile while her stomach jumped with a thousand flying reindeer. "Of course I'm sure, Mamma. It's time for me to try the world outside the Pole," she assured her mother. "Papa wouldn't have agreed if he didn't think I was ready for it."

Mary jumped in. "How can you throw away a perfectly good male, like Elvin the wagon wheel maker, for only a chance at a life you aren't sure you want? Elvin won't be single forever you know."

Krista crossed the room and took her mother's hand into her own. "Elvin, however stable he may be, can't give me the life I want. Not the travel or adventures I'm seeking. Look at the way Noll stares after Candy. The way Chrissy and Nic play and laugh together. I'm so happy they all found love but now it's my turn to try and grab the brass candy cane."

Tears filled Mary's berry blue eyes. "Of course you do,

my dear." Loving arms wrapped tight around Krista's waist. "I've forgotten how wonderful finding that life can be and how scary."

With another quick hug, Mary dropped her arms and stepped back. "Now, what are you going to pack to start this new phase of your life?"

Tears threatened to overflow Krista's eyes at her mother's acceptance. Did she really want to go and leave the security of her family's love for the unknown?

Of course she did. Romance and love were in full bloom throughout the Claus household. Her brother was happily settled down to a wonderful warm woman. Chrissy and Nic were already talking about starting a family. Holly was so in love with her new husband, her eyes glowed with happiness.

With everyone but Joy and herself settled down, Krista knew this would be a good time to ditch her snowshoes and try out her wings.

And the first place on her agenda was warm and sunny Key West, Florida.

"I'm not going to need too many things from here, Mama," she said, thinking of the shorts, tank tops and bathing suits she intended to buy once she reached someplace warm enough to buy them.

An indulgent smile bloomed on Mary's face. "Now, Krista, don't go throwing away all your old things. There is a chance, a slight one mind you, that you won't like the humid hot weather."

Not like hot weather? What wasn't there to like? She wouldn't be dressed up like a polar bear twelve months out of the year. She'd actually be able to have a tan. Most important she'd be able to stay outside for more than an hour at a time.

Granted being an elf made it nearly impossible to die from exposure but her magical blood didn't prevent her from freezing.

She patted her mother's arm. "Don't worry, Mama. I'm not throwing anything out. Just packing things in boxes. You'll need this room sooner or later for one of the grandkids bound to come along."

Joy lit Mary's eyes brighter than the lights on the tree. "Oh do you think so? I wonder..."

Krista let her mother wander off in a hazy daydream of babies and plans.

Two more trunks lined the walls of her mint green and pink bedroom. It was fussy and overdone but she had loved it as a child. Now she couldn't wait to get out and decorate her new place as an adult.

There were so many places to see and experience; she couldn't wait to get started. And if her heart wilted a little at the thought of seeing the world alone, she pushed it aside. Krista was determined to have only happy thoughts. For once she was determined to live up to her name.

Chapter Five

"Not a snowballs chance in Texas, Nick." Jack said in a determined voice. His jaw clenched tight to prevent further discussion.

Nick, as usual, heard only what he wanted to hear. "Now, I know I could have brought her with me then dropped her off but it wouldn't be fair to Krista. She's so anxious to get started with her plans. I didn't have the heart to make her wait."

More like he lacked the courage to break his little girl's heart, Jack thought. "I can't take her. I won't take her. That's final, Nick."

It was ludicrous. To think Nick wanted him, Jack Frost, to snow fly Krista all the way to LA. From there she would catch a plane to wherever her final destination was.

Oh he would have loved for Krista to fly anywhere with him but that would involve touching her. Something Jack could and would never do.

Nick would be forced to give up on this one.

"Now, Jack," Nick protested. "Why should I make her take a commercial flight all the way by herself to Juno? Then have her hop on another plane for a six hour trip when you could get her to LA in a shorter period of time."

Mouth open to refuse, Nick started again. "Just think of the worry you'll save her poor old mother. Mary ain't as young as she used to be."

The last part his friend whispered as he looked around the room.

"What's the matter, Nick? Afraid the poor old woman will hear that comment and bash in your head with her eggnog bowl?" He teased.

Chest puffed up in pride, Nick winked. "Darn tootin, son. That woman throws a mean punch bowl."

Before Jack could settle back down in the brown leather armchair, Nick was back poking.

"You know I wouldn't ask unless it were important, don't you? I mean she is my baby, my youngest child." Nick came to sit beside him in the matching chair "Krista's never been more than a few hours away from home. Never ridden a plane, never driven a car. I'm afraid for her, Jack."

Oh that was too much. "If you're so bloody worried about the girl then refuse to allow her to leave."

That was a fine plan. If Nick forbade Krista from moving, Jack would have more time to gather memories of her smiles and laughter.

The smiles Jack loved would be no more if Krista were forced to stay at the Pole. What reason would she have to smile if her body were in one place and her spirit another?

It was the thought of Krista's unhappiness that made Jack's decision. "I'll take her."

The world-renowned chuckle filled the room and Nick slapped him on the back. "I knew you'd come through for me son. Now, let me go tell Krista of our plan. Why don't you check out the new ornaments on the tree?" With those hasty words, Nick bolted from the room as fast as his red stocking feet would allow.

Krista didn't know.

If she didn't know he was her escort, it could be she'd refuse to go. After all, she didn't know him well. The journey alone with him might make her uncomfortable.

Shaking the dreary thoughts off, Jack made his way to the large tree in the corner. As usual lights shone brightly off the tall pine but this time there were new ornaments decorating its limbs.

The balls were sea green and brighter than the lights of the tree.

He was drawn into the color and the wispy scene he

could almost make out on its surface.

It looked like a couple. One man and one woman locked in each other's arms, surrounded by piles of presents and toys wrapped in big red bows.

The woman had silky looking mink hair, which trailed over the man's arm wrapped around her waist. She leaned her head against his chest, a look of love and happiness on her face.

The man had icy blue eyes, jet-black hair and such a joy and contentment on his face; it took Jack a few seconds to recognize the man.

It was he with his arms wrapped around Krista, surrounded by children's toys.

He stared harder, willing the glowing orb to give him more information. He saw the mirage couple kiss until two children interrupted them. A boy with black hair and green eyes and a little girl with her mother's satin hair and her father's silver blue eyes.

It wasn't until wetness dripped across his hand that Jack knew he was crying.

Quickly he drew himself away from the happy scene. A quick look around assured him no witness saw his momentary lapse of control.

There was no future with Krista and certainly no children of his loins.

When he peered back at the ball again, he saw only his wistful expression.

"Everything all right in here, Jack?" Nick called from the doorway.

Hastily Jack moved away from the tree. "Everything's fine, Nick. Did you settle things with Krista?"

Part of him wanted Nick to say no. Krista had refused to travel with Jack. Then he'd be off the hook through no fault of his own. The other part of him, his heart, sped in anticipation of being in Krista's company alone and prayed for a yes.

Nick nodded his snow-white head. "Oh yes, she's

upstairs packing now."

"Packing?" jack questioned.

He nodded again. "Yep, don't know what she needs to pack though. Not like she can use her winter coat where she's going." Nick pushed away from the door and made his way to the tree.

For a minute, Jack was terrified his friend would see the same image within the green globe as he had. But when Nick failed to make a comment, tension eased out of Jack's body.

With a shake he brought himself back to the conversation and away from the damn tree. "Nick, you know I can't take anything else. Flying Krista with me will take all my concentration as it is."

At once Krista's father agreed. "Oh, I know, son. Whatever she feels she needs will be shipped to her. I wouldn't ask you to drag a woman's baggage halfway across the country."

"Now, Papa, you know I wouldn't ask Mr. Frost to drag both me and my stuff anywhere." Krista spoke from the door.

Both men looked up, startled at her sudden appearance. Jack drank in the sight of her. From the top of her silky brown colored hair to the tips of her sensible tennis shoes, she fed him like a beggar at a banquet.

"You okay with traveling like this?" he asked, to give her one more opportunity to back out.

Instead she smiled and made his heart speed and his pants tight. "Of course, I'm sure. I can think of nothing better than flying through the night with the stars surrounding me."

"Um...yeah...that's great." He managed to reply. He was glad one of them looked happy about the journey.

Jack had a feeling he'd spend most of the trip trying to remember why he couldn't touch her and rip her clothes off.

"Whenever you're ready," he told her.

Once again she beamed a smile at him that warmed

his soul and raced his pulse.

"I've got everything I need for now in my backpack. Is this okay to bring?" she asked, holding up a bright pink bag with shoulder straps. At least she had sense enough to get one she would have to carry.

"Yes," he answered her. "It should be fine."

"Great." Another million watt smile and Krista turned to her father.

"Papa, come give me a hug and tell me you'll see me soon."

Nick's voice came out husky. "Of course you'll be seeing me soon. Not like I could keep your dear old mother away."

"Her dear old mother is going to bean you in the head with a candy cane if I hear that one more time."

Mary Claus's voice preceded her into the room.

At once Nick turned bright red to match his shirt and tried to back peddle. "Now, honey, you know I didn't mean that the way it sounded."

A perfectly arched eyebrow rose. "Oh really? And exactly how did you mean it?"

"Well now see...I'm was just telling your youngest that you'd miss her. Figured if I threw in something about us being old...well then she might reconsider this moving business." He explained with great relish.

His wife didn't buy a word of it. "You old fart," she said with laughter in her voice. "You'll do the worrying between the two of us and you know it. Poor old woman, my ginger bread house."

Jack looked back at Nick, surprised to see the color still high in the older man's face.

"Yes...well...ah...ahh...ahhh...CHOO." Nick didn't get far before a fit of sneezing stopped him in his tracks.

Mary was by his side in an instant. "Nicky," she placed one hand on his forehead and another on his arm. "Are you feeling off? Maybe you're getting what the reindeer did?"

Nick shook off her concern gently. "Nonsense, my

dear, I'm fit as a fiddle. Besides, I'm immortal. I don't get sick."

"Blitzen is immortal as well but that didn't stop him from tossing his sugar cookies all over the barn." She reminded him.

The words bleached the sunny color out of Nick's cheeks and he swayed.

Jack remained motionless while the women rushed to Nick's side.

He brushed off their concern and hands. "I'm fine the both of you. Garland to gingersnaps, woman, I told you not to mention that bugger of an ailment in front of me."

Mary Claus looked amused at her husband's weak stomach but concerned with his lack of color. "Dear, why don't you ease my nerves and go see the healer?"

The older man's response was a surprise to no one. "Don't need no cold fingered healer, Mary." He spared Jack a glance. "No offense, son."

Knowing Santa, Jack motioned away the apology. "No offense taken."

Nick grimaced at his wife's fussing hands. "Mary, now you stop that." He pushed her palm away from his sweat-beaded forehead. "I tell you it's all the fluffy smelling stuff you put around here."

"Nonsense. I'm using the same things I've used for years."

"Well, if you don't quit your fidgeting with me, you'll make the kids late."

It had been a number of years, if ever, since Jack had heard himself referred to as a kid. He held back his smile at the term.

"Oh dear, I'm so sorry, Jack, Krista. Your father keeps me in a tizzy half the time. If he'd look after his own self half as well as he does those reindeer..." she trailed off and linked her fingers with Nick's.

Jack saw the small squeeze shared between the two and felt envy clawing its way past his throat. "Yes, well, we do need to be going."

Krista turned to him with a smile. "I'm ready whenever you are." She assured him brightly. Her green eyes shone with anticipation.

"You'll remember to phone when you land and before you board that plane?" Her mother asked as a question when they both knew it was an order. They made their way out of Santa's study, through the hall and toward the front door.

Krista gave her mother a fierce hug. "Of course I'll call." She promised with a quick kiss to Mary's cheek.

"Humph, said she would, didn't she." Nick mumbled as he made his own grab for his youngest child. Jack could see the sheen of tears in her father's eyes.

In contrast to the hug she'd given her mother, this one was gentle and careful. "Love you, Papa."

"Love you too, snowflake." He whispered back pressing a tender kiss to Krista's temple.

Jack watched as she stepped away from her parents. "Thanks for agreeing to let me tag along." Krista eyes shimmered with unshed tears.

For some reason Jack had to turn his own head away and clear his throat before he spoke. "It's not a problem."

"Bye, Mama, Papa, give my love to everyone and I'll see you in a few months." She waved while walking backward in the snow until her house and family were out of sight.

"Oh, I do hope Papa will take care of himself." She spoke in a low tone to herself.

Jack forced himself to speak. "You can always delay your trip until you're certain of Nick's health."

With startled green eyes, Krista met his gaze. "And have him complain that I was coddling him? No," she laughed tightly. "I'll have to trust Mama to watch out for him."

"Okay then." Jack was at a loss for other things to say.

Then they reached their destination. A low short cleared field empty of buildings, trees or shrubbery. The perfect place to call the north wind that would carry them on their journey.

"Are you positive I packed light enough? I'm sure there are one or two things I could live without." Krista gave a nervous glance to her backpack and him.

"There is nothing in your small pack that would delay or jeopardize our journey. The north wind is coming and eager to carry us to our destination."

At his words the wind picked up swirling around them, tugging at Krista's clothes and hair. She laughed as the wind surrounded her.

"I feel like a child caught in a snow globe," she told him.

He didn't say anything just looked at her. The wind whipped color to her cheeks making them rosy and bright. Her eyes shone brighter than any evergreen and her lips looked juicier than any berry he'd tasted. And he was twice as hungry to taste the lushness of her mouth.

He shook the dangerous thoughts away. Instead, he held out a wide leather strap for her to grasp. "Wrap this around your waist and fasten it securely." He instructed her while double-checking the fastening on his end.

When she did as he asked, Jack called forth more cold wind, asking for the right of transportation and giving thanks for the wind's generosity.

As their feet lifted into the air, Krista's laugh rang through the night and sent shivers of desire up and down his spine.

It was going to be a long night and an even longer journey.

Chapter Six

The land flew by in a blur of white wonder. Krista couldn't believe she'd lived in this place all her life but never saw the exact beauty of her home.

"You are truly blessed to see so much wonder any time you choose," she told Jack over the blowing wind.

Though a greater distance separated them than Krista would have believed, Jack heard her words. He gave a small smile and turned his face back into the wind.

What was it with Jackson Frost that fascinated her? He'd never so much as touched her hand but Krista was enraptured with him all the same.

From the tips of soot black hair, to the ice blue of his eyes, Jack was every inch the alpha male she'd read about in her romance novels.

He was decisive and carried an air of authority around his person as other men might an expensive coat. His word was such that no one questioned his orders when he gave them. Those were rare times indeed when his orders were questioned.

The last time in Krista's memory was the great blizzard of 1874. Everyone had given up in defeat saying there was no way even Rudolph could guide the sleigh for Santa. The wind was too fierce, the snow too blinding and the sleet too heavy.

Out of the blue, Jack showed up. He assured Santa and his team that he would guide the sleigh and control the wind for them.

As impossible as it seemed, no one questioned his word. Everyone had jumped to obey his slightest order, even the moody Donner.

Now she could see the strength and control it took for

him to guide and control the wind. More than ever, Krista was amazed at his strength and determination. The man never gave up and never admitted defeat.

There were other stories and rumors about him. Most told over low fires in hushed voices in the darkness of night where such tales made better entertainment.

She'd never had much use for gossip, but Krista had gobbled up every word anyone had said about Jack. There were more tales of Jack saving the day or night. He'd come in where no one else dared and saved whatever situation he found.

But now when she was alone with him for the first time in her life, Krista found words tangled in her mouth. She wanted to talk with him, to find out where he went when he left the Clause's house. No one ever seemed to know where he lived or spent his free time or if the elf even had any free time. Then again, he must or he wouldn't be flying Krista to LA.

About the time she gathered her nerve to ask where he lived, the wind stopped and they started a fast tumble out of the sky.

"JACK!" Krista managed to scream as wind rushed in her open mouth choking off her next words.

The night tipped and flashed before her terrified eyes. Krista couldn't see Jack or the leather tethering them together. Her vision consisted of fast falling snow and she knew the ground rushed too quickly up at her.

After minutes, which seemed like hours, Krista was roughly jerked up and strong hands grabbed for the tie around her waist.

"Krista, hang on. I'll get us down. Hold on to my sweater." Jack shouted in her ear past the rushing noise of the wind.

She didn't ask what happened or why, Krista knew better than to ask questions Jack would answer later. For now she grabbed on to the back of Jack's soft black sweater and held on for dear life. In the midst of her fear, Krista took the time to inhale the soft piney clean scent of

Jack's skin and was grateful for that one small experience of him.

Instead of the snow covered land coming full force at them, they slowed to a gentle drift. When their feet were a few feet above the chilly dirt, the wind gave way and gravity dropped them down with a soft thud.

Snow covered Krista from her snug leather boots to her cherry red scarf when her legs gave out and she slid on ice into a nearby snow bank.

She sat up and spit cold snow from her mouth. All her parts seemed to be in working order. Caught up in her body check, Krista didn't notice Jack until she heard his harsh voice tremble with her name.

"KRISTA" His voice held the faint note of panic as he ran from snow pile to snow pile, hastily throwing piles of the wet slush over his shoulders.

She could see his gaze and the misery reflected in those beautiful ice blue eyes made her feel guilty for keeping silent for so long.

Giving up her hiding place, Krista waved both arms in the air to gain his attention while shouting his name.

"Jack, over here." She stretched both arms to her side and fell back in the snow.

He was at her side in seconds and ran lean, rough hands along her sides and down her legs. "Krista, love, where are hurt? Did you hit something when we landed?"

Though his touch was fast and impersonal, Krista felt a shock of desire and heat race through her blood. If it felt this good when he wasn't even trying, how much better would it be if he was bent on seduction.

Shaking her head to rid those thoughts and answer him, Krista pushed herself back to a sitting position.

"I'm fine, Jack. A bit on the wet side, but I'll live." She was touched by the concern warming his normally frigid blue eyes.

At her words, Jack immediately pulled away and stood. "I am relieved you are not hurt."

Krista smiled at his formalness and held a hand up

for assistance in gaining her feet.

Instead of reaching for her, Jack took one look at her bare skin and backed away.

"I...um...must scout our location and find out why the wind as deserted us this night." He stumbled away in a rush.

Grumbling to herself, Krista stood on her own, brushed the snow off her rear and glared in the direction her travel buddy had rushed off in. "Well, it's not like I really needed the help."

The look of horror on his face irked her. "It's not like I've got cooties, you know." She yelled to the path he'd taken.

"Men, you can't live with them and you can't bake them into gingerbread cookies."

Picturing Jack as a toasted cookie man went far in appeasing Krista's hurt pride. Yep, the first thing she'd do with her Jack cookie was bite the head off. Then she'd lick the icing off the chest until she reached his waist. There she knew the skin would be hot to her lips as she trailed her tongue down one muscular thigh and straight to his...

"Stop it." She muttered, hands in her hair. "Wrong direction and very wrong thoughts."

Jackson Frost was not the man or elf for her. If he had been, he would have made a move or taken notice of her years ago.

Kind indifference was the best way to describe Jack's treatment of her. He was tolerant and withdrawn most of the time. In no way could she take that to mean more. Anything else was a product of her own lust filled fantasies.

But damn those images were making her hot in more ways than one.

****

The wind had failed him. Such a thing had never happened in all of Jack's existence.

He turned to face the North Pole, summoned the magic to call the wind and nothing happened.

"Jingle my bells!" he cursed aloud while looking around.

Nerves shaky from his near miss with Krista's skin, Jack wanted to be as far away from her as inhumanly possible. She was a temptation. He didn't know how much longer he'd be able to resist. But if his willpower gave out and he allowed himself the luxury of feeling her flesh then Krista would be in danger.

As much as he longed to make a feast of her body, nothing was worth risking her life.

The thoughts led him in mental circles, frustrating him further. With his enormous willpower, he shoved the distracting thoughts of his traveling companion away.

Instead Jack focused his attention on their unplanned landing ground.

There was nothing to see except snow and more snow. The stuff fell in blankets coating the ground and covering Jack's footprints almost before he made them.

The cold wouldn't kill him or Krista. At least he was almost positive the freezing temperature wouldn't do her permanent harm.

The elven blood that ran through her veins would protect her from the worst of it for a short time. It was the longer exposure he was worried about. Had she ever tested her magical limits?

Swearing under his breath, Jack turned his back to their unknown location and went in search of Krista. As much as he longed to keep the physical distance between them, the mental images made her almost a part of him.

When he reached the area he'd left Nick's daughter, the space was empty. Snow had gobbled and concealed whatever footprints might have been.

"Krista." Jack shouted into the stillness of the night.

No answering cry or greeting reached his ears in return.

Once more he raised his voice while trying to keep the panic leashed. "Krista!"

This time his voice answered back in the form of an

echo.

"Krista."

"Kristaaaaaaaa."

"KKKKRRRRIIISSSTTTAAA."

"Rudolph's red nose!" The curse was carried into the wind and shouted back at him.

"Where in the land of magic did the woman go?"

There was nothing to show her location or even a direction where she might have ventured.

"And did I not tell her specifically to stay here? Here in this location?"

The snow gave up no answers to his questions.

Jack reached the point where he would bury his pride and make contact with Nick when the sweetest sound in all eternity reached his ears.

"Jjaacckk."

There was no way to tell where Krista's voice was coming from. The sound bounced from one snow pile to another before he could get a fix on her location.

"Krista, show yourself so I may rescue you." A rescue that wouldn't be necessary if she hadn't wandered off in the first place, he acknowledged to himself.

A small head popped up over a tall mound of snow.

"You bellowed?" she asked as the rest of her tempting body came into view.

Jack gave a small shake of his head. "I don't bellow." He informed her tersely.

"Yeah, whatever." When only a few inches separated them, she wrapped her hand around his upper arm and pointed to where she had come from. "Over that mound is a cabin. I didn't get that close before I heard you bell…um…calling my name." She corrected quickly with a small smile playing across her lips.

"Did it at least look secure?" He questioned her while trying to distance himself from the burning touch of her small hand.

She gave him a duh look. "I didn't get that close, Jack. But it had a roof, and three walls that I could see."

Every step Jack took back, Krista followed resulting in an awkward, jerky dance. Not only was it irritating to retreat from such a small woman, but also if the amusement in her eyes was any indication, she knew the game he was playing.

"Fine, I'll go for a closer look." Giving up on subtlety, he firmly pulled his arm away from her grasp. Then he moved quickly toward the direction she'd come from.

"Wait." She cried out to his retreating back. "You're not leaving me here. I'm the one who found the place."

As if finding some abandoned shack in the middle of nowhere gave her rights, Jack mused. "You'll stay here until I know it's safe." He shot back, not breaking his fast stride.

"Oh, I sure as mistletoe will not."

The quick steps of crushing snow that followed after him were the only noises breaking the night. But still Jack didn't feel comfortable taking Krista to a place he couldn't guarantee her safety.

He made one last ditch effort to stop her. "Krista, I do not know what lies in the building. I will not be able to assure your safety until I assess it myself."

He knew his face was set in its accustomed neutral lines so when Krista broke out in laughter, Jack was stunned.

"What do you find so amusing about our situation?" He demanded, letting ice coat his words.

"You." She laughingly informed him. "Do you honestly think there's some terrorist group hiding out in the wilds of Oregon on the off chance Santa Claus's daughter will drop by? And if there is, what is their big plan? Hold me hostage until my father gives them presents instead of coal?"

When she put it that way, his excessive safety measures did seem a tad extreme. There was no way he was letting her know that.

"Fine, but you will do as I say." He turned back to the mound, started the short climb, aware of Krista's every easy breath behind him.

"You will do as I say." He heard her mumble in a deep voice.

Was she mocking him? He'd never heard anyone mock him to his face before. Sure, elves and pixies did it behind his back when they thought there wasn't a match's chance in snow, he'd hear them. Never would he have thought Krista so bold as to mock him to his face...er back.

"Something you wish to say?" he asked keeping a tight reign on his temper and hurt. Jack doubted Krista would repeat her softly issued words to his face.

"I said," Her voice grew louder. "You will do as I say." Again she pitched her voice low in a poor imitation of his.

"You mock me?" This couldn't be happening. He was the strongest, oldest and fiercest warrior in the community. No one mocked him directly.

"I mock you." She retorted in a strange accent.

He could only stare at her, mouth wide open and catching the fast falling snow.

"I mock you, I irritate you and most of all I annoy you. Yeah, I got that message a long time ago." She assured him in a light tone.

Annoy him, where in the twelve days of Christmas did she get that idea?

He was about to ask when they reached the rise of the small hill.

In front of them exactly as Krista had said, stood a small ramshackle cabin. There was indeed a roof with a chimney sticking out, along with the mentioned three walls. Jack was almost certain the fourth wall would be found in back. There was no way the house could be standing as straight and tall without it.

As they walked closer, the snow no longer blinded his eyes to the cabin's true state. It was indeed a small structure. At a rough guess he put the dimensions around eight or nine hundred square feet. Not large enough for a family to live in but perfect as a hunter's weekend getaway.

"Think it's safe to go in, double-oh-tinsel?" Regardless of what his answer might have been Krista pushed past him, up the steps and opened the front door.

In a burst of speed, Jack rushed in front of her, willing to take whatever blow might come. There was nothing but the sounds of their breathing and the soft fall of snow.

He peered cautiously around the frame. It was an open floor plan with stairs leading to what Jack assumed was a loft for sleeping, as he saw no bedding in the main area. With hesitant steps he tested the boards to see if they would bear his weight. When no creaking or groaning came from the wood he placed his full weight down.

Turning to instruct Krista to use caution, he was shocked as she pushed past him and strode inside the small house.

"Krista, perhaps some caution would be wise." He tried to advise her.

Again she gave him a mocking smile. "Still afraid of those Santa sadists?"

He did not like the battle light in her beautiful green eyes. But years of reserve kept his mouth closed.

Understanding Jack wouldn't respond, she twirled around the room touching things here and there.

"It's a nice place, don't you think?" she questioned without waiting for his reply. "Looks too nice for a hunter's retreat. I wonder if it's a lover's rendezvous."

Krista seemed to give the idea some serious thought. Her brow puckered with lines, lips thinned out and one foot rhythmically tapped a pattern on the hardwood floor. He had no idea what she searched for.

Then again ever since they had become stranded, Krista's attitude had been changing. She was more assertive and less happy-go-lucky. Jack wondered if it was the result of separation from the origin of her powers.

"Yes," she said nodding her head. "I think this is a

place a man and woman would definitely sneak off to."

"Or it is simply a retreat for a single person."

In no way did he want to be stranded in some lothario's love shack with Christmas Claus. His restraint was under enough pressure just standing beside her. Throw in ideas of lovers and sex and Jack was a goner.

Quick as a wink, Krista scampered up the ladder and yelled down to him. "I was right. It's a love nest. Only one big bed with a silk bedspread, not to mention a nice big fireplace."

The groan Jack kept to himself but the rest he made sure Krista would hear. "I think it would be best if I placed a call to your father."

Chapter Seven

It would be a hot day at the North Pole before Krista let that happen. She didn't need Jack calling her Daddy in to save her.

Free falling to a fast death really shakes up the priorities in a girl's life. Krista knew for sure she didn't want to miss out on the excitement of being stranded in a lovely, secluded mountain cabin with Jackson Frost.

Sometime between imminent death and nearly wetting her pants, Krista learned life was short even for the long-lived. There were things she'd always meant to do but put off for a better time.

Here was her giant kick in the ass wake up call. She needed to do all the things she'd planned later, now. And it just so happened seducing Mr. Jackson Frost was fast approaching the top of her list.

"No." She let her hips sway backing down the ladder. "You will not call my father. He has enough to do tonight. Plus, he's not feeling well. Why bother him?" Krista made sure all her reasons were valid and justified. No way was she letting Jack know her intentions until it was too late.

Krista watched his amazing blue eyes narrow until she was sure her body was the only thing in his vision.

"If I do not call your father, then how can I get you out of here? The wind refuses to heed my calls." The tight clenching of his jaw let Krista know how much that bothered him.

Out came the questions praying on her mind. "Why did the wind fail and drop us here? Has this ever occurred before?"

It wasn't polite to ask and thirty minutes ago she would never dream of questioning the big bad Jack. Now she didn't see what the big deal was. Since she was almost turned into a permanent flat snow angel, Krista felt she deserved some answers.

It was amazing. She watched as Jack thought of and discarded many versions of the truth. She could see him picking and sorting them out in his mind. His eyes squinted the slightest bit, his nose flared and those luscious kissable lips narrowed.

"I have never experienced the desertion of the North wind before. I do not know what may have caused it."

It was simple, to the point and Krista believed the truth.

Brownie points for the snowman.

When she brushed past him on the pretense of looking out the room's one window, shivers ran up her spine and heat flooded her veins.

"So what do you want to do for the next twenty four hours?" Krista asked in what she hoped was an innocent voice and expression.

****

The leather covering his raging erection would bust soon. Jack turned away. He made a useless adjustment to his pants, hoping something would calm his libido.

The heat and hunger in Krista's eyes did nothing to slow his ardor. A vision of naked skin, hot mouths and greedy hands passed through his mind leaving him all but shaking with desire.

It was wrong, these feelings he had for Nick's daughter. His number one concern should be for her safety and comfort. All his erection could think about was the comfort of her warm body surrounding him.

Deep breaths and Jack's own internal cooling system allowed him to turn.

Too caught up in internal warfare, Jack had missed Krista's movement across the floor. His body caught up before his mind.

There she was, in his personal space, invading his senses with her smell and heat. All the previous minutes of deep breathing, cooling breezes and reasons not to touch this woman went down in the flames of his desire.

Trying to back away without Krista knowing he was running away wasn't easy. "I think I'll check the outside for wood." He told her lamely, neatly sidestepping her outreached hand.

"Jack, wait." She called after him.

But Jack didn't want to take any more chances alone with her. Those eyes and lips not to mention her lush curvy body would tempt better men than he to cast aside scruples and take what he wanted.

If only it wouldn't mean Krista's life, Jack would happily toss his scruples, honor and morals for one night in her arms.

"Damn it, Jack, I said wait."

Shock had him stopping.

Christmas Spirit didn't curse. She didn't yell or lose her temper. Yet, Krista had done all three.

What was happening with Nick's daughter?

****

Warm flesh met Krista's hand briefly before Jack pulled away from her touch once more.

How could she seduce the man if he wouldn't stand still long enough to try? He didn't even like the feel of her flesh against him.

"What is your problem?" she demanded.

Krista was shocked at herself. Never before had she been able to get angry with anyone. To show something other than happiness, goodwill and kindness to others was literally out of her nature.

Suddenly one small fall from the sky and Christmas Spirit was no longer. Long live Christmas Kick-butt!

The transformation must have shocked Jack as well because he looked at her with a strange light in his eyes and no sharp retort on his sexy lips.

"Yes, Christmas?" he politely inquired while moving back several steps.

Oh, that couldn't be good, she knew. No one ever

called her by her first name. Unless she'd done something wrong or her special brand of help was needed.

She didn't think Jack was in the mood for a spirit lifting nor did he look in need of her help.

"I believe you bellowed at me, Christmas?" The tone was cordial and even polite but Krista felt compelled to back away several steps.

Oh yeah, she was in huge trouble.

"Um, yes, Jack." She stumbled over her words. How did one go about asking for sex? Should she come right out with it? Tell him his body made her mouth dry and toes curl?

"Yes, Jack..." he prompted her.

"I was wondering what we'll do for food?" she finally spit out.

Mentally she smacked her head. Stupid, stupid, stupid. Without a doubt Jack would think Krista was the most ignorant elf in the pole.

Asking about food for an elf was the equivalent of asking a camel if it needed water in the desert.

Not her brightest moment.

Instead of treating her like a refugee from the South Pole, Jack answered her. "If you get hungry, I can try and locate a town nearby to secure supplies."

"NO!" That came out louder and harsher then she intended. "What I mean is, should we look in the cabin before you do something so drastic?"

He couldn't leave. If he left then surely he'd contact her father and her one chance would be over.

Jack flashed a strange look and Krista wished she were better at reading people's faces.

In all the years she'd known him, Krista had never once been able to see through that ice calm expression. And now, more than ever, she wished to know what was going on in his mind.

"Why would we need to look through someone else's belongings when we will not be staying?"

They had to stay, Krista's heart screamed. This was

THE chance to get closer to the winter king.

She tried again with fake calm. "I just mean it can't hurt to stay a while. I mean, Papa's not feeling so hot and tonight's his big night. I'd hate for him to lose time just to pick me up. Especially when there's no reason to. We have shelter and warmth if we need it. Neither one of us have to worry about food too much."

As excuses went, Krista thought the ones she used were pretty valid. She hoped Jack thought so too.

Expression still stuck in neutral, Jack gave her a long look. "Yes, I supposed it would be rude to have Nick stop his route for something so minor. I'm sure my power will be back before too long and I'll be able to finish our journey."

Krista truly did feel bad about Jack's missing power but not guilty enough to change her plans.

"Great," she enthused, almost clapping her hands but stopping the motion just in time. "I'll take a look around here if you'll gather some wood for a fire."

A nod of his head and Jack was out the door.

Krista slumped against the counter in relief. She'd won the battle but now it was time to prepare for the war.

****

If he had to put a label on it, Jack would say Krista was acting strange. He would normally put it down to nerves at being alone with the big bad of the North Pole. Except for the heat in her eyes when she thought he wasn't looking.

Christmas Spirit Claus had looked at him, Jackson Frost, with lust in her eyes. The man every elf, human and other species avoided at all cost.

The woods around the small cabin held a veritable treasure of broken wood and branches. He mindlessly picked up the various pieces while turning over the startling information in his mind.

What would possess a smart, kind and loving woman to want him? He wasn't known for his social skills. Jack was as frosty as his name. Until Krista was around, then his body heated into flames. It was all he could do not to press his lips against hers and mold her lush curves against his hardness.

Oh yeah, he had it bad. Unfortunately, the lust on both sides would go unrequited. No matter how badly his hands ached to touch her skin, he would never know the pleasure of her body.

A small startled scream broke through his concentration and Jack was running through the woods and back to the house.

He arrived in time to see Krista hanging off the side of the chimney.

Even from the distance he saw the look of relief in her eyes when she spotted him.

"Jack." She waved an arm and caused the brick to break away.

Panic flashed through Krista's beautiful green eyes when her anchor gave way and sent her sliding down the roof's steep slope.

In a flash of speed Jack was by the eaves, mentally dispersing the snow. He wasn't worried about the fall; Krista could live through worse. It was the sharp iron picket surrounding the house that would kill her.

In seconds that seemed like hours, he watched Krista's fall in slow motion. As her body cleared the house, Jack braced himself for her weight.

With a whoosh and oomph, Krista landed in his arms like she belonged there. Strong feminine arms went around his neck and she buried her face against his neck. Her warm breath heated his insides as well as his flesh.

With a move to release her, Krista cried out. "NO! Please don't let me go yet."

He hushed her with a soothing tone. "No, I won't let you go, but I need to get you inside to check for any damage."

A small nod was her only reply.

In an unconscious move, Jack leaned down and brushed his lips against the top of her head, neck and finally pressed his lips to the soft skin of her cheek.

"Oh Jack." Her breath wafted against his flesh. "I was so scared. As soon as you appeared I knew you'd help. You caught me before I knew I was falling."

There was something important in her words he should pay attention to. But the relief mingled with the adrenalin rushing through his system blocked everything but Krista and the feel of her in his arms.

"You were foolish to risk your safety." He admonished her while walking swiftly to the door.

She leaned back enough to give him a small rueful smile. "I was trying to check for nests before lighting the fire." She winced when he repositioned his arm around her waist. "I go with Papa all the time and nothing like this had ever happened to me before."

"You've always had your father's magic to back you up." He explained softy as he moved into the living area of the cabin.

Krista gave a small murmur of agreement. Her next words shattered his world.

"You feel so warm against my skin. Why is that? I thought you were supposed to be permanently like an ice pop."

With realization dawning, Jack nearly threw Krista on the couch and back away. Horror spread through his body.

"What have I done?" he whispered out loud.

Not understanding his fear, Krista's face screwed up in confusion. "You haven't done anything but save my life." When he didn't answer she moved off the couch and toward him.

He couldn't help it. He backed away until his spine hit the counter separating the kitchen from the rest of the open space.

"Jack, what's the matter with you?" she demanded.

He shook his head not wanting to put into words the fears running through his mind.

"Please, talk to me. I can't help if I don't know what

to fix." Her tone took on a pleading note.

"Krista, don't touch me." He was ready to climb over the blasted counter to get away from the hand she raised to him.

"What in the twelve days of Christmas are you babbling about, Jack? I just touched quite a bit of you back there and everything is fine." He watched with a breaking heart as puzzlement turned to embarrassment.

"Oh, I get it." She turned away from him her shoulders slumped and footsteps heavy. "Don't worry Jack, I didn't read anything into those few kisses."

She thought he was rejecting her. The absurd thought almost made him laugh. If only she knew the truth.

"It's not your touch I find offensive." He tried to explain to her while maintaining a safe distance. "There are other...issues here, things I cannot explain."

With her back still turned she spoke again but all the joy had gone from her voice. "It's okay, really. I understand; I'm not your type."

This time it was Jack who followed her across the room. In any other circumstance he'd find this chase amusing but not when Krista's life was at stake.

"Are you feeling okay? You're warm enough? No tingling in your back or..." Where in the name of winter had he touched her? He couldn't quite place each touch. Vague thoughts of feeling her warmth against his flesh caused his body to harden.

At his questions Krista finally turned to look at him. "Of course I'm chilly, Jack. It's the middle of winter, we're in a cabin with no heat and I just slid off a roof covered in snow. My clothes are wet, I've made a fool of myself and we're stuck here until tomorrow night."

The look she shot him was typical female. But one he'd never seen cross the Spirit of Christmas's face. She was irritated.

Underneath the anger was hurt. Jack would rather cut out his own heart than cause this woman a second of pain.

He could live with her scorn or pity. What he could not live the next few centuries with was the knowledge that she thought he'd rejected her.

It was time to share his secret. At the thought of putting the truth out there for her ridicule or sympathy, Jack's stomach twisted.

"Krista, there are reasons I can never touch you again. Very valid ones, I assure you." Maybe he could get away with only telling her a partial truth.

"Oh yeah, I know your valid reasons." She marked the air in quotation marks.

He heaved a sigh of defeat and motioned her to sit on the couch. "Please. I want to get this out and over with."

With a suspicions look in her eyes, Krista grudgingly sat down.

He was about to open his mouth when he saw Krista's body shake. "What is it?"

"I'm cold. I told you my clothes got wet from the snow slide." She explained around chattering teeth.

"Donner's balls," he cursed. "Go upstairs and see if there is anything to change into. I'll gather the firewood I dropped in the woods. There will be a fire going by the time you get back downstairs," he assured her, already making his way out the door.

****

Jack Frost had a secret. Or at least he wanted her to believe there was some other reason he had to avoid her touch.

While she appreciated his thoughtfulness in trying to placate her, Krista knew the truth. Jack didn't want her. The more she tried to touch him, the quicker he'd backed away.

Yep, she was repulsive to the one man she desired. Even with her newfound resolve, Krista couldn't overcome the poor man's distaste of her. It wasn't like she was going to force herself on him.

The thought of having Jack tied down and at her

mercy succeeded in making her smile as she shivered her way up the stairs.

"If only my sisters could see me now." She muttered to herself.

The loft was large, running the length of one side of the cabin. Inside the closet, Krista lucked out and found a pair of men's sweatpants and shirt.

Shoving off her wet clothes, she shivered in the cold air. The cotton top felt delicious across her naked skin. She hurried and tossed her underwear on top of the other clothes. No way was she wearing wet underwear under dry clothes.

Besides, what did it matter? It wasn't like Jack would see her out of the ugly gray sweats anyway.

Pulling on a pair of men's thick wool socks, Krista twisted her damp hair into a knot on the back of her head and went back down the steps.

As good as his word, Jack knelt in front of a blazing fire, steadily feeding it small sticks.

Knowing this might be the last time to look her fill, Krista didn't make any noise on the last few steps. She simply drank her fill of him.

Jet-black hair fell over his face giving him a rakish look. She couldn't see those ice blue eyes but knew they'd be intent on the job he set before himself. Everything Jack Frost did, he did with his whole self. She gave a sigh of regret knowing she'd never be the sole object of his anything.

The sigh caught his attention and he turned swiftly to face her.

"Are you all right?" He rose swiftly to his feet, those glacier blue eyes stared intently at her, searching her face for something.

"Yes," she said, exasperated with the kid gloves treatment.

He took a few more hesitant steps in her direction. "No frozen limbs or numbness?" he questioned while his eyes lingered on her lips.

Feeling nervous and still aroused, Krista licked her suddenly dry lips. "Why would I be numb?"

Like a penguin shaking his feathers, Jack jerked his body back. "No reason."

It was a lie. She read the hesitation in his eyes before he spoke the words.

"I don't believe you." She held a hand out to forestall any protest. "It doesn't matter. Weren't you going to share your big bad secret before I got the shivers and shakes?"

All right, so it wasn't very nice of her to taunt him. She'd never been cruel to anyone in her long life no matter how much she wished to be.

With Jack, it seemed like the curse/blessing of her name didn't exist. She'd take advantage of the freedom while she could.

Jack seemed to understand her thoughts. "I seem to be the only one immune from your holiday goodness."

A small shrug was the only answer she had to give him. She didn't understand the lack of cheer in her voice or heart either.

"I've found the pantry fully stocked with a vast selection of canned goods. Would you like me to fix you something to eat? There is also a large selection of refreshments, if you are thirsty." Jack turned his back and quickly walked into the kitchen.

A small rumble from her stomach made a lie out of her earlier boast that she could do without food. With another shrug she decided she was too hungry to care and followed his very nice backside into the kitchen.

All the cabinet doors had been opened and she saw Jack had been right. There was enough food to feed the two of them for months.

It was a strange selection of potted meats, cheeses, beans and vegetables. Krista would have thought a hunting cabin would hold only a few emergency rations. Whatever the case she was grateful for the enormous selection.

Perusing her dinner selections, Krista got to the last

door and gave a delighted laugh.

The interior of the cabinet was far wider and deeper than the others and fitted with specific racks to hold the many bottles of wine and liqueur.

"Hmmm," she murmured. "I wonder what vintage goes best with pork and beans."

"It is good you can keep your humor about you after such an incident." With muscled arms crossed over his wide chest, Jack looked every inch the warrior he was rumored to be. All that was missing from the picture was his trusty steed and sword.

She smirked at the thought of Jack riding to the rescue on the back of a reindeer. She replaced the mental image with that of a polar bear and couldn't stop the grin from splitting her face.

"You have found something else to amuse you besides the dinner selection?" The tone was more formal. In fact, since she'd come down the stairs, Jack's voice had grown colder and more withdrawn.

What the heck, she thought, deciding to be honest with him. "I was picturing you riding to the rescue on the back of one of Papa's reindeer then switched it to a huge snowy white polar bear. The thought made me smile."

A perplexed look shot across his features. "You would picture me rescuing someone?"

"Of course, aren't you the great protector of the North Pole?"

It was his turn to shrug. "I do what is necessary."

She very much doubted that. Jack was the type of man to go beyond what was asked of him.

"So are we hungry for potted meat, canned tuna, canned chicken or can-o-surprise." She asked holding out a silver can with a missing label.

"Choose what you like, I am not hungry at the moment." He turned back to the living room to tend his fire.

"How rude," she said with a grimace. She really wasn't interested in eating the can of mystery. Instead, she set the can down and explored the liquor selection.

Ten minutes later, Krista walked into the living room with a bottle of wine in one hand and two glasses in the other.

"You ready to exchange deep dark secrets?" Maybe she shouldn't have had those sample sips before she finally selected a bottle. The alcohol made her tongue loose and her inhibitions non-existent.

With the fire roaring at his back, Jack looked like some medieval warrior. His coal black hair hung in his eyes and Krista's fingers itched to brush it back. The glow of the fire enhanced his already rugged features making him look even more dangerous and sexy.

"You would have me hear your secrets as well." Though his tone was neutral, Krista could see tension tighten his shoulders and around his lips.

"Sure why not." She replied and flung herself down on the wide couch cushions and closed her eyes. "Would you like me to go first?"

When he didn't reply, Krista turned her head; forced heavy lids open and found Jack staring at her.

"What?"

He gave a small shake of his head. "No one has ever shared confidences with me before."

Careful to keep her face neutral while her heart broke for him, Krista chose her words with care. "I can't imagine why. You are a man of honor. If you give me your word that you will not speak of what I tell you, that's all I need to know."

His assurance was immediate and sincere. "You do me a great honor with your trust. Whatever you might say will go no further than my ears."

He spoke of her honor and Krista wanted to wince. She was using his against him or would be soon.

Instead of calling a halt to this ridiculous game she started, Krista found herself saying, "Great, same goes for me. If you want to unburden yourself, I'm all ears."

This time she didn't give him a chance to reply.

Krista opened her mouth and jumped off the ledge. "My deepest secret is my greatest desire." Coward that she was, Krista had to turn her head from Jack's all seeing gaze. Emptying the rest of the wine in her glass was a good way to gather courage and time she mused as the rest of the potent sweet wine flowed down her throat.

"You, Jack, have been my desire. I've wanted to be your lover since I knew what the word meant. I've dreamed and fantasized about you more times than I can count. I'd picture your lips touching mine; taste the flavor of your tongue in my mouth. Imagine the cool heat of your naked body rubbing against mine and the pleasure of having you thrust inside my body until we both exploded with pleasure."

****

In everything he'd imagined Krista might confess; Jack's own imagination hadn't even come close.

She had fantasized about him making love to her. The thought almost stole his breath away because he could see the picture clearly in his mind.

He'd run calloused hands down her shoulders to caress her breasts, use his teeth to nip gently on the luscious nipples he knew lay beneath the ragged sweatshirt she wore. Swirl his tongue around her bellybutton before pushing her legs wide and feasting on the sweetness he knew glistened between her lush thighs.

"Jack!"

Krista's voice broke the sensual spell his mind wove from her words. For a split second in time he couldn't remember why they both shouldn't make those fantasies a reality.

The truth slammed into him second later and he groaned under the weight of suppressed desire. His cock throbbed beneath the confines of his leather pants. He wanted more than anything to release it and find paradise in Krista's body.

"What?" his tone was surly and reflected the downward slide of his mood.

Her voice matched his as she swung her legs off the couch and stood to face him. "I just bared my soul to you. All you can do is close your eyes and groan? Thanks a lot, Jackson. I know why people don't confide in you. You make a lousy sounding board."

She marched past him in a furious sway of feminine outrage. Without thinking, his hand shot out to stop her. Skin on skin contract stopped the breath in his body.

Krista turned cold eyes from his hand to his face. "I thought you couldn't stand the touch of my skin." She said in a bland voice and tried to shake off his grip.

Jack knew he had to remove his fingers from her wrist. To let the touch linger any longer would surely spell her doom. Yet, even as the words passed through his mind he couldn't make himself loosen his hold.

"I shouldn't be touching you." He tried to explain while watching his own fingers rub gentle circles on her silken skin.

"Oh yeah, that's a great way to impress a woman. Tell her you can't touch her while caressing her arm." The sarcasm was sharp and exact, like an icicle through the heart.

Once more he attempted to explain. "My touch brings harm and death to all who encounter it."

The shame of his words hung heavy on his shoulders and it was the truth behind the words that allowed him to release her.

Jack expected Krista to bolt up the stairs and place a mental S.O.S to her father. Anyone else would have after hearing the truth of his curse. Then there was the way he unconsciously had placed her in danger not once but twice.

But Krista being Krista moved to him instead of running for her life.

With a scornful voice she asked, "Where did you get an idiotic idea like that?"

So much for playing on her sympathy, he thought, but out loud said, "I've known it to be true since I was created."

"Created?" she scoffed. "You weren't created, ice-cubes for brains, you were born, just like the rest of us."

Oh how he wished that were true, but he knew nothing other than being in this form. He had no memories of a childhood or family. No idle thoughts of growing up anywhere with a home or pets.

Krista shook him out of lost memories. "Jack, whatever it is get over it."

Strange, every time he imagined telling Krista his deep dark secret he's always pictured her beautiful face full of pity and sorrow for what they would never share. Never once in all his imaginings did he see Krista with the expression she wore now.

She looked pissed off and irritated. Not a good look for the embodiment of Christmas Spirit.

"I hate to burst your bubble, Ebenezer idiot, but you've been touching me since you started this lame excuse and I'm not dead yet."

There were only so many insults an elf could take and Krista had pushed him way over his limit.

"I can't just get over it." He told her hotly, going to stand toe to toe with her. "I've had to live with this blizzard of a curse for my entire existence. I'm an elf not a eunuch, woman. You think I haven't tried to bed a woman before? No go." Part of his brain was telling him to shut the Blitzen up. The other half was rejoicing at finally being able to spew the venom from his soul to another living being.

"I touch a woman and her body instantly freezes. Doesn't do much for foreplay let me tell you. I sure as hell don't get second invites."

He'd finally gotten through to her. Jack could tell by the stunned expression on her face. Horror widened her holly green eyes and red blazed across her cheeks.

Once again he misjudged everything about Krista. Instead of the sympathy and understanding, the elf responsible for ensuring good will to men and spreading the holiday spirit hauled back and punched him in the face.

Jack heard his nose crack from the force of her fist and felt the warm dribble of blood coat his mouth and chin. The pain he easily dismissed but the shock of seeing the Spirit of Christmas swearing and shaking her hand left him speechless.

Unfortunately that gave Krista the opening to vent.

"You inconsiderate, egotistical, snow for brains male." She paced away from him only to whirl back with one finger pointing in his chest.

He winced not from pain but from the selfish pleasure he took in Krista's every touch, regardless if the touch was given in anger.

"How dare you pop out with 'I've tried to bed other women,' especially after I just got through telling you I," poke "wanted," poke "you," poke. "In," poke "my bed."

Her words stopped the mindless pleasure drowning him with her touch. "What have other women got to do with you? I never did anything with them. One thing has nothing to do with the other."

Krista's cheeks went from cherry red to scarlet flame. Jack stepped back. He may not have spent much time with women but his instinct told him to abandon sleigh.

"You don't want me. You won't touch me because of some stupid issues you have with your mother or your uncle being your aunt. Frankly, I don't give a candy cane's stripe what your 'issues' are." He watched in fascination as Krista tried to pull herself back but she was too close to the edge to back away.

Jack's stomach lurched as tears swam into her evergreen eyes.

"Do me a favor and call Papa for me. I don't want him to know I'm upset or why." She took a deep calming breath and backed another few steps away from him. "As far as I'm concerned this night and conversation never happened. We never touched and I never spilled my guts to you."

With a twist of her foot, Krista turned and walked to the stairs.

That was it. She was leaving. This torment and torture of desire, longing and love would end when Nick came to fetch his daughter.

Good, he thought, waiting for the relief to lighten the tension in his shoulders.

She stopped at the base of the stairs and he would have made it, Jack was certain he would have called Nick. The old man would have flown down here, and picked his wayward daughter up. Then Jack could get on with the rest of his long, cold and lonely life. He would have done exactly as she asked if Krista hadn't spoken the words that tore his heart out.

Instead, she muttered under her breath. "I'm jumping the first man I see in LA. I'll have a week long marathon of hot monkey sex with a different man each night."

She made it to the first step before Jack caught her arm and spun her around. "I will permanently freeze off any man's cock if he tries to touch you."

"You have no right to dictate what I do much less who." She was glorious in temper, eyes flashing hot. Desire burned him with ice-cold intensity.

"I don't need the right when I have this."

There was no chance given to prepare. Jack's mouth swooped down and took Krista's lips in a kiss that stole his breath, mind and fear.

Damn his curse. Damn her for pushing his restraint. She was his now.

****

Thought and reason flew out of Krista's head at the first touch of Jack's mouth. Anger melted away in the first thrust of his tongue. This is what she wanted, had always wanted. Jack unleashed and making love to her was better than any late night fantasy.

With a moan of acceptance, Krista threw her arms

around his neck and dug her hands into his silky black strands. She couldn't get enough of touching him, tasting him.

While his mouth devoured her in a taste of mint and male, Jack's hands were busy running the length of her back down to her ass.

Krista had a moment to wonder if Jack's curse was true because her body was burning with a freezing fire. Then he deepened the kiss, feasting on her mouth like a man starved. And she forgot everything but Jack's mouth, hands and body.

She wanted that glorious hard body on top of hers, thrusting into her with all the ice and fire that came with it. Krista wanted her hands on his bare flesh. She needed to feel the flex and play of his muscles as he touched her. She wanted to take everything he was and give him back the same.

When Jack's hand moved under the bulky sweatshirt and found nothing but skin, he raised his head and cursed. "Are you trying to kill me, female?"

She shook her head no, and eagerly went back for his mouth. His kisses were addicting and she needed another fix of his taste.

When he moved out of reach of her lips, Krista pressed her hips against his. She thrilled to find the hard proof of his desire burning against her hip, and reached one hand down to caress the steely length of him.

A muttered oath escaped his lips. "Not here. I'll not take you against the wall like some untrained human."

Vaguely aware of his words, Krista used her other hand to slide under the silky cotton of his shirt and rake her nails through his chest hair.

"Take me to bed, Jackson." She whispered against his neck before nipping his ear lobe.

"Damn me for a fool, Krista, because I can't tell you no."

In a flash of elfin speed, Jack had her in his arms and up the stairs in a matter of seconds.

The look of heat, wariness and desire in his eyes caused Krista's heart to catch. Please don't let him stop now, she pleaded silently.

Instead of walking away as she half expected him to do, Jack sat next to her on the bed. "Are you sure of this, Krista? Once done we can never undo the act," he warned in a gruff tone.

Since her throat was clogged with desire, Krista could only nod her acceptance.

"You're not having any ill effects from my touch?" he persisted. "No numbness or cold spots?"

Finally able to swallow past the lump in her throat, Krista spoke. "The only coldness I feel is from missing the heat of your body."

A confused look came and went across his face, replaced with an all male knowing grin. "I can't allow that, now can I?" He said shifting so that he was lying next to her on the soft bed, one arm around her, one leg pressed between hers.

He kissed her again, his tongue taking slow possession of her mouth, as his free hand gently tugged her sweatshirt from her body. When the garment cleared her head, he tossed it over his shoulder and stared at the skin he'd uncovered.

Shyness nearly over took her until she heard Jack's quick intake of breath. "Perfect," he said softly, bending down to take a hard nipple in his mouth.

She reached between them to yank at his sweater, needing to feel his skin against her own.

Jack moved back enough to let her tug the sweater from his broad shoulders. It sailed across the room to join hers. Then he was back. His mouth moved hotly across her skin as he licked and nibbled his way across her body.

Krista had a small glimpse of his bare chest before he pressed their bodies tightly together. He had smoky black hair on his chest and more muscles than she'd ever seen.

With sheer force of will, Krista untangled one hand from his head. She used that hand to touch him lightly at first, then harder. His back was so smooth, the hair on his chest soft. She could feel his hand sliding down her stomach, past the barrier of her loose pants. The sensation was incredible. She moaned out loud.

Like a switch had been flicked, Jack pulled out of her arms and off the bed.

"Are you hurt? What happened?" He didn't give her a chance to answer before he was rambling on. Jack's hands impatiently tugged on his black hair as he paced the foot of the bed. "I knew I shouldn't have given in to this madness. No matter how badly I want you, it was selfish to give into you."

When the urge came over her, Krista gave into it and screamed. Instantly Jack was at her side.

"Where does it hurt?" His hands moved quickly over her limbs. He checked for blood or ice spots, she guessed.

Krista didn't have the patience to correct him gently. Her body was wet and ready, yet Jack acted like they had been doing nothing but sipping eggnog.

For the second time that night, Krista resorted to violence and smacked Jack upside his head.

He looked up from his examination of her right arm and frowned. "What the name of the Rudolph's red nose did you do that for?" He asked as he dropped her arm and rubbed the side of his head. He sent her a cold glare. "You need to tell me where the pain is."

"The pain is in my head," she replied, and wanted to hit him again. She, who had never resorted to violence in her life, wanted to beat this man to ground up ginger.

At her answer, Jack looked confused. The line between his eyes grew more pronounced and his lips flattened. "Why is there pain in your head? I did not touch you there."

Just like that heat flared back into his eyes. She knew he was remembering just where he had touched.

She fought off the sugary warmth the heated looked caused. "The pain is in my head because you are one brick short of a chimney."

Jack shook his head, the baffled look still on his handsome face. "But you cried out," he defended himself.

"Yeah," she answered in a huff, and pulled the comforter around her semi-naked body. "I moaned."

"Exactly, you moaned." He stopped as the words sank in. "You moaned?" This time he made it a question.

Krista moaned again but this time in exasperation. This was never going to work. Jack was too worried about some weird curse. She was the worst kind of fool for even trying.

"Never mind, Jack, you were right. We should never have tried this. Please make the call to Papa." She wondered if she could stay wrapped in the safety of the bedspread until her father arrived. Then again she really didn't want her father to know about what almost happened between her and Jack. It was humiliating enough that she knew.

Jack caught the edge of the spread with one hand and pushed her to lie down on the bed with his other. Quickly he followed her down and pressed his hard body against her own.

"You moaned because I gave you pleasure?" It was more of a statement than a question but Krista sensed he needed to hear the answer.

"Yes." She wished she could hide under the covers instead of on top. How did she talk herself into doing something so embarrassing?

Jack still didn't look like he believed her. "My touch caused you to writhe on the bed and cry out in enjoyment?"

"Are you hard of hearing all of a sudden or do you enjoy watching me turn the six shades of mistletoe?"

His face showed surprise at her response. Clearly he expected her to lie underneath his half naked body and discuss what turned her on.

Men, no matter the species, were idiots. She turned her face away from his, not wanting to see the smug satisfaction spread across his face.

Jack refused to allow her even that privacy. He cupped her cheek in one warm, solid hand and turned her back to face him.

"I don't ask to feed my pride or ego, Krista. I ask because my first thought at the sound of your cries, was that I had caused you pain. To cause you pain would be beyond the worst injury to myself."

His husky voice sounded so sincere and Krista wanted desperately to believe him, but fear kept her mouth shut.

"My little blizzard," he murmured and kissed her cheeks softly. "You must remember I haven't had the best of luck in the area of oth-"

He stopped himself in time. Krista knew what the next words out of his mouth would have been and she appreciated that he caught himself so quickly.

"Why did you call me that?" The term was familiar to her but not the context in which he used it.

Jack raised his head from where his lips had been trailing a heated path from her neck to her chest. "Call you what? My little blizzard?" He questioned and returned his mouth to the slope of her breast.

"Yes." She cut off the moan that was desperate to escape her lips but Krista would rather ride in her father's sleigh naked than go through another misunderstanding with Jack.

With his mouth full of her nipple and his hand wandering past her waist, she didn't think he heard her question.

But the talented male raised his head long enough to send her a heat filled look with blazing hot blue eyes.

"A blizzard is deceptive at first, coming in as nothing more than a few beautiful flakes. If you don't pay attention you are caught up in its beauty and it can swallow you whole. You are like that beautiful storm, my Krista. The calmness you project deceives many into believing there is nothing of importance beneath your surface. Then when it is too late, you've stormed past their defensives and swirled them in your wake."

The words he used were flattering but she wasn't sure he intended them as a compliment.

When his finger dipped in the wetness between her legs, Krista found she didn't care.

Jack matched the thrusting of his fingers with his tongue dancing in her mouth.

Moans and whimpers of pleasure tried to rise, but Krista refused to allow them release. The plunge of his fingers inside her body sent exquisite shafts of pleasure shooting through her. She felt her body climb to a release that would surely kill her. No one, not even an elf, could survive this much pleasure.

Jack's touch set her on fire. The way his talented lips and tongue flicked and sucked her breasts made her movements jerky and frantic. She turned her face into the pillow to muffle her screams as the pleasure over took her.

Before the last scream of pleasure died from her lips, Jack yanked her face out of the pillow.

Still riding the high of her orgasm, Krista watched with drowsy eyes as Jack's face came into focus.

"Don't," he whispered against her lips, softy tracing their outline with his tongue. "I may have been a fool once, but not again. The only way you will get me to stop our pleasure is to come out and say it."

A feeling of emptiness filled her when his fingers left her body. She watched in stunned fascination as Jack used one hand to paint her nipple with the juices of her body. Then he brought it to his nose and inhaled.

"You smell sweeter than any berry wine." To Krista's complete shock, Jack moved the hand from his nose to his mouth. He licked and sucked the wetness from his skin. "You taste creamier than any eggnog. I could get drunk on the taste of you alone."

The change in Jack stunned her. She had always dreamed of hearing passionate words tumble from his lips. She never dared to dream he would be this sensual.

"Then taste me and take me, Jack. I want to feel you inside my body." She opened her legs to cradle his cock where she needed it the most.

Krista maneuvered her hand between their bodies. She worked his zipper down, and then touched him, covering him with her hand.

Jack went supernova. His body jerked, breath hissed out of his lungs in a quick rush and his mouth devoured hers.

Before she knew what was happening, Jack was gone. In a brief flash he was back, naked. Krista tried to look over his body but he was back on top of her before she could blink.

He seemed to understand her disappointment. "Later," he whispered in her ear while placing love bites along the outer rim. "When the madness has left us both, I'll give you free reign of my body. For now," he spread her legs wider with his knees. "I need to be inside you more than I need my next breath."

Instead of responding with words, Krista lifted her legs and wrapped them around his hips.

He took himself in hand and pushed the first few inches into the wetness he'd created. This time it was Jack that moaned. "Krista…sweet…so sweet."

"Yes, Jack." She freely moaned right back. Oh how she wanted this, had dreamed of it for years. Now it was coming true.

She opened her eyes to watch his expression as he made them one. Sweat beaded his forehead and upper lip. Strain caused his arms to shake with the effort it took to hold himself back.

She'd waited too damn long for Jack to hold back on her now. He'd pushed in a few inches, pulled out then pushed back in those few inches only.

She wanted all of him, hard, fast, and now. "All of you, Jack. I want to feel everything."

Her words jerked his head up. Startled blue eyes met determined green ones. "Krista, I don't want to hurt you. I need and want you so much I'm afraid I'll lose control. The first time should be something you always remember with pleasure, never pain."

His words alone almost pushed her over the edge. "Yes, that's exactly how I want it. How I want you. Lose your control, I promise you won't hurt me. It's feels like I've waited for you my entire life. Now, I'm tired of waiting."

Jack searched her eyes. Whatever he found there must have reassured him because he gave a sharp nod of his head. "Your wish is my command."

Krista grabbed on to his muscular ass, felt the flex and pull of his muscles. With one hard thrust, he broke through the last barrier separating them.

She screamed again, as pleasure washed through her, the pain a barely noticeable blip in her body. The feel of Jack's body so deep inside her caused her inner muscles to contract and Jack groaned.

"So tight," he whispered. "So hot...perfect...so perfect."

Krista could do nothing more than hold on to Jack's body as his rhythm picked up and his strokes became harder and faster.

There was a building inside her, a wave growing with each pleasurable thrust of his cock inside her. Krista wanted to run from it and to it all at the same time.

"Let go, my Krista. Come with me." His masculine voice took on an urgent tone and his breathing grew harsher. He trembled just as she did, resting his brow on hers as Krista took him deep, held him fast.

His hands sought hers, fingers tangling. She felt him rock inside her, his struggle to keep the pace even. She could feel his heart thudding in his chest, watched as the blood pounded in his veins.

She dug her nails into his shoulders as the wave crashed down upon their bodies, drowning Krista in perfect pleasure. She felt Jack shudder above her, cry out her name one last time and then the hotness of his release inside her body.

She came back to herself to find Jack's body blanketing hers, his shaft still deep within her but not as hard, breath heavy in her ear and his heart pounding against her own.

Krista tried to catch her breath. "That was..." Words wouldn't come to mind. That was so much more than she had expected of her first time.

A soft nuzzle of lips against her breast, and then he raised his head. "Everything." He leaned down to brush a kiss as soft as a snowflake against her swollen lips.

Yes, she agreed silently, it had been everything from her fantasies come true, just like Jack was.

It was going to break her heart to let him go.

How could she trap him into staying with her? Right now he was enamored with her body because hers was the first he'd touched. But someday he might come to resent her for keeping him by her side.

Before today he'd never shown the slightest interest in her. This had to be a passing fancy for him. And if it wasn't...

There was a reason for the old saying, 'If you love something set it free, if it comes back to you it will always be yours. If it doesn't, it was never truly yours to begin with.'

Krista would set Jack free. She'd allow him time and freedom to roam the world and seek his pleasure.

But first she'd have this weekend and all the lovemaking she could cram into it.

****

Jack never felt such contentment as he did now with Krista's generous breast acting as his pillow. He'd known sex between them would be good, but never in all his imaginings had he dreamt of something this incredible.

For the first time in his memory, his mind and body were at peace. No nagging questions pestered his mind, asking what was wrong with him, or what he had done to deserve a loveless fate.

Now he knew the fault wasn't in him but that each woman he tried to become intimate with wasn't Krista. She made all the difference.

He should move off Krista. With his body on top of her delicate one, she probably couldn't breathe. Quickly, he slid both arms around her and flipped them so she rested on top. Her head burrowed on his chest.

Her hair was soft and thick in his fingers. He marveled at the freedom he felt to touch her anywhere. The thought itself was a turn on, but add to that the fact he was still snuggled inside her welcoming warmth, and he was hard again.

Krista must have felt the stiffening of his body. She raised her slumberous eyes and smiled. "You can't be ready so soon."

With one hand Jack pulled her down for a steamy kiss and with the other he stroked and tweaked her hardening nipple.

When breathing became an issue, they raised their heads as one. "I look at you and want. There doesn't seem to be a time when my body doesn't respond to even the thought of you."

He nipped her lips, then moved on to the salty satin of her neck until he reached her plump breasts. Taking her berry crest into the warm heat of his mouth, he started a slow gentle rhythm inside her.

Their earlier release eased his way and the movements were smooth and fluid. Jack groaned at the feel of her wetness enclosing him like a tight fist.

Sex was better than he thought it would be. Sex with Krista was becoming addictive.

"This is more than I ever dreamed it could be," he told her as his thrust gained strength.

Her body stiffened on top of his, losing the easy pattern they had fallen into.

"Wait, Jack." Krista sat straight; the movement pushed him all the way inside her, deeper than he'd been able to go before. "We forgot protection."

For a second, Jack was too caught up in lust to understand. When comprehension dawned, he smiled and lightly bit her nipple. "We can carry no diseases. Ill health is not an issue for us."

With the issue resolved in his mind, Jack clamped both hands on her hips, trying to guide her down into his upward thrust.

"No, Jack." She cried, her voice husky with need and pleasure. "I could get pregnant."

The idea should have wilted his cock. His heart stopped and his movement ceased. Jack stared up at Krista's beautiful face. The face he'd loved and longed for all her life. The picture of her rounded stomach filled with his child sent burst of heat and happiness through his body.

He remembered the scene at Nick's house. The vision in the Christmas ball. He'd been standing with his arms around Krista and children had come running in. There was nothing more he'd like to see than that vision come to life. And he could make it happen.

His seed might be forming a child even as they spoke of it.

The thought, the idea was enough to push him over the edge.

Jack pulled Krista tightly to his chest as his hips pounded a savage rhythm in her. His balls tightened and knew he was close to coming.

He shoved one hand between their bodies and found the center of Krista's desire. With one finger he circled her clit, with another he rubbed in time with his hips.

She came with a sharp cry, screamed his name and convulsed around him. Jack followed behind, shouting his pleasure as his body spurted forth his seed.

****

Krista still couldn't believe it. Jack had come not once but twice in her body. She could feel the wetness of him dripping down her leg. And after she'd told him of the possible results.

She knew he didn't do it out of love and desire to have a child with her. He did it because this was his first few times with a woman and he couldn't help himself.

Well, tough cookie cutters. Maybe Jack didn't love her but she would be damned to the South Pole before she let him get away with dumping her and her child.

The more her anger grew the less she could stay still. Jack snored behind her, one arm tightly around her waist as if clutching her to him. Only in her dreams would Jack want to hold her tight.

She'd gotten herself in a mess. Krista really wished her sisters were here to talk to. Then again, they'd tell Noel and he'd threaten Jack; there would be a fight and all the details would come spilling out.

No, her family couldn't be involved. It would only complicate the situation.

What she needed was a plan to escape both Jack and her family. If she could hide out for a few weeks, until she knew whether or not she was having a baby, she'd go from there.

If there was a child...a secret smile formed on her lips. A boy with Jack's black hair and her green eyes. A son with his father's sense of adventure and his mother's gift of peace. Oh what a joy such a child would be, too bad he'd never know his father.

If she truly were pregnant, she'd explain to her family that she's met a man, thought it was love and found out it wasn't.

It was as close to the truth as she dared. She had met Jack, did believe herself in love and found out Jack wasn't in love with her.

He had spoken no words of love or emotions. He'd praised her body, her movements. He'd loved everything about her or so he said, but he never once said he loved her.

A small voice inside her head reminded her that she hadn't spoken the words either.

With a firm hand, she mentally pushed the voice aside. There were plans to be made and things to prepare for. The biggest thing was to avoid the man holding her so tightly in his sleep.

With as much speed as she dared, Krista lifted Jack's arm from her stomach and scooted across the bed.

Once free of the mattress she turned to look at her first and only lover.

With his black hair tousled and face relaxed, he looked carefree.

Krista took a mental picture to store in her memories for the years to come when she would no longer be here to see him.

Krista did wish him happiness and love. Something she sensed he'd had too little of. She hoped one day, he'd find a woman worthy of his heart.

Spears of jealousy stabbed her chest at the thought of Jack with another woman. Krista didn't know who the woman was or even if she existed but she hated her all the same.

It was the thought of hate that jerked her out of her thoughts. Krista had never hated anyone in her life. She was all that was good, calm and peaceful in the holiday. She was the one who took hate away from others and showed them the true joy of the season.

But she couldn't deny the kernel of darkness dwelling within her mind and heart. Someday she would be able to exercise it; until then she would ignore it.

Silently she gathered the sweatpants and shirt from across the room. Walking as quickly as she dared on tiptoes, she opened the door and had one foot outside when a deep voice stopped her.

"What is so important that you must rush from our bed into to the coldness of the night?"

She turned back.

Jack sat leaning against the headboard with the sheet pulled just past his waist. His muscles flexed when he stretched his arms. Krista felt her mouth water.

Did he ask a question? She couldn't remember with all the warm delicious flesh showing. Her fingers itched to run down the muscles of his stomach and follow the dark trail that led just below the sheet.

"Krista," Jack waved a hand. "I asked why you left our bed?"

Oh darn it, reality was back.

Since she couldn't face him with a lie in her eyes, Krista turned to fiddle with the doorknob. "I got hungry. I was going to the kitchen to get something to eat."

She turned back and saw his head tilt to the side. "Why are you lying to me?"

****

He'd always had an instinct with Krista. He'd known when she was sad even though she smiled to the world. He could tell when excitement fueled her body. Mostly he knew when she was lying.

Krista wasn't any good at. She'd never had practice before, Jack knew. It stood to reason she would know what a dead giveaway her guilty expression was.

He watched part amused and part hurt as she tried to recover herself.

A small strained laugh forced itself out of her lips. "What gives you the idea I'm lying?" She shuffled her feet, and dug one toe in the thick rug covering the floor.

All Krista needed was a sign on her head. She couldn't be more obvious, at least to someone who knew her.

With a sigh of regret, Jack gave up the hope of staying in bed and making love. He understood the determined expression behind the guilt on his lover's face. Whatever was on her mind was more important than finding out their favorite sexual position.

A quick flick of his hand tossed the sheet away from his waist. Krista's sharp intake of breath eased Jack's shaky ego. She liked the look of him nude, he mused. It was good information to know.

He ignored his clothing thrown across the room and

stalked to Krista's retreating form.

"Wait a minute, my little blizzard. I want to know why you're making up excuses to leave me."

Another phony laugh bubbled from her lips and Krista's eyes couldn't stay focused on one thing. She licked her still kiss-swollen lips. "Umm, I told you. I was feeling hungry. Why would I lie about that?"

"Your body tells me you are leaving more than this room." He flatly told her.

He watched as her chin lifted and her eyes flashed. "It's really not a concern of yours where I go, Jack."

That was it. Jack had put up with a lot in his long life, including celibacy until a few short hours ago. He would be damned to a penguin if he let Krista get away with this. She was running from him and what they shared like it didn't matter.

She had been the one to break the curse over his body and heart. He was not something she would just walk away from. What they shared dealt with more than physical connections. Jack touched Krista's soul and saw all the possibilities in his life he'd been missing.

He understood Krista wasn't a means of escaping his former way of life but of enhancing it. Everything looked and sounded more interesting if she was part of it.

Jack Frost was in love. His icy heart had melted with Krista's first gentle touch.

His grip was gentle but unbreakable when he stopped her from walking out of the bedroom.

"You are very much mistaken on that part, Christmas. Everything you do, say and feel is very much my business."

The tone was gruff but Jack knew his eyes held all the emotions pouring out of his soul.

Krista gave a jerk to her arm. "You don't own me, Jackson Frost." She sputtered when he pulled her into the circle of his arms.

"Tell me why you wished to leave me. Did I not please you? I know I lack experience but I felt your pleasure squeezing me tight. So that cannot be the excuse. Given enough time, I will show you all the bedroom tricks I've read or heard about." He told her in a confident voice.

Instead of fighting his hold as Jack had expected, Krista gave a deep sigh and rested her head on his naked chest.

"You know it has nothing to do with your experience. I'd say we're evenly matched in that area." Her breath ruffled his chest hair. "I don't want to be the one pining for you at home while you go sow your frozen oats. I want a life that I can count on. I want...no I deserve what my parents have. I won't settle for less."

"Krista, how could you not know what this meant to me? I've never touched or been touched by anyone. You've released me from the prison within my body."

To Jack, the truth was obvious. He didn't understand why Krista didn't understand it was love that had set his touch and body free. Without his ability to love her, he would have died a lonely old man with nothing but dreams.

Krista must return at least some of his feelings. If she didn't, how did she break through the icy barrier that always came between him and other women?

"That's just it, Jack." She pushed away from his chest and finished dressing. "I'm the first woman to have sex with you..."

"We made love," he interrupted.

She waved a hand to dismiss the difference. "Fine, but it doesn't change the facts."

He felt the melting ice around his heart begin to harden once more. She was rejecting him.

"And what are the facts?" Ice drifted off the vapors of his voice.

She paced as she talked, agitation in her every step. "I'm the first person you've..." she hesitated over the words. Jack was feeling childish enough to hold his silence.

"You know..." again her hand waved, this time between their two bodies. "Been with."

"I am aware of that."

"So I think maybe you need to explore the world a bit more."

He arched one black brow and rubbed the bridge of his nose. "Explore?" What in the name of Frosty's black hat was the female babbling about? "I agree; exploring could be fun." He thought of exploring the swells and valleys of her body. He could become addicted to exploring.

Until she spoke again. "You'll go out into the world and see what it holds for you. I'll do the same."

"You want me to screw other women?" How dare she suggest he do such a thing? He'd break the bones of any human male that dared touch her.

The swift intake of breath caused him a moment of satisfaction but heartache over ruled any pleasure. She didn't share his feelings. That was all Jack needed to know.

"There's no need to be crude, Jack." Hurt layered in her voice.

"I was honest not crude." Why had he ever let emotions cloud his once perfect judgment? The ice had encased him but left Jack protected at the same time.

He pulled the coldness around him like an invisible cloak. "As you say, Krista, maybe experience would sort me out."

He turned with whatever dignity he had left and walked out the bedroom door, back to his lonely and much colder life.

****

She would not go to him. He deserved a chance to discover life after celibacy.

"Set him free," the words became her mantra as she finished getting dressed.

Her life and gift were all about letting people be true to themselves and their hearts. Why should Jack be any different? Didn't he deserve the chance to find out if there was more to life than one female elf at the pole?

Krista was a mature elf. Jack would have his chance to bed other women. Then when they both had more experience, maybe they would meet again and re-evaluate their relationship

She loved him so she would let him go.

"Oh crap on a cookie cutter! I'll be a reindeer's aunt if I let that elf run wild with mortal women." Krista's common sense all but shoved her out the door.

There was another part to the mortal saying she'd forgotten.

"If it doesn't come back to you, hunt it down and tie it to your bed."

For once Krista was incomplete agreement with the mortal women.

She had an elf to hunt.

****

Jack made it all the way to the front door before common sense hit him like an icicle to the heart.

Ego had prevented logic. He really was an elf in love.

In all their arguments Krista had never denied having feelings for him. She told him he needed to find out about life outside the pole. But never once did she say anything about her life.

Okay, there was the one remark about bedding other men, but that could have been sheer bravado.

If he walked out the door it might be years before he saw Krista again. But then too much time would have passed and she might love another.

Damn him for a seven-toed troll. Jack wouldn't allow his one chance at happiness to desert him. If Krista didn't love him now, then he'd love her more until she did.

He turned, sped up the steps and ran straight into the object of his love.

"Krista," he started.

"Jack," she said breathlessly at the same time.

Both elves backed slowly away from each other,

emotions rich and ripe in the air.

Questions were asked with seeking eyes. Answers were given in hesitant body language.

"You first," Jack offered, as his heart pounded within his chest.

She looked flustered by his offer. "Um, right…okay."

Krista looked at the floor, the ceiling, and the wood grain in the stairway banister. She looked, in fact, everywhere but at him.

"Is there something you wish to say?" he tried to help her start.

"Yes," she took a deep breath. Jack couldn't help but admire the way her sweatshirt rode up and showed the delightful stretch of flesh between the materials.

"I was going to hunt you down and tie you to the bed," she said in a rush.

Jack wasn't sure what to think. If she intended to join him there, then he was all for her bondage game. But if she wanted to leave him alone to suffer, he would dissuade her. "Huh," was the only answer he felt safe with.

With the first declaration out in the open, Krista gained speed and confidence. "You see I had it all wrong. I thought if I loved you, I had to let you go. If you came back it meant you loved me too. But then I thought, who gives a dumpling if you come back. I want you now."

"I see."

Krista's logic was confusing and completely jig sawed but somehow he gleaned hope from her message.

"So you were coming to hunt me down?" The spark of hope grew brighter and bigger in his chest.

Hands on hips, chin tilted, Krista glared at him. "You bet your stocking, buddy. I don't care if you are the big bad of the North Pole. You were able to touch me for a reason. So I'm going to be the only woman you ever touch. First, last and always. Got it?"

Oh how he loved her like this. Green eyes flashed temper and wariness, chest heaved with nerves and temper, and her lickable, kissable lips pursed with pique.

"I believe I understand. Now would you like me to explain why I was coming up those stairs as you were racing down?"

The thought must not have occurred to her because her face lost its mulish expression. "You were…um…"

"I came back up to tell you I loved you. I don't need to sow my frozen oats with other women to find that out. I've loved you for more years than I can recall."

Hope shone brightly out of her evergreen eyes. "Really?"

"Really," he said, and closed the distance between them. "Why do you think it's taken me all this time to be able to touch someone?"

"I don't know. I don't care." Fiercely she wrapped her arms tight around his waist.

"My heart was as cold as the ice I create. It took someone with a special gift to unlock the warmth of my heart. Someone with the gift of Christmas in her soul."

"Oh Jack," she whispered, and lifted herself to touch his lips with her own.

Yes, Jackson Frost had finally found his Christmas Spirit and he was never letting her go.

About the author...

It came as no surprise to anyone when Allie decided she wanted to write humorous adventure-filled romance stories. After all her life has been one of constant adventure. From surviving the wilds of oft-flooding South East Texas where she lives to growing up in Saudi Arabia where her brother tried to sell her to Bedouins (for what amounts to less than $1.50), it's been non stop. And she loves every minute of it.

When not writing the stories of all the people in her head, Allie can be found fighting off her demonic cat, chasing a dog with a penchant for purple underwear, avoiding the kitchen and grocery stores at all costs, and trying not to think about her next deadline.

Far From Silent Night

Bev Oz

Chapter One

Holly removed her hand from its resting place under the red velvet blanket and brought her wrist within inches of her face. The snowfall was so hard she could barely make out the time on her watch.

Two minutes. He had already been down there two minutes.

That much time might be needed for a house with two adults and five kids. But this house—no, cabin - was small, and only one guy lived here. Something must be wrong.

She shifted her bottom on the leather seat and strummed her fingers on the shellacked wooden sides of the open sleigh. Though her nails weren't long, the tips drummed out a fast cadence mimicking that of a death roll on a snare drum.

What could be taking him so long?

A blast of wind whipped through the trees and blew icy snow pellets in her face. She winced and clamped her eyes shut. How did humans deal with such intense cold? Being an elf sure had its advantages. If her adopted sister Chrissy were here instead, the poor girl would be frozen like a Popsicle out in this weather.

She turned her back to the pelting gusts and checked her watch again. Narrowing her eyes, she could just make out the time. Three minutes. That was just too long. According to the Naughty and Nice list, they should already be at the next stop by now.

Images of her father splayed out on the floor of the cabin raced through her mind. A pool of his deep red blood that matched the color of his suit and hat was spreading out from his chest.

The man who lived in this tiny place probably had a gun and had shot Daddy. She hadn't heard a gunshot, but that didn't mean anything. Maybe the guy had a silencer.

She huffed. The moisture in her breath instantly formed a frozen mist and then blew away.

Why did she stress like this whenever Daddy was away? The whole shoot Santa Claus paranoia was absolutely over the top and ludicrous. Yet that knowledge never helped. It didn't stop the intense pressure pushing down on her chest or her heart from beating like the Energizer bunny on crack at being left alone for so long.

According to Daddy's list, the man living here, David White, had been good all year. The guy's name and address was even underlined in red ink and had three asterisks. Whatever that meant.

What in the world was Daddy doing down there?

Holly threw off the blanket and tugged at the white fur lining the bustier top of her Christmas elf uniform. The outfit was too tight, and she was practically spilling out of the damned thing. Either her boobs were getting bigger or she was eating way too many Christmas cookies. Probably both.

With her hands gripping to the sleigh, she jumped onto the steep angle of the roof. Her feet and legs sank into three feet of snow. She lifted her thigh-high black boots as high as she could get them and shuffled her way around the reindeer toward the chimney.

As she passed Blitzen, the stupid deer shoved her butt hard with his nose. She slipped and the weight of her body teetered back and forth on her pointed boot heels. She frantically waved her arms like deranged windmills, trying to stay upright, but gravity won out. She fell flat on her back, buried in the snow's depths.

Blitzen shook his head and snorted. The sleigh bells attached to his harness jiggled in mock laughter.

Frustration warmed Holly's blood. If the arrogant reindeer didn't watch himself, he might have an 'accident' and end up on the Claus family dinner table. The egotistical flying nuisance would not be missed by many, except maybe, Dad. Not even the other reindeer liked the alpha-deer bully.

Holly pulled herself up and brushed off hunks of snow attached to the velvet of her uniform. “Paybacks are Hell, Blitzen.” Pushing by the wayward deer, she grabbed hold of the chimney. She turned back and gave Blitzen one last glare. “No matter how much Santa likes you, he loves me ten times better. I’m his daughter. You are replaceable; I’m not. Put that in your corn and chew on it, buddy.” Then, laying a finger on the side of her nose, she slipped down the chimney.

The inside of the rustic cabin was dark. Holly blinked, adjusting her eyes to the lack of light. She scanned the small room, seeing nothing but a couch, rocking chair, and a coffee table. “Daddy?” Her whisper was barely audible over the blowing storm outside.

From behind the sofa came a low groan.

Fear-induced adrenaline flooded Holly’s belly. She dashed behind the couch and stopped cold.

Santa Claus lay motionless on the floor.

A black dog the size of a small pony lie beside Daddy. The Great Dane lifted his head from where it rested on her father’s lap and moaned. He tilted his massive face and perked his silky ears as though asking what he should do.

Bending to Daddy’s side, Holly could feel the heat radiating from his body before she even touched his cheek. His skin was on fire.

“Holly?”

He sounded weak, confused. For the first time ever Daddy seemed helpless and frail. Her stomach tightened, and air wouldn’t fill her lungs. Surely he would be all right once he got some rest.

“Don’t worry, Daddy. I’ll get you home and into bed.” Holly grabbed hold of his too-warm hands and helped him to his feet. “You’re sick and you’ve got a fever, just like everyone else at Christmas Town. We never should have allowed you to come out tonight.”

“My sweet child. Just see me to the sleigh.” He

staggered to the stone fireplace.

The large canine joined them, apparently not wanting to leave Santa's side.

"There's a good lad." Daddy rubbed behind the animal's ear. "When we get home, we'll have Noel take over and finish the job. It's Christmas Eve, we can't let everyone down."

Holly bit her tongue. Noel might be a changed person these days, but trusting him to complete the Christmas run might be more than big brother could deliver.

Santa placed a chubby finger next to his red nose, and they both rose up the chimney. A blast of snowy wind met them at the top, nearly knocking him down.

Though the reindeer didn't move a muscle, their gazes followed Holly as she helped Daddy into the sleigh.

Santa slumped on the leather bench. His eyelids hung heavy and his face was a bright shade of pink.

"My bag. I need to go back and get it." Making a great effort, he scooted himself forward, but quickly sat back. Santa swayed in the sleigh's seat. "Holly, my dear, my bag is still below. We can't leave without it."

Go down there?

By myself?

Like a vice, terror gripped her heart and squeezed mercilessly.

What if something happened and she couldn't use her magic to get back up the chimney? What if the over-grown pony waiting by the fireplace decided to have her for breakfast? What if the guy living here woke up and caught her?

Holly glanced at her ailing father. Slumped in the corner of the sleigh, he looked so weak.

There was no other choice. She had to take care of this situation herself.

She forced a smile and swallowed hard. "Okay. I'll go get it." After tucking the velvet blanket over Daddy's waist and placing the leather reins on his lap, she added, "Then we'll go home."

Daddy struggled to keep his eyes opened and nodded. "Hurry. There's much left to do this Christmas Eve."

Turning her face back into the blowing storm, Holly scooted by the patient deer and stopped at the front of the reindeer team. "Listen up, guys. Santa's very sick. We've got to get him back home A.S.A.P."

All eight reindeer lifted their heads. Concern filled their big brown eyes.

Blitzen jerked his snout high, pulling at the reins. The sound of sleigh bells filled the blistery night's air.

"I'm going to go back inside and get Santa's sack. Then we're heading straight to Christmas Town." Bolstering her courage with a deep draw of cold air, Holly closed her eyes and scrambled down the chimney.

The Great Dane stood waiting at the fireplace. Once he saw her, he barked and set his tail a wagging. The whip-like appendage whacked against the cabin wall. The loud banging sounded as though he was trying to chop a hole through the rough-hewn logs.

Holly's heart pounded in her chest. How the heck was she supposed to find Daddy's bag and slip out with Fido making enough noise to wake a passed out New Year's drunk?

While patting the dog on the head, she scanned the room. Anything to get the animal to be quiet. Last thing she needed was to wake up the homeowner. Goodness knows what kind of trouble that would cause.

Daddy's big velvet bag lay draped over the rocking chair. All the way on the other side of the living room near the only interior door in the entire cabin.

Holly's shoulders slumped and she rolled her eyes. Nothing about this evening was going right. Except maybe that the door by the chair was closed. Quiet as a mouse, she tiptoed on the ends of her boots, careful not to let the heels clump on the floor.

The mammoth dog barked and raced ahead. When he tried to turn his tremendous body back her way, he slipped on a woven rag rug. Rather than moving forward, momentum carried him backward. His entire muscular body slammed into the closed door.

"Chaos, what in the Hell are you doing out there?"

Holly froze mid step, her hand reaching out to grab the couch for balance.

The raspy voice came from the other side of the door, and it didn't sound full of Christmas spirit.

A short burst of clatter and jingling bells came down the chimney, and then faded.

Panic seized every muscle in her body. Her breath lodged in her chest, and her muscles locked tight.

Daddy left her behind.

Chapter Two

The first bark startled him.

The second bark and crash had David up and out of his nice warm bed before his eyes were even open. He threw back the door, tripped over Chaos, and landed on his face with a horrible thud.

Ohhhh… that's going to leave a mark.

He reached up and placed a cool hand on his aching cheek. Thank God he wasn't on television right now. Falling on his face in front of millions of couch potatoes would have ended up being played over and over on not only his reality show, but every entertainment and news program in the United States. Last thing he needed now was to have his mug plastered over the airwaves. Too many people looking for his stupid ass already.

David lifted himself up on his elbows and squinted into the inky darkness.

What the…

Some kind of red blur whizzed past the couch and flew up the chimney.

He shook his head, wincing at the intense throbbing in his cheek. His weary mind must be playing with his vision. After pulling himself up to a sitting position, he rubbed his eyes. Time for a visit to the ophthalmologist.

Something heavy thumped up on the roof. Then, what sounded like an anguished scream of "Blitzen" pierced through the roaring storm outside.

Blitzen?

David checked Chaos.

The big black dog jumped to her feet, both ears at the alert. Her long, wet tongue hung out and her tail wagged so hard her entire body shook.

The noises weren't just his imagination. He actually had heard something.

David rose from the floor, scrambled out the front door, and plowed into a three-foot high pile of snow. The icy barricade immediately stopped his pajama-covered legs, but the rest of his body continued forward with enough force to bend him forward at the hips. His face and bare chest made a less than graceful swan dive into the frozen white powder.

Why, oh why, did every Christmas have to be this way?

"Daddy!"

The feminine yell was clear this time, and had definitely come from his roof. Who in the world would be calling for Daddy in the forests of Colorado during a blizzard?

David pulled himself up the snowdrift barring his doorway and crawled on the surface of the hardened mound. Intense cold stung the bared bottoms of his feet. The blowing winds were on the attack, barraging the entire area with pure white. When he was far enough out, he cupped his hands around his eyes and fought the gusts long enough to see a petite, barely dressed woman standing next to his chimney.

She faced the North, looking away. She jumped several times and waved her hands as though trying to get someone's attention.

The poor girl had to be freezing. Though he could only see her from the back, it was clear the little Christmas elf dress she was wearing didn't cover much skin. The short red skirt lifted with each gust of wind, revealing a well-rounded bottom in white panties. Black leather boots reached her thighs, protecting at least the majority of her legs from the frigid weather. Other than the red hat covering her head, there wasn't another stitch of clothing in sight. No coat, muffler, or mittens anywhere.

David raised his eyes to Heaven and sighed. Since

being cast as the star of television's Marry a Single Guy, a lot of desperate women did some crazy stunts to attract his attention. Each of them clinging to the hope she might be his choice for a wife and win a million dollars.

This particular act of stupidity topped them all.

Though he was at the cabin to get away from the show, the women, and the press, he didn't have much of a choice of what to do with this lady. If he didn't do something fast, the provocatively dressed woman on his snow-covered roof would end up dead.

David stood on the packed snow and waved his arms in the air. "Hey! You found me. Now get inside before you turn into a human ice kabob."

The woman turned her head and her jaw dropped. She let out a shriek and raced behind the chimney.

"It's colder than the North Pole out here." Freezing himself, he wrapped his arms around his chest and jumped around on his bare feet. "Get down here now before I have to come up and get you."

The woman peeked around the bricks, her eyebrows shot up on her forehead and her eyes widened.

A long, stinging shiver ran over every inch of his exposed skin. "Damn it, woman, don't make me lose my temper. I might seem like a nice guy on TV, but I've got a nasty streak a mile long." His heated words came out on a frosty puff of air.

She frowned, squinching her nose, but nodded.

The petite little thing scooted down the top of the cabin to its lowest hanging point. Her agility and balance on the snow-covered roof was amazing, especially since she was wearing sexy thigh-high boots. Those leather things couldn't be easy to maneuver in.

How the heck had she gotten up there?

David raised his hands and latched on to hers. Much to his surprise, her palms and fingers were toasty warm and soft. He grabbed her waist as she jumped the four feet to the top of the snowdrift. She was light as cotton candy, and looked just as tasty.

He momentarily held her against his bare chest, adjusting his balance to keep them both upright. His icy body relished the heat radiating from hers. The slight movement shifted the small top to her dress downward, pushing the curvy tops of her breasts high on her chest. No nippleage, but not far from it.

An arrow of lust struck his gut. Thank the merciful stars the temperature in the blowing storm was below zero, keeping his boy nice and cool. If the weather were warmer, he would not have been able to control an embarrassing tent in his pajamas.

Gawking at the beautiful alabaster mound-tops staring him in the face was tempting, but his training as a gentleman won over. He raised his gaze, taking in her sassy short brown hair, sweet round cheeks, and fearful blue eyes. In her little Christmas outfit, she really looked like one of Santa's elves. A terrified elf with a curvy body found in most strip joints, but an elf all the same.

With great care as to not cause the dress any further strain, he put the woman down on the snow.

She didn't move and she didn't say a word. Her big glittering eyes did all the speaking necessary. She was genuinely scared.

Maybe his last comment about his nasty temper was a little over the top. Now he felt like a total jerk. Though he didn't want this woman here, neither did he want her afraid. Some kind of damage control was needed—and fast. "What's your name?"

"Holly."

Her quiet voice trembled. Every limb of her body shook, but she was wonderfully warm to the touch. Could the jittering be from fright?

"Okay, Holly. Come on inside." He lowered his voice even further and gestured to the open door. "I promise I won't hurt you."

She hesitated, but bobbed her head and then scooted down the drift into the cabin.

Chaos immediately stood by her side and nudged

Holly's leg with her big wet nose. The dog's long, narrow tail swung back and forth with enough force to knock the petite girl down.

Holly smiled at the overgrown mutt. She hunched down on her knees and drew the Great Dane close, wrapping her arms around the dog's thick muscular neck.

David stared at the odd scene. Chaos' reaction, or lack of reaction, was definitely not in character. For as long as the dog was his pet, David had never seen her get so friendly with a stranger. Rather than growling or barking like mad, the Dane was cozying up. She was practically jumping in Holly's lap.

David jumped down the snowdrift into the house, and fought the battling wind to get the door closed. Once inside a blood-curdling chill ran from his iced-over bare feet to his snow-covered bare chest. He hugged himself to build up some warmth, but his teeth started chattering. "Exxcusssee mmmee wwhile IIII ggget mmoore ccloothes oonn."

He dashed into the bedroom and rummaged through his dresser until he found his favorite University of Texas sweatshirt and a pair of jeans. As soon as he threw on the clothes and his well-worn slippers, he quickly brushed his teeth, and scooted back into the living room.

The warmth from a roaring fire in the fireplace and the smell of brewed hot chocolate stopped him in his tracks. "When could you...How did you?" Stunned into silence, he couldn't think to say much more.

"You don't even have a Christmas tree." Holly pushed a cup into his hands. "I'm left behind with a guy who doesn't even bother to celebrate the season right. Not a single holiday trimming in sight."

Her watery blue eyes forecasted tears to come.

Confused, David put the hot mug on the table and ran a hand through his hair. He was having difficulty wrapping his thoughts around the entire surreal chain of events, let alone making sense of what was upsetting her. He hadn't been in his room more than a minute. How could she have built a fire and made cocoa in that time? He didn't even own hot chocolate mix. And what was up with the waterworks? "Listen, Holly. I have no idea what's going on here." He cut a glance around the inside of the cabin, peering into the shadows. "If we're on camera right now, I want to know. Last thing I need is America watching me have a momentary lapse in sanity."

Holly's lips trembled and she sniffled. Two large teardrops rolled from her big baby blues down her round cheeks. She waved a hand in the air, pulled out a handkerchief, and dabbed her eyes.

He blinked and looked again. Correction. She pulled the white hanky out from her sleeve. The small piece of cloth had to have come from her sleeve. Right?

David frowned. Her outfit didn't have any sleeves. She was wearing a short, red velvet sleeveless dress and black leather boots that reached curvy, toned thighs.

The entire look was hot. She was hot. The whole Holly package was the stuff of Christmas dreams come true. But regardless how incredibly tempting she looked, the fact of the matter was there was just no place in that getup to hide a handkerchief.

How had she done it?

David dropped on the couch. Nothing about what he saw tonight made sense. Unless...He snapped his fingers. "Wait just a minute. I think I've got this all figured out." He glanced her way. "This is sweeps week for the networks, isn't it? Wasn't the last woman, the Las Vegas stripper who tamed lions, crazy enough? Now they send me a single female magician as a Christmas present?"

Holly stopped crying and blew her nose with the hanky.

Like a tuba being played for the first time, the loud noise reverberated, filling the cabin with sound.

Chaos twitched her ears and tilted her big head. She uttered a high-pitched whine.

When she finished her blowing, Holly waved her hand. The used handkerchief disappeared. "I have no idea what you are talking about."

"Don't mess with me, honey. I can tell when I'm being played." David jumped from the sofa and looked behind a painting on the wall. Nothing there. No wires. No microphones. No camera equipment. How were they broadcasting this? "Where did they put the goods? I know they're here somewhere."

"Are you mad?" Her look of high-browed confusion and fright quickly morphed into agitation. "Can't you see I've been abandoned in the middle of the Colorado wilderness?"

"Oh! Sure. Your daddy, right?" He crossed the room and opened every cabinet in the efficiency kitchen. Still nothing. "I suppose you and your daddy were just out snowmobiling in the middle of a blizzard on Christmas Eve. Then all of a sudden, he slipped you off the back and bailed." He stopped his inspection long enough to stare at the woman attempting to make him a mockery on national television. "Just what kind of idiot do you take me for?"

Brows wrinkled, she opened her mouth to speak.

David cut her off. "Don't answer that question."

Holly shrugged and waved her hand at the room. "Honestly, I don't know who you are or what's going on here."

"Everyone in the United States has seen me on television for the last six months." He slammed the cabinet doors with a succession of bangs, and then lifted himself on the small dining room table to examine the light fixture. He took a moment to shoot her a narrow-eyed look. "Don't act as though you don't know what I'm looking for."

Holly balled her hands into fists and planted them on her hips. "I'm Santa Claus's daughter. When Daddy was here this evening, he passed out in your cabin because he's sick with the flu. I put him in his sleigh to take him home, but Blitzen, that stupid reindeer, ran off without me. And, I live on the North Pole in Christmas Town. We don't watch a lot of television up there."

She bent forward, glaring. Even more of her ample cleavage showed. David fought the urge to stare at the well-rounded, high and tight globes.

"So, no," she continued. "Other than what little I know of your Christmas wishes, and the fact you are on my father's 'nice' list with asterisks, I really don't know that much about you."

Without a doubt, this pretty woman was one of the wackiest yet. The casting staff for the show must have really worked overtime to pick her from the throngs of women trying to meet him. "Yah? Well, I'm the abominable snowman."

Daggers shot from her piercing eyes.

She pointed directly at the glowing flames in the fireplace. With a flick of her wrist, the roaring disappeared. She glanced at the cold hearth and then nodded. When she looked back, a satisfied grin spread across her face.

She raised her chin. "Does that prove I'm Santa's daughter?"

David sighed and turned back to look through the wires of the light fixture. "You forget, sweetheart, I've met a lot of celebrities, including some talented magicians. I've seen them make things like giant African elephants and the Statue of Liberty disappear." He glanced up. "Didn't mean they were Santa's nephews and nieces."

"Hmmph!" Holly crossed her arms and stamped a foot. After a moment of thought, she straightened her back and leveled her shoulders. "Alright. How about this?"

Once again she pointed, but this time to the corner of the room. In the blink of an eye, a Christmas tree and all the trimmings appeared. The multi-colored lights of the small bulbs illuminated the dark space. The entire room instantly radiated holiday cheer.

David had to admit the ol' tinsel Tannenbaum trick was one he hadn't seen before. Many a magician could make things disappear in thin air. Making things appear from nowhere was a whole 'nother ball of wax. Especially when the item materializing needed to be plugged into one of the cabin's few electrical outlets.

Still, this lady Copperfield found hollering on his roof thought she was Santa's daughter. She might be an awesome magician with a pretty face and a hot-to-trot body, but crazy was crazy. "Not a bad little trick. It'll take me weeks to figure out how you did that. But pulling a Christmas tree out of your hat doesn't prove anything other than your ability as a prestidigitator."

A smug smile spread across Holly's face. She cocked her head toward the glowing tree. "That's no ordinary Christmas tree, David White. I think you might want to take a closer look."

From his vantage point on the top of the kitchen table, he looked over the tree in the corner. The well-decorated, brightly lit Douglas Fur appeared much like any other he'd seen. But curiosity tempted him enough to temporarily give up the search for hidden television cameras. David dropped from his perch, brushed by Chaos and the crossed-armed Holly, and walked across the small living room. He stopped before the tree and turned. "Just what exactly am I looking for? A letter of reference from Santa Claus on one of the branches? Maybe a birth certificate from the North Pole Hospital?"

She threw down her hands. "Just inspect the ornaments on the limbs."

David raised his own hands in front of his chest and waved. "Alright, alright. Gheesh. A little testy, aren't we?" Without taking his gaze off Holly he reached for a tree decoration and plucked it off the branch. "For someone who says she's Santa's daughter, you sure have a short fuse. I thought everyone from Santa's household was jolly."

"Anything look familiar?" she asked.

"Now how could I possibly recognize..." He stopped short and swallowed hard. Upon inspection, he did recognize the hideous porcelain object. The orange and purple reindeer ornament was exactly like the one he painted when he was in the Boy Scouts over twenty years ago.

Unbelieving, David pulled another familiar decoration from the tree. Blue and silver glitter from an antique glass ball flaked off on his fingers. The fragile globe was a gift his great aunt Gertie had given him as a small child.

Great Caesar's ghost. She really was Santa Claus's daughter. The woman was an elf.

A tight knot formed in the pit of his stomach. A flash of vertigo caused him to sway like a drunken sailor. Before he could brace himself for the impact, David fell flat onto the hardwood floor.

Chapter Three

Anxiety pushed down on Holly's chest and pressed so hard she couldn't breath. The good-looking but conceited dummy had realized the truth and passed out. She never should have shocked him like that. After all, he was only human.

She ran over to David's side and waved her hands in front of his face. "Holy Christmas morning. Are you okay?"

He didn't move.

Was he dead?

Chaos got up. With claws clicking on the boards beneath his paws, he trotted over to his master. The large dog sniffed David's sandy blonde hair, and then licked his master's face with a big, slimy tongue.

David stirred to life and grimaced. "Ughh. Chaos, what have you been eating? Your breath smells like rotting garlic chicken." He put down the old Christmas ornament and half-heartedly swatted at the big pet. "Go away, you overgrown mutt."

Globs of slobber oozed and dripped from the Dane's jowls, covering David's sweatshirt with runny, wet spots. The big, black dog shook his head with incredible force, sending juicy hunks of spittle everywhere.

Holly jumped back and covered her face. "That's disgusting."

The shaking continued in small sections throughout rest of his body, and didn't end until his backside had had enough and his tail finally came to a sudden rest between his long ebony legs.

Finished with resuscitating his master, Chaos returned to his spot on the woven rag rug. After circling himself several times, he stopped and plopped down.

Holly bent over David and placed her hands on his face, needing to touch him—make sure he was really unhurt. His short whiskers pricked against the sensitive skin of her palms. Shivers of electric current sent goosebumps up her arms.

She looked into his roguish brown eyes. “Did you hurt yourself?” She slid her fingers over his cheeks, relishing the feel of his skin against hers. “That was some fall you took.”

“I'm fine.” David stood then shook his arms and hands. A look of pure disgust was etched on his handsome, unshaven face. “I may need a bath now.”

A vision of David standing in a shower fully naked flashed. Warm water splashed over his head, down his broad chest, and further south. Rich sudsy lather dotted his long, muscular body like whipped cream.

She licked the top half of her lip, but came to an abrupt stop.

What was she doing? David was handsome, sure. But, he was a stranger and she was miles away from her family. She might never get back home. Never see Daddy, Momma, or any of her brothers or sisters again. “If it will put you in a better mood, I suggest you do. Or do I need to spend some more time proving that I'm Santa Claus's daughter?” She bit her lip, but the words were already out.

Why had she said that? Never in her life had she openly provoked another person. A few reindeer, yes, and more than once. But never a human. Before her brain had fully engaged, her nervousness got the better of her. Her mouth had clicked off safety and blurted out.

“Nope.” He wiped a glob of gook from his cheek with the sleeve of his sweatshirt. “You've done enough. I'm pretty well convinced.”

“Here. You may want to use this.” She snapped her fingers, producing a clean, wet towel, and then tossed it to him.

David raised an eyebrow as he caught the towel in the air. He ran the towel over his face and the wet spots on his shirt. When he finished, he jerked his thumb at the Christmas tree in the corner. "How did you know what my family's tree looked like? It was destroyed in a fire years ago. This copy is a dead ringer."

Holly walked over to where the tall, rugged man stood, and plucked the towel from his hands. "I read your mind and reproduced it." She wiped at a spot he'd missed on his chin, and a tingling sensation fluttered across her stomach. If only he hadn't put on the sweatshirt. She would have traded a year's worth of peppermint sticks to rub his broad, hairless chest. Even if to clean off dog slobber.

Reaching out, David gently grabbed her wrist. With care, he removed the cloth from her grip, and turned her hand over, revealing her palm. "You look just like a regular person. Very fit and very pretty." For several seconds he flipped her hand back and forth. "I imagined anyone related to Santa to be, well, kind of chubby and extraordinary. You know, someone with pointed ears and a stomach that jiggles like a bowl full of jelly."

An odd rush of warmth rose from her chest to her face, burning her cheeks. Never in her two hundred and fifty years of life had a handsome stranger ever given her a compliment. "So I take it you really do believe me."

From her hand, David lifted his gaze to hers. A quirky grin lightened his face. "Yah, I do."

His voice was more of an undertone, and she almost missed his words. She was too distracted, lost in the dark pools of David's eyes. Her elven senses picked up his compassion and strong passion. He had a great capacity for love and faithfulness. With the exception of Chrissy's new love, not often had she read these characteristics from human men.

She heaved a heavy sigh. "Thank the holiday spirit. If the tree hadn't worked, I wasn't sure what else I could do."

"Well now that I know who you are and that I'm not on camera, give me a chance to start all over." He shifted his hand from her wrist to her palm and shook. "I'm David White, struggling author from Texas."

His touch was warm and reassuring. The cold anxious feeling twisting her belly and squeezing her chest since Daddy's sleigh flew off melted away. "I'm Holly Claus, lost daughter of the big guy from the North Pole."

"I owe you an apology, Holly." David ran a hand over his stubbled cheek. "I've been hiding from the media. The last thing I wanted to see tonight was someone at my doorstep, or on my rooftop."

"Are you running from the law?" A naughty thrill pulsed through her. From what her sisters had told her, bad boys were exciting and dangerous. Rough men and rough lovers.

Another wave of heat flushed her skin.

"No, not the police. Though dealing with them might be considerably easier." He bent, picking up the antique glass ornament, and replaced it on the tree. David regarded the decked out tree for several moments, and fingered a few of the hanging decorations.

Apparently, whatever he had to say was even worse than being on the lam.

"I thought you might have been a reporter or someone who wanted to marry me." David turned back, a hint of a blush staining his high cheekbones.

Holly's breath caught in her throat, almost making her choke. "Marry you? I don't even know you." Was David a psychic? Had he read her graphic naughty thoughts of him in the shower, or picked up on her attraction?

She took a small step back, her gazed raked over him from head to toe. Even though his blond hair was a mess, his face was scruffy, and he wore horribly wrinkled jeans, he was still remarkably sexy. And, the best part of all, he was tall and lean, with good-sized muscles. A very different look from the typical short dumpy male elves in

Christmas Town.

Her thoughts raced back to their brief embrace outside. The crush of her breasts against his well-defined pecks had taken her breath away. The memory of their touch caused a rush of sensations, and every nerve ending vibrated with electricity. Unfortunately, her body didn't register what her mind already knew. She couldn't stay around long enough to get to know him better. Getting home, back to her safe zone, was the priority now.

She heaved a heavy sigh. "Don't get me wrong, you seem like a nice enough guy."

He waved his hands in the air. "I know, I know. Any normal person who hasn't seen my show would think that sounds egotistical. Unfortunately, it's not. It's been my crazy reality for the last six months."

Holly leaned against the armrest of the small plaid couch and rubbed her forehead. "I'm confused. What show? Why is the media after you?"

David's cheerful grin disappeared and his brown eyes dimmed. He suddenly looked tired, as though all the joy had been sucked right out of his body.

"Last Christmas my ex-fiancé dumped me. Said my children's books were silly and I would never get published." He plopped down on the couch and rubbed his eyes. "Right after New Year's Eve, my best buddy signed me up for a television reality show called Marry a Single Guy. He thought the exposure would be good for my writing career, and I might meet the girl of my dreams." Looking up, he added, "I was lonely and not quite in my right mind, so I went along with it."

That he hadn't already found someone was a surprise. David was handsome, reasonably intelligent, and seemed genuine. As far as she was concerned, a perfect tri-fecta. "I take it you got on the show."

He rolled his eyes. "Boy, did I. Worst mistake of my life. The network put cameras and microphones in every conceivable nook and cranny of my house and car. Where they couldn't put some type of recording device, they sent a camera man to follow me around." David frowned. "The whole thing was a disaster."

"I can imagine. I've never been on television, but I have a pretty good idea what you've been through. Being Santa's daughter isn't exactly low profile." Dating the elf that changed careers from toy maker to dentist had been food for public fodder in Christmas Town for weeks until they broke up. And, how many times had her brother Noel caused a scandal for the family? His insistence on being called Leon and riding around in the chromed-up, supercharged Ducati was infamous.

"To make matters worse, the show's producers constantly set me up with strange women they knew I wouldn't like. Just to get the show's ratings high." David patted at the space on the sofa next to him. "Here, take a seat. Standing on those heels can't be comfortable."

For a second or two she couldn't move. The couch was little more than a large love seat. Her body trembled with excitement at the prospect of sitting next to him. But her mind fretted and nagged. She should be trying to find a way to get home. She didn't belong here.

Holly smiled, attempting to cover her nervousness and indecision.

Since Daddy left nothing bad had happened. She was unhurt and nothing threatened here. Plus, every time she allowed her overactive imagination to run wild, she usually ended up feeling foolish. Being close to someone, especially a friendly, good-looking someone would be all right—until her family found her.

Decision made, Holly sat on the overstuffed sofa. Her bottom sank pleasantly in the soft cushion, her thigh brushed against his. Crossing her legs would shift her body away, so she wouldn't be sitting quite so close. But, being near him was...well, nice. "And were they?" She cringed. Her voice cracked like a hormonal teenage boy.

"Huh? Oh." He lifted his gaze from where their legs touched. "Yah, some of the highest. I hit instant celebrity. Was on every talk show and every magazine cover."

His face flushed a deep shade of red. He tugged at the banded collar of his sweatshirt.

"It was fun for a while," he continued, "but things got out of control. Women chased me twenty-four hours a day. The press stalked me wherever I went. Finally decided I had had enough and came here. Unless Hell freezes over, I'm never going back to that craziness. Never."

David raised his arms high over his head and stretched. When he lowered them, one returned to the armrest. The other he draped across the back of the couch, behind Holly. "When I saw you on the roof, I thought the network execs found me, and you were the latest woman thrown my way."

Breathing was impossible. With her heart racing a mile a minute and blood rushing through her veins to her head, passing out herself didn't feel too far away.

She reclined into the sofa, steadying herself, and licked dry lips. "Don't worry. I promise not to chase you."

"That's too bad." He leaned toward her, his brown eyes never leaving hers. "You actually seem like the kind of girl I might like."

Before she could form another thought, he reached his arm over her shoulder and pressed warm lips against hers. She closed her eyes, allowing all of her senses to bask in the moment. He smelled of clean linen sheets, and his mouth tasted like winter-fresh mint.

He pulled her closer, wrapping her further into his hold. For the first time in a very long time, she felt completely safe.

Chapter Four

What he was doing was beyond him. The sexy woman—no female elf - in the red, fur-lined, next-to-nothing Christmas outfit was Santa Claus's daughter. He was supposed to be staying away from women, even elven women. The entire female species were nothing but trouble. Hadn't he had enough craziness?

Apparently not.

His ability to think straight was lost when the pretty little thing held his face after he blacked out. She smelled so good, a cross between vanilla and gingerbread. When she sat next to him and touched his leg with hers, all his resolve against women flew away like the winds blowing outside his door. Pure molten lava had run through his veins at that moment, and nothing seemed better than giving in to heated, lust-driven impulse.

He had to kiss her, to see if she tasted as delicious as she smelled. And, man did she ever.

David licked his lips, savoring the last of her sweetness. "I tell you what. If that is how all of Santa's daughters kiss, we regular guys are really missing out on some good stuff."

He bent to kiss Holly again, but she used her hands as a barrier, keeping him away. "What's the matter? Did I say something wrong?"

Her bright blue eyes widened.

"Oh, no. It's just . . ."she tucked a short brown lock of hair behind her ear and looked away.

With one hand, he cupped her chin and turned her face to his. He searched her baby blues, looking for some clue of what was suddenly bothering her. "It's just what?"

She glanced at her hands, refusing to look him in the

eye. "Did you kiss many of girls on your show? I mean, I imagine you did if a lot of pretty women were after you. I couldn't blame you if you did. Big temptation."

Finally, a woman with a real conscience. David held back a grin.

Holly, evidently, wasn't like the girls he had met on his program. Those 'ladies' literally threw themselves at him, not caring what they exposed on national television, or that they made complete asses of themselves. True, all the skin and trampiness made for excellent ratings, but those girls did nothing more than turn him off. Not that he wanted someone frumpy or unattractive. Just someone pretty and nice. Someone he could actually connect with.

He brushed a thumb down her cheek. Her creamy skin was amazingly soft and warm. "I only kissed two girls while I was on the program."

A frown tugged at the corners of her mouth. "Only two? That's hard to believe."

David nodded. "Yep. Only two. My mom and Chaos over there."

At the mention of her name, Chaos raised her head and twitched her ears. The big black dog scratched her own head with a long back foot, then lay her head back down on her front two legs.

"This is so embarrassing. I should have noticed. I guess I'm just a little of sorts being in a strange place." Holly looked to where Chaos lay on the floor, and then turned back. "Chaos is a girl?"

This time Chaos not only perked up her head, she also let loose a huge, whiny yawn.

David did his best to hold back his own, but the forces of nature would not be controlled. Not only did he yawn, he stretched his arms, slightly flexing his biceps. Heck. Didn't hurt for Holly to know he was packing some pretty big guns underneath the sleeves of his sweatshirt. Might even warm her up to him a little more. A few more of her sweet kisses would be one of the best Christmas presents he got this year.

"Yes, she is." David twitched his eyebrows and pantomimed a cigar in his mouth, a la Groucho Marx. "So is my mother. At least, that's what Mom tells everyone. I can't speak from personal experience."

Holly laughed a laugh that could only be described as a melodious tinkle from a small silver bell. Pure music to his ears.

He now had a new mission in life. Hearing more of her gentle laughter.

David returned his arm around her shoulder. "Seeing how we're stuck here for a while, why don't you start the fire up again and whip us up some more of your hot chocolate. I'll entertain you with amusing anecdotes from previous Christmas disasters. Trust me, I've got dozens."

****

Holly glanced out the sliding glass doors. Heavy snow flew past, and was piling up on the deck. The blowing winds whistled and howled in the night air.

David was right. They certainly weren't going anywhere tonight. Not in this blizzard. If she were lucky, Noel or her father would find her sometime tomorrow—after all the Christmas presents were delivered and the weather wasn't quite so bad.

If she was lucky.

If they could find her.

What if her dad or brother couldn't find her? She'd left her special cell phone in her bag on the sleigh. No way she could call Christmas Town on a regular phone to let them know where she was. Dad was so sick when he left, he may or may not remember this stop. She might be stuck south of the North Pole forever, never being able to see her family and home again.

The familiar press of anxiety was back again, with a vengeance. Holly sucked in and exhaled several deep gulps of air, filling her compressed chest. "I need to get home." Her lungs ached so badly she barely got the words out.

"Whoa now, little princess. What's wrong?" David

pulled her closer and rubbed her arm. "You seem upset."

The urgent need to have something familiar around was nearly paralyzing. The only thing keeping her from falling into a full-fledged panic attack was David. His gentle manner and compassion were the threads tying her to sanity.

What could she do?

As much as she enjoyed David's company and wanted to get to know him better, the last thing she wanted was to share her dark concerns. Having people laugh at her or throw pity her way was worse than hand-packing sand in Etch-A-Sketches. But, this far from home, she was completely out of her element, with no way of knowing what to do next.

David was literally her lifeline. She had to trust him to help her.

Holly gulped, swallowing her pride. "I…I always feel anxiousness whenever I'm left alone or I'm around people I don't know. In reality, it's more like panic."

She shifted her gaze to the twinkling lights of the Christmas tree—too embarrassed to look David in the eye. "Ever since I was a little girl and Daddy left to deliver toys, I was afraid I might never see him again." She looked back and drew in another deep breath, quieting her racing heart. "I worried myself sick thinking about what might happen to him. Unfortunately, I now get a little freaked out when I'm not around familiar things or family."

"I see." He leaned back, creating a space between them. "Do I freak you out?"

Actually, he didn't. David was great. Besides being funny and quirky, he had her thinking thoughts she hadn't had in a long time. Way too long. Like what that scruffy beard of his would feel like rubbing against the inside of her thighs, and whether or not the rumors about human men having bigger penises than elven men were true.

Plus, being around David felt better than snuggling

up in Mom's old quilt. Very warm, very safe. His bulging muscles kept him from being as soft as the blanket, but that old quilt sure couldn't kiss like David. And, for the brief moment their lips touched and he'd held her, she completely forgot about the situation and her fears. Hard to obsess about being away from family and things familiar with two strong arms holding her tight.

Holly shook her head and smiled. "No. You don't make me nervous at all. You're wonderful. The best thing to happen to me in a long time." She took his hand. Her palm looked so small against his. "I just don't know how or when my family will find me, and take me back home."

He entwined his fingers with hers and squeezed. "Don't worry. I'm not family, but as long as I'm around, I'll make sure you're never alone." He reached for her and held her close to his chest.

She leaned into his warm, tender embrace and closed her eyes, shutting out any feelings of anxiousness. Other than the storm blowing outside, his steady, regular heartbeat was the last sound she heard.

Chapter Five

From the cabin's deck, David watched the sun set over the snow covered mountains. Above, deep, dark blue faded to pale yellow and orange in the cloudless sky. The woodsy smell of pine rode thick on the wind.

David lifted his face, feeling the last of the sun's rays warm his skin. He breathed in the frigid, fresh air, enjoying the cold tingle in his lungs.

On his granddad's property everything seemed clearer. Little wonder why this little log cabin in the mountains had been the first place he thought to come when his life started spinning out of control. Here, the insane rat race of television and the media didn't exist. Here, the trees and the rocks didn't know him from Adam. He could walk around unrecognized and live his life in peace. Here, women weren't clamoring to meet him and banging down his door, trying to get in.

A smile spread from ear to ear.

Nope. No women up here in the mountains. Just an abandoned, sexy-as-all-get-out female elf with a heart of pure gold.

He glanced through the sliding glass doors. Holly sat on a rug next to the Christmas tree, wearing a pair of his sweats and an old football jersey. Chaos was curled up next to her. The dog's big black head lay in Holly's lap.

Heat rolled from his chest to his gut. Heaven help him, the woman was smokin' hot. Just seeing her walking around in his too-big jersey was enough to make him want to jump her petite bones.

She had been at the cabin three days. Though his goal in coming here was to get away from women, being around Holly and getting to know her better had him rethinking his objective. She was the first woman in a long time that he could talk to and hang out with without feeling used or uncomfortable.

With little else to do, they had swapped stories—her elf tales were particularly incredible—exchanged dark secrets, and spent late evenings together in front of the fire kissing. Every time he was near her, tasting her sweet lips and feeling her soft curves, his restraint had been put to the test.

Up to now, he had taken things slow with Holly. Partially because of her fears. She trusted him to care for her until she found her way home. Partially because she was a nice girl. The kind a guy takes home to meet mom. The type of woman he had been looking for. Well, except for the elf part. Hadn't anticipated being attracted to Santa's daughter.

No doubt about it, he wanted her, and sleeping on the coach again, horny, hard, and frustrated wasn't something to look forward to. Just how long did he have to be the good guy and keep his hands to himself?

What was he thinking? He was holed up in Granddad's cabin for two reasons. She, or at least her kind, was one of those reasons.

Holly stood, brushed off her backside, and made her way across the small living room to the porch. Chaos was only two steps behind.

David's jeans suddenly became uncomfortable. He adjusted his boy and raised his gaze to the heavens. He was more pathetic than he realized. How could just watching Holly sashay from one room to another give him a hard-on? Even the cool mountain winds couldn't keep 'little Elvis' down.

He couldn't go on like this. His self-control was fading faster than this evening's sunset.

The sliding door opened and Holly stepped through. "Hey, stranger. What's going on out here?"

Though she was usually very warm, the cold air was definitely having an effect. Two pointed nipples poked through the flimsy cotton jersey. They were practically screaming to be noticed, saying, "Hello David. Can we come out and play with you?"

Why you sure can, little ladies. Just let me help you out of that old shirt.

The ache in his groin intensified. His stiff penis pressed without mercy against the unyielding denim of his pants. If he didn't get some relief soon, he'd surely go mad. He was already having imaginary conversations with her boobs, for crying out loud.

He checked the shirttail covering the front of his pants, making sure his bulge was hidden. No need scaring the girl with his mighty monster. "Nothing much. Just checking out the scenery." If she knew the view he was taking in was her large, ripe breasts, she would probably snap those fingers, magic up a pair of gardening sheers, and cut his big boy right off. She didn't look like she had any Bobbit in her, but one never knew.

Holly moved past him and leaned over the railing of the porch. "It is beautiful here. Reminds me a little of my family's place. Course, not as many trees up that way." She turned back. "We all live a big house a few miles from Christmas Town. Not too far from the toy shop."

Her cheeks were tinged pink, and her blue eyes danced as she smiled.

He had met many a beautiful woman on the show who primped and dressed to the nines. None of those girls looked as incredible as Holly did at that moment. Standing in front of the setting sun, she seemed to glow, inside and out.

Man, oh man, did he want her.

Moving closer, he circled his arms around her small shoulders and drew her close. Her petite frame felt so right in his embrace. She smelled like fresh baked cookies, making his mouth water for just a taste of her sweetness.

He pulled back, searching her face for some kind of sign. Was she still anxious about being away from her family? Did she want him to take the next step?

The signal wasn't in her face, but everywhere else. Her heart pounded so strong and fast, he could feel the beats thrum throughout her body.

She tilted her head, closed her eyes, and parted her luscious, ruby lips.

She wanted him, too.

Desire fanned the flames smoldering in his gut, setting his blood on fire. With rough hands he cupped her face and bent to kiss her. He pressed his lips hard against hers, claiming her mouth with his. Using his tongue, he further spread her lips, and sipped the flavors hidden there. Could there be anything more delicious?

Holly broke the kiss and moved in closer, loosening each button on his oxford. Once she had the shirt completely unbuttoned, she opened the flaps and rubbed the palms of her hands over his pecs. "I love your chest. It's so smooth."

The icy breeze chilled his skin, producing small goose bumps, but he was too hot for her to care.

"You aren't too cold, are you?" She latched her fingertips onto one of his nipples and gently pinched.

David moaned as a bolt of lightening flashed from his chest all the way to his jingle balls. His penis swelled to the size of a Thanksgiving Day Parade balloon. "Not a big . . I mean, bit."

Little Miss Christmas elf had a streak of naughty in her, and he loved it. She had him so wound up he couldn't speak straight.

His hands reached under the jersey, feeling their way up the sides of her curvy hips and tight, flat stomach. Her skin was like mink, warm and soft. "Let me help you out of this." He continued up her body, dragging the shirt up and over her head.

She stood still before him, giving him much needed time to take in her lovely body.

"Do you like what you see?" she asked.

David let out a long draw of breath that immediately

crystallized in the frigid air. "I can't imagine anything or anyone more beautiful. You are a wonder."

She smiled. "I can't imagine being anywhere else right now than with you."

Like handing him a passkey, her words gave him permission to forge ahead and unlock her innermost passageways. By the time he was finished this evening, he would investigate every one of her winding paths and intimate corridors. No inch of her body would go unexplored.

To gain a better vantage point, he moved to her side. With one hand he supported her back, the other slid palm side up beneath a generous breast. He gently squeezed and kneaded the heavy floating globes, doting upon the womanly flesh, which filled his hand completely.

Holly closed her eyes and arched her back, thrusting her chest high. The hardened pinnacle of her nipples crested the alabaster mounds.

David brushed the pad of his thumb over one rosy peak, making small circles. His hands busy, he employed his mouth, lightly sucking her exposed neck.

She groaned and shuddered. The small quake reverberated down her entire body.

Encouraged by her response, he shifted his position and lowered his head, covering her peaches and cream breast with his mouth. Like a ravenous man bent on satisfying his cravings, he sucked and nipped one swollen tip and then the other, but still wanted more. "I've got to have you, Holly." His voice sounded raspy and urgent, even to his own ears.

Her knees faltered and she fell into his embrace. She opened her eyes and flashed big baby blues. "Then take me, David."

He didn't need to be told twice.

David whisked Holly off her feet. With long strides he made his way from the porch to the bedroom. Though the log cabin was small, the journey across the short span was taking too long. He wanted her now.

When he reached the bed, he laid her on the dark blue comforter. Before he had a chance to kick off his shoes, she sat up and grabbed the top of his jeans. With clever hands she ran down the row of metal buttons on his pants, liberating each fastening as she went. Pants loosened, he quickly pulled the garment off his legs and set it flying to the corner of the room. Having gone commando that morning, he now stood butt-ass naked in front of the girl who was turning his insides out.

"Now you, my dear." He untied the bow of the sweat's drawstrings and tugged the elastic ends until her silky legs and feet fell out.

She lie on the plush down comforter in only a pair of white panties. A shining lone star on a field of blue.

For a ridiculous moment, he was reminded of the Texas flag. He was tempted to salute, and then realized he was. Little Elvis was paying his respects the only way he knew how.

Starting at her toes and working his way up to her hips, he brushed his fingertips against Holly's velvety smooth skin. The muscles beneath his touch were lean and tone.

A runner? Perhaps. Definitely an athlete of some sort. Had to be with legs like hers.

When he reached the top of her cotton panties, he tucked his thumbs under the elastic waist and slowly pulled the material down. Inch by inch, the white undies revealed more of her flat abdomen until the dark mound of her hidden treasure was visible. Suddenly impatient to feel her warm, supple body next to his, he dragged the underwear off the remaining portion of her legs and tossed them over his shoulder.

The melodious sound of her giggles sent ripples straight to his heart. There, an unfamiliar but pleasant warmth pulsated. He placed his hand on his forehead. The room filled with bright flashes of light, while an incredible sense of joy and happiness washed over him.

"David? What's wrong?"

He looked down, taking in this most marvelous woman. "For the first time in over a year, I can honestly tell you there isn't one thing wrong. Everything is fantastic."

Bending at the waist, he spread her legs with his hands and leaned into the available space.

She ran her fingers through his hair, and then held his head, preventing him from moving any further. "Just what did you plan on doing down there?"

With a finger that he wet with his mouth, he spread the delicate folds of skin and located his target. Her glistening pink nub. She was wet and ready. "Give me just a few minutes, darlin', and you'll find out."

His thumb circled her swollen clit, and she gasped and wiggled. Not wanting to give her a moment to stop him, he pushed himself forward and flicked his tongue up, over, and around her moist kernel. Her juices were tangy and delicious, like fresh tangerines, his favorite winter fruit.

"Oh, David."

Her angelic voice was little more than a breathy whisper.

Hearing her call out his name in pleasure was incredibly satisfying. He felt hearty, powerful, and more than just a little bit sexy.

He continued with his tender torture, increasing the pressure with each lick and suck. When the rate of his loving hit a feverish pace, she cried out. Her body quivered.

Raising his gaze up the length of her naked body and over her twin peaks, he checked her reaction. Was he a stud, or what?

For a moment, Holly covered her face with her hands, and then suddenly flung her arms wide. "That was incredible!"

"Oh baby, you ain't seen nothin' yet." He stood, flexing both arm muscles until his less than spectacular biceps and pecs bulged. "I'm just getting warmed up."

Taking a running leap, he jumped in the bed, landing next to her. He grabbed her and pulled until her head reached his chest. She was so petite her feet only touched his ankles. “Come on up here, little lady. We gots lots o'lovin to make this evening.”

Holly obliged, wrenching and squirming until her mouth hovered over his.

Like the flutter of a butterfly's wings, she showered his lips, nose, and cheeks with tiny pecks, while her breasts brushed against his upper chest. When she pushed herself forward to kiss his forehead, he lifted his head, latching onto a perky nipple.

Just as he prepared to suck the hardened pebble until she begged for mercy, the sound of jingling bells filtered into the bedroom from outside the cabin.

Every muscle in Holly's lithe body froze.

David turned his head, pointing an ear toward the ceiling. What in the world…

Something fell on the roof with a loud thud and then a scraping noise.

“Holy moley.” Her eyes grew as big as dinner plates. “I think my dad is here.”

Chapter Six

David's head fell back against his pillow. "You've got to be kidding me. Now?"

"I wish I were." Holly whispered. She jumped off David's chest and scrambled around the bedroom, searching for the clothes he had tossed aside. "Hurry. Get up and get dressed. He'll be down in a second." Panic gripped her heart and squeezed. Daddy would kill them both if he found them like this.

She scanned the wood floor. "I can't find my underwear."

"Over there." David pointed to the top of an old rocking chair. Popping out of bed, he ran to a corner where his jeans lay in a heap on the floor. "Man, oh man. And I thought my past Christmases were bad."

Finding her sweatpants, she quickly pulled them up and tied the strings. "Just put your clothes on. It will be alright." She hoped. Truth was, there was no telling how Daddy might react. She was two hundred and fifty years old, after all. Even in elf years she wasn't exactly a kid. Still, dads were always dads.

The sound of heavy footsteps crossing the roof thudded from above.

"Oh, crap." Turning left then right, she hunted for her shirt. "Is your jersey still outside?"

David stopped running around the room long enough to fasten his pants' buttons. He nodded toward his dresser. "Look in the bottom shelf. There's a t-shirt in there."

She threw open the drawer. At least fifteen shirts were stuffed into the little space. "Which one?"

"It doesn't matter. Just pick one." He thrust his arms

through his oxford and frantically started buttoning.

Holly grabbed a burnt-orange and white t-shirt from the pile and pulled it over her head. By the time she smoothed down the material and ran her fingers through her hair, a knock sounded at the door.

Attempting to strike a casual pose, she rushed to the kitchen and leaned her hip against the table. She picked up a coffee cup left over from breakfast and slid her fingers around the cold ceramic. Sucking in a deep breath, she filled her lungs, and then slowly blew out the air. She was ready. Mostly.

David stepped to the door, shook out his arms and hands, and then squared his shoulders.

Poor thing. Not only was he preparing to meet her father for the first time, he was about to come face to face with Santa Claus—the real McCoy.

When the second knock sounded, David opened the door, letting in a draft of cold air. Instead of Daddy's imposing, rotund figure filling the doorway, Noel's long and lean form stood on the welcome mat. As usual, he sported his trademark black leather jacket and black boots.

"You David White?" Noel crossed his arms and raked over David with a steely glare.

Big brother did not look happy.

David mirrored Noel's showdown pose. "Who's asking?"

Holly rolled her eyes. Did all men have to complete this 'my pecker is bigger than your pecker' ritual when first meeting? "I'm over here, Noel." She put the cup down, strode over to the door, and gave her brother a heart-felt hug. "It's so good to see you. I thought you guys forgot about me."

A smile stretched across Noel's handsome face. With his blond hair falling into his eyes in complete disarray, he looked more like a bad-boy surfer than Santa's troublemaking son.

"I would have been here sooner, but the whole

damned town is sick. I stayed back to take care of the reindeer." He placed his hand on Holly's head and ruffled her hair. "Figured you'd be plenty freaked out by now, being off on your own. Mom's afraid you'll come back wearing a straight jacket."

"Actually, I'm great. Never been better. David's been kind enough to care for me." She linked her arm in David's. "After the initial shock and some rough introductions, I really started to like being here."

Noel's smile faded. He narrowed his eyes and looked back and forth between David and Holly. "There's a glow about you, sis, that makes me want to wring this guy's neck."

"Gheesh. Who came up with the notion the Claus's were a jolly, friendly bunch?" David dropped his arms and pointed a thumb toward Noel. "The man who wrote that Christmas poem was way wrong."

These two were certainly hitting it off.

Holly stepped in between the testosterone and raised her hands. "Okay, guys. That's about enough."

David frowned, but made a grand sweep of his arm into the cabin. "Please, do come in. I'll make some tea and we can talk for hours about how you want to beat my face to a pulp."

The side of Noel's lip rose. "If you've so much as touched a hair on my sister's head, I won't just stop at your face." He curled his hand into a fist.

"I said, that's enough." Her words came out on a growl. What was going on with these knuckleheads? They were behaving like ten year olds on a rough playground. "Noel, why don't you come in? I would really like for you to get to know David. He's a great guy."

"No time, Holly. I wasn't kidding about everyone being sick. They need us back, quick." He reached into his jacket pocket and pulled out some spouted greenish-yellow corn.

When the obnoxious odor from the germinated grain wafted up, Holly's eyes watered. She turned her head and pinched the end of her nose. "Get that nasty stuff away from me. Daddy should have outlawed that stuff years ago."

David coughed. "What the heck is that? It smells like spoiled Limburger cheese."

"Jet fuel for reindeer. Gives them a sugar booster." Noel stuck his hand back in his pocket. "Also gives the deer a terrible case of the runs. Don't want to stand under those big flying babies after they've eaten a basketful of the stuff. Not pretty."

"Yah, I'll bet," David replied.

"I'd love to yuck it up with you, but we gotta roll." Noel bent, plucked Holly off her feet, and started walking. "Lot of sick folks needing our help." With a twitch of his hand, they were standing near Daddy's sleigh.

"Wait! Put me down." Everything was happening too fast. Not more than ten minutes ago she was preparing to make love to the only man who made her feel comfortable being on her own. Now her brute brother was whisking her away, and she might never see David again.

Her stomach churned. A lump the size of Yule log formed in her throat.

Holly pounded Noel's leather armored chest. "I'm not ready to go. I didn't get to say good-bye."

"Then send the dude a postcard." He dropped Holly onto the red leather bench, and then jumped in himself. "We're outta here."

Noel grabbed hold of the reins and flicked his wrists, causing the long leather strips to snap. The reindeer responded and leaped from the snow-covered roof. In a flash the sleigh was flying high.

Before she could turn around and wave farewell, they were halfway back to Christmas Town.

Chapter Seven

Holly walked among the pieces of furniture in her family's home, dragging the pads of her fingers across the smooth damask upholstery covering the ornate Victorian couch. She leaned her head back as far as it would go, taking in all four floors of the vaulted ceiling. Like an intricate wood spider web, thick support beams spanned the entire length of the grand living room and criss-crossed each other at various points. From these junctures hung antique brass chandeliers lit with dozens of glowing candles, basking the room with a warm glow.

Everything in this room, this house, was familiar. From the savory smells of roasting turkey and baking pies floating in from the nearby kitchen, to the views of the frozen landscape outside the large picture windows, there wasn't a thing out of place or different. But, for reasons Holly couldn't explain, nothing here felt right. She had lived in the big old place for over two hundred years, and now felt like a stranger in her own home.

One week had passed since coming back from her brief stay with David. The people who had fallen ill with the flu were back to health, and Christmas Town was up and running like clockwork again.

Since her return, Holly hadn't been left by herself for more than a moment. Now that everyone was well, the house was teeming with family and friends, talk and laughter filling the air. Yet, even with the constant flow of people, she never felt so alone.

Holly peeked into the yellow and white kitchen.

New paragraphNoel stood next to the sink by Candice, tossing popcorn into her mouth. Chrissy and Nick were cooking together at mom's big old-fashioned stove, both wearing Kiss the Chef aprons. Jack Frost and Krista were sitting at the table, their hands linked together over the lace-covered top. Everyone had someone, and they looked so darn happy.

An all-consuming emptiness panged in Holly's chest. Somewhere deep down, a piece of her was missing, like a big gaping hole. Though she had never noticed the void before meeting David, the ache throbbing there now was near unbearable. Her heart felt as though it had been torn in two.

"If you keep wandering around this room like that, you'll wear the rugs thin."

Daddy's deep calming voice sounded from behind.

Holly turned and forced a smile. "Hi, Daddy."

"What's wrong with my little girl?"

She looked away, not wanting him to read her eyes. "I'm fine. Just a little tired."

He tucked a short tuff of hair behind her ear and then smoothed a hand across her cheek. "I know your heart, Holly. You're a long way from being fine."

The forlorn emptiness within bubbled too close to the surface. She felt absolutely wretched and lonely. Her lips trembled as she tried to speak, but the words simply wouldn't come. Tears formed in the corners of her eyes and fell down her face in hot streaks.

"There, there now, my dear." He pulled her close and held her tight. "That bad, eh?"

She nodded, releasing the hold on her emotions. Tears flooded her eyes and her nose started running. "I don't know what to do, Daddy. He said he wasn't interested in women. He was in that cabin to get away from them and his show. But I really like him." She couldn't catch her breath, and her body shook with the effort. "I thought he liked me, too, but I haven't heard from him at all." The last word croaked out on a sob.

"My child, how could he possibly contact you?" He stopped his gentle rocking back and forth, and took a step back. From his pants pocket he produced a white handkerchief and dabbed at her cheeks. "Other than sending a letter to Santa, humans don't know how to reach us up here."

Holly's shoulders fell. "I know, and that makes me miserable, too." A fresh batch of tears welled. She took the hanky from her father and mopped up her wet face.

A shriek sounded from upstairs, and then footsteps pounded down the old wooden stairs.

Joy ran into the living room, a piece of paper clutched in her hand. "Holly, you have to see this." She smoothed the wrinkled paper and thrust it forward.

The sheet was a printout of a website. Holly scanned the words on the paper and stopped when she read David's name. She looked up. "Joy, what is this?"

"It's a news site on the internet. They update their information about every ten minutes. I was reading a story about a woman who donated a kidney to save her dog's life, when this popped up." Her sister jumped several times and clapped her hands. "David is holding a press conference in Denver. He's supposed to be announcing his choice for a bride."

"What?" Holly shifted her attention back to the printout and read further down. "Nearly two weeks since his disappearance, missing Marry a Single Guy, David White, has come forward. In minutes an impromptu press conference will be held in Denver's Civic Center Park. Speculations of his impending conference abound. Many feel he will announce his selection for his bride, and the winner of one million dollars."

The paper slid from her grip. "He didn't tell me he was serious about anyone and he was thinking about getting married. He thought I was there because I wanted to marry him." Confusion swirled through her thoughts like weightless flakes of snow caught up in a gust of air. Holly sat on the couch and leaned her head back on the soft upholstery.

"You know. . . If I was a man looking for a woman, but didn't know how to contact her, I would use any means I could to get her attention." Daddy put his hand on Holly's shoulder and squeezed. "Sounds like David's making an attempt. You may need to go to him."

Holly glanced over to the kitchen, noting the shining smiles and bursts of laughter ringing from the bright room. Her brother and sisters and their mates were still busy happily chatting and cooking. With all the loud talk and banging of pots and pans, they hadn't noticed the exchange in the living room.

Was it wanting too much to wish for what they had? Someone to share her day-to-day moments with?

A bright spark flickered. Maybe Daddy was right. Maybe David was trying to reach her the only way he knew how.

Poor David. Making the decision to go back in front of television cameras, to be seen in the homes of millions of people, must have been torture.

Holly looked up at her father and placed her hand over his. "Dad, will you take me?"

He shook his head. "No, my dear." Pointing toward the kitchen, he added, "That corn your brother fed the deer gave them all diarrhea. They're all too sick to pull a sleigh or fly, except Blitzen. He was too smart to eat that souped-up feed."

"But, if Blitzen isn't sick, Holly could ride him there, couldn't she?" Joy asked.

"Well, yes. I suppose she could." Santa searched Holly's face and frowned. "I'm sorry, Holly. If you want to go, you'll have to make the trip on your own."

Panic and dread hit her with a one-two punch.

To see David again, not only would she need to leave her home and family again and fly by herself half way around the world, she would need to ask that arrogant bastard, Blitzen, for a ride.

Like a rhinoceros completing a gymnastic routine in her belly, the heavy weight in her stomach flip-flopped, and then landed with a crash.

Joy sat and pushed against Holly's leg. "What are

you going to do? The conference starts any second. If you leave now, you can just make it in time."

Holly shot up and paced the long runner carpet in the living room, wringing her hands. "I'm not sure. I honestly don't know if I can do it." She stopped and grabbed her stomach, clutching the sides of her waist hard. "I think I'm going to be sick."

Chapter Eight

David craned his neck around a columned wall at Denver's outdoor Greek theater and scanned the crowd waiting in the frigid cold. Hundreds of bundled-up women ranging from just barely legal to sixty huddled together in the available seating, and more women were making their way across the park's snow-covered lawn.

Several girls held homemade signs high over their heads. A few read, 'choose me' or 'I love you, David!' One announced, 'I'm all over David like white on rice.'

David groaned.

The very last place on the planet he wanted to be was here, in front of the cameras and all these crazed women again. But he had little choice. And desperate times called for desperate measures.

He narrowed his eyes and looked through the throng for the one familiar face he hoped had come, but she wasn't there. He did happen to notice a woman take off her coat and pull off her shirt, revealing a behemoth pair of boobs that couldn't possibly be real.

He groaned again. Yes, he was a desperate man.

"It's time, David. We're ready to roll."

David nodded at the pudgy producer from the show. The man's fat little face was bright pink and his greedy brown eyes shone bright. Little wonder. This broadcast was pulling in more viewers than all of his other shows combined. People all the way to Japan were watching.

As he walked across the stage to the podium, thousands of bright camera bulbs flashed, and the crush of girls screamed. The sound was deafening.

A woman broke through the barrier of guards and ran to him. Before he could defend himself, the deranged girl grabbed at his coat and ripped off one of the small pockets. She turned toward the crowd and waved the torn material like a trophy.

The cries and shouts from the crowd shook the solid rock stage.

Four guards rushed to the woman, who was now sprinting to the exit. They overtook her right before she could make it down the entrance ramp.

What the Hell was he doing up here? He must be out of his ever lovin' mind.

Shaken, David raised his hand over his eyes, shielding his face from the onslaught of light. He tapped the microphone, producing an ear-piercing screech. For just a moment, the hordes of women were relatively quiet.

"Thank you all for coming out in this cold to be here today." He tried to continue, but the noise coming from the seating and lawn was just too loud. He motioned with his hands for quiet. "I'm here to tell you I have..." David glanced up.

In the sky, a small brown spot appeared and grew large. Within seconds the rough shape of a rider on a large deer was clear.

David's palms sweated and heart pumped wildly in his chest.

Holly.

She had come.

Every head in the crowd turned. A collective gasp rang through the cold air.

Before he realized what he was doing, David was half way across the stage, waving his arms above his head and shouting. "Here. I'm over here."

The giant reindeer landed next to David, a beaming Holly held the reins. "Hey, stranger. Want a lift?" She reached out a hand.

David hesitated. "Can that reindeer carry two people?"

The big animal turned his head and snorted with a jerk.

"Better get on before you offend him any more," she shouted. "Getting him to come here in the first place cost me a year's worth of sugar cubes."

Taking a running leap, David jumped behind her onto the back of the big reindeer, and held on to Holly's waist for his life.

As the massive animal prepared for take off, the show's producer, a dozen security guards, and several hundred angry women rushed the stage. The reindeer was barely off the ground when the first guard reached them. The man grabbed at David's foot, but missed.

The reindeer kicked his long legs several times, and quick as lightening they were flying.

David closed his eyes, unable to look at the earth speeding by miles below. He rested his head on Holly's back, never letting go of the grip he had around her small frame. "Where are we going?"

"I'm taking you to my family's house in Christmas Town. No one will be able to find you there," she said over her shoulder.

Wind passing by tugged hard on his legs and coat. Keeping his balance on Blitzen's bare back wasn't easy. If he didn't know better, he was sure the big reindeer was twitching his hide, trying to get David to fall off. "And how long is this going to take?"

"Look up. We're already here."

"What?" Unbelieving, David cracked one eyelid opened, and then the other.

To his right, snow-covered mountains lined the horizon. He turned to his left and saw a rustic lodge the size of a small hotel and a nearby barn big enough to shelter half the animals in Noah's arc.

Blitzen slowed and came to an abrupt stop at the side of the barn. The sudden stop was so jarring, both Holly and David fell off the animal's back into a pile of soft snow. Blitzen snorted, shook his head, and trotted off toward the shelter, dragging the reins behind.

David pulled Holly into his embrace. "You hurt?"

"No. I'm great. You?" She smiled up at him.

A flood of warmth washed over him. Just having her in his arms made his heart swell. "Never better."

Holly nuzzled her face in the curve of his neck and kissed the sensitive skin there. "Listen, before you go and meet the big guy, let me tell you, I'm not ready to marry you."

He raised an eyebrow and crooked grin tugged at his mouth. "You're not?" He wasn't either, but he couldn't help but wonder where this conversation was going.

"No. Not yet." She grinned. "But Mom and Daddy have prepared a room for you at the house. You can stay as long as you want. Forever if you like." She pulled her body over his and kissed him hard on the mouth.

She parted her sweet lips, allowing his tongue to probe and explore. But he wanted more, much more, than just her mouth. She was giving him the room he wanted. No pressure. Enough time to discover if she really was the one.

He broke the kiss. His breathing was rough and uneven. "If I stay, what will I do?"

Holly's chest rose and fell as she filled her lungs with air. "Daddy's looking for someone to write children's books. He had planned on meeting with you when he was at your cabin. He wanted to talk about you taking on a job here. That's why you had the asterisks by your name on his list. Says he's trying to get more kids' heads out of their computer screens and into books." She bent and kissed him again.

He stopped her and gently pushed her back. "And what do you want?"

She smiled and pinched his cheek. "Just what I got for Christmas. You."

About the author...

Mention poker, men with Scottish accents, and anything to do with ghosts, and you'll have Bev Oz's full attention. Anyone who knows Bev can tell you those three subjects are very telling of her personality. She's a highly competitive, otherworldly nut who likes alpha males in short kilts. Much of these traits and interests are woven into her sometimes wacky, but always highly entertaining stories, which range from sweet romances to highly sensual romanticas.